CROSSINGS

BOOK TWO

CROSSINGS

THE STEEL ROOTS SERIES

J L MULVIHILL

SEVENTH STAR PRESS

Cover art and illustrations: Anne Rosario
Cover art and illustrations in this book copyright © 2014 Anne
Rosario & Seventh Star Press, LLC.

Editor: Amanda DeBord

Published by Seventh Star Press, LLC.

ISBN Number: 978-1-941706-98-5

Seventh Star Press
www.seventhstarpress.com
info@seventhstarpress.com

Publisher's Note:
Crossings is a work of fiction. All names, characters, and places
are the product of the author's imagination, used in a fictitious
manner. Any resemblances to actual persons, places, locales,
events, etc. are purely coincidental.

Printed in the United States of America
First Edition

FOREWARD

Though I am sure I don't have to tell you that this is a work of fiction, I would like to remind you of this once again. I find that it is my duty to inform all who read this that hopping trains is not only against the law but very dangerous and you could die if you try it. Please do not try it. If you end up in jail or worse, then you won't be able to finish the series and that would be a tragedy. All kidding aside though, please do not try to train hop. Remember it is illegal and deadly and I do not encourage such activity.

Sincerely,
J L Mulvihill

DEDICATION
To my sister Kristen, I love you dearly.
Now and forever you will be in my heart.

CHAPTER 1

$\mathcal{P}$anic overcomes me as I slowly wake; I don't know where I am. I can feel the strange environment around me without even opening my eyes, and I know this is not home. Even when I sometimes fall asleep under the oak tree in the yard, I feel safe in my own surroundings, but here I don't have that feeling. I keep my eyes closed and listen for a while. I can hear chickens in a yard not far from me, but they are not my chickens. Funny how I would know my own chickens; my chickens have their own distinct sounds linked to their personalities. Thinking about my chickens triggers my memory and I recall the events in my life the last few months, remembering that home is gone, forever, and so are the chickens; even my favorite chicken Myrtle who flew into the apple tree to sleep every night. Myrtle is probably someone's dinner by now.

I sniff the air but I can't smell the sweet pungent odor of decaying oak leaves that fall every year and blend in the soil, or the cool, wet algae smell of the pond. What I smell here is old wood, dry dirt, and burnt air like a smoldering fire. Around me are faint sounds of breathing and I remember the workinhouse and being cramped up in that stuffy room hearing everyone breathing all

1

night and smelling their breath and body odor. However, where I am now is not like that, I'm outside far from the workinhouse. I feel a chill going across my skin and down into my bones so deep that I hug myself for warmth.

"Are you ok Abby? Are you cold?" asks a sweet loving voice. It's not Granny's and it's not Papa's voice but a girl's, and I recognize Freckles' gentle tone.

"I'm ok," I say, as I open my eyes and see the greying sky above me.

"Shh, it's not time to wake up yet. I'm still sleeping," I hear Charlotte say.

A soft purring breaks the momentary silence and we all break out in soft giggles as Boots comes crawling out from under the covers and does his long cat body stretch.

Freckles, Charlotte, Boots, and I are lying by the fire in the back yard of Momma Sampson's house. It all comes back to me now, the horrors of the night before and the weeks and months before. The nightmare that I have found myself in now, with nothing to call my own except for what I hold in my satchel, Papa's spyglass, his map, the clothes I wear, and my friends. I wouldn't have been able to make the trip this far without my friends, but as I sit up and shake the cobwebs from my mind, I realize that I may have to continue my journey alone.

While Freckles and Charlotte are still with me, Charlotte is not prepared to do the kind of traveling I must do which will require a lot of walking and probably hopping on trains. Her ankle is getting better but she's not strong enough. I have a feeling that Freckles will want to accompany Tom on his journey north, to get the children we rescued from the mine home to their families.. Charlotte won't want to be left behind, and if she can ride in the wagon then there is no reason why she can't go with them.

We haven't heard from Lyza and Julian yet, and I doubt that anyone will for a while. There is no telling how far the river would have taken Raine, or her body, when she fell off the train into the water. I really don't have time to wait for Lyza and Julian to get back; at least I don't want to take the time. I have no idea which direction to search for Papa so I must try every location on the map until I can get some kind of answer about where he was going and what he was up to, or who took him. Searching for Papa will take time, and I'm not sure how much time I have.

As for Jim, well I have Boots, his cat, but I don't know what has become of Jim since the Hobo Jungle. I hope the Crushers didn't catch him. If they did, I'm sure he'll manage without my help. After all, the guy is pretty old and has done for himself all these years before he met me. Of course, I do owe him some form of debt because of Papa, but I can't help him if I don't know where he is.

Sleep is out of my reach now so I get up, stretch, and make my way to the house to use the water closet, as Momma Sampson calls it. Tom is still asleep with the older boys in the wagon; they had it rough and really should spend a few days here to rest. However, all these people staying here at Momma Sampson's house could get her into trouble. If any of the Crushers came by here and saw all these kids they would know something was up and take us all back to the workinhouse. Momma Sampson would be charged with being a System breaker and get thrown either in the clinker or a workinhouse. It will be best for all of us to leave and give her some peace and quiet.

After I wash up, I go to the kitchen and find Momma Sampson already at the stove cooking. She turns her head and nods toward a coffee pot sitting on the table. There are scattered tin cups around it, and I pick one and pour hot steaming black coffee into the cup. I glance around the table until I find the sugar bowl but I don't see any milk for the coffee. I turn to ask Momma Sampson if she has any milk and she is holding up a bucket to me.

"If you want some milk you're gonna have to milk the cow first," she says, smiling slyly.

"Sure," I say. I'm no stranger to chores and I know how to milk a cow, it's just been a while.

I take the bucket and as I go out the door I hear her say, "Mind you treat o'le Bessie nice now or she won't do for you."

"I got it, I've milked a cow before, Bessie will be fine," I say.

"Bessie ain't the name of the cow, Bessie is what I call the milk'n machine," she says, laughing.

"Oh. Well then, what's the cow's name?" I ask.

"Cow don't gotta name she just gonna be steak on my table when she stops given milk so I don't see no point in naming her," she says.

"Good point," I say shutting the door behind me.

The day is growing brighter and I'm feeling almost like my old self, doing something I used to do back home. I'm wondering what Bessie is and if I will know what to do with it. I guess I'll just figure it out when I get in there. I see Freckles and Charlotte getting up and I nod to them as I walk by.

"Where you going?" asks Freckles.

"I'm getting some milk. Momma Sampson is making breakfast so she might need help in the kitchen," I say.

"Ok, we're going," says Freckles. Charlotte just nods her head sleepily and I see the boys in the wagon starting to move around.

I get a hot stone out of the fire using a couple of sticks and put it in the bucket. Then I stop by the water pump on the way to the barn and fill the bucket halfway. The cool water from the well hisses and bubbles when it first hits the hot rock. I take the rock out and toss it aside and finish filling the bucket up more.

In the barn, I close my eyes a moment and it's as if I'm home. The smell of sweet straw, old wood, manure, and animal sweat dominates my nostrils. I guess most barns must smell like this, what else should it smell like? Except this barn is missing one key ingredient, the smell of chemicals, hot metal, and burnt air that permeated from Papa's workshop.

Momma Sampson's barn is average size and could hold several animals and wagons but it's filled with all kinds of junk instead; broken chairs, wagon wheels, fence posts, chicken wire, crates, tubs, old doors, and an assortment of odd metal objects here and there, which appear to be pieces of buildings or signs or something. As a whole, the building looks like an indoor junkyard, a complete kid's playground, and I find myself fascinated with every artifact I come across.

She doesn't have many animals, only a cow and a mule in their stalls next to each other. I know the cow doesn't have a name but I wonder if the mule does, after all, she's not planning to eat the mule, is she? The animal seems quite friendly as I approach the stall and it comes up to nuzzle my hand. I look around until I find some feed and pour it into its trough, and then I check the water. It's low but it will keep until I'm done milking the cow.

The cow is not as curious as the mule and acts very indifferent to me as I come into her stall to milk her. Our cow back home, Sophie, used to require me to pet her and even brush her like I did the ponies before she would even allow me to think about milking her. I guess she was a bit spoiled. This cow appears to lack all prospects of a personality.

I find some towels obviously set aside for washing and drying and start the whole procedure. I feel a little frustrated because couldn't I have at least had the cup of coffee before I milked the cow? I'm thankful at least that Momma Sampson has a milk'n machine even if it's an old one, a cranker at that.

I attach the suckers to the cow's teats making sure they are secure and flip the vacuum switch. She starts a moment then realizes what is going on and relaxes into it. Maybe this won't take as long as I thought. I start cranking the handle, and it's not long before milk is flowing through the tubes and into the bucket. I'm halfway through the milking when I hear my name being called.

"I'm over here," I call out.

"We brought your coffee," says Charlotte.

"Momma Sampson said you would be a while and no one can have breakfast until you're done," says Freckles.

"Well, I'm milking, it takes time," I say, thinking that I was in a good mood until now.

"Don't be mad," says Charlotte

"I'm not mad, I'm just frustrated, that's all," I say.

"About what?" she asks.

"I know," says Freckles. "You're mad cuz I was sweet on Thomas."

"No, it's not that. He's nice but I've more important things to worry about than boys. I have to get going, I have to get back on the trail and find my papa," I say. They both get quiet as I finish the milking and pull the bucket out from under the cow and stand up.

"Here. I'll take it," says Freckles, taking the bucket from my hands.

"Ok, thanks," I say and unhook the milk'n' machine from the cow and give her some hay and check her water before I'm ready to leave.

As we walk out the door to the house, I get the feeling from the silence that Charlotte and Freckles have something they want to say to me but don't know how to say it.

"So what is it?" I ask finally before we get too close to the house.

"What is what?" asks Charlotte.

"Why are you two so quiet? What's going on?" I ask, stopping and turning to them both since they had been trailing behind me.

"Well," Freckles hesitates, "we think it would be best if we went with Thomas to help him with the kids."

"Oh, is that all" I say with relief.

"You're not mad?" asks Charlotte.

"Of course not, I was thinking that myself. You can't be train hopping with your ankle like that. Riding in a wagon is way better for you, and I think Tom could use both your help," I say, smiling slyly at Freckles.

"Thomas. I like to call him Thomas. It's more dignified than Tom, and after all, he is a hero," says Freckles.

"Ok, anyway, like I was saying, it's ok with me if you both go with Thomas," I say.

"That's a relief," says Freckles, "but what about Lyza and Julian?"

"And Raine," says Charlotte.

"Well yeah, Raine," says Freckles.

"I don't know. I guess we can leave word with Momma Sampson to let them know where we are going. The problem is none of us really knows where we are going. I mean, I do because

I have the map but I'm not sure which direction to go first or what I will find," I say.

"Let's have breakfast and then we can look at the map and maybe plan something out," suggests Charlotte.

"That's a good plan, I'm starving," says Freckles.

"Me too," I say.

CHAPTER 2

We continue walking to the house and find Momma Sampson has some of the kids helping her with breakfast. Surprisingly, everything runs smoothly and I get the impression that Momma Sampson has dealt with lots of children before. After breakfast, Tom gives everyone a task of either cleaning up, or packing up for their trip. While the kids are all doing their delegated jobs, the three of us go out to the barn to talk and look over the map. I remember what old Jim said about not letting too many people see the map but I feel that Tom is part of our group now and can be trusted. Besides, the way Freckles is making goo-goo eyes at him, I get the feeling he will be around for a while.

In the barn, we go up to the loft and open the loft door for light and fresh air. There is no furniture up here and very little hay since Momma Sampson only has two animals to feed. We settle on the floor with the map spread before us. As I look down at the map and Papa's handwriting my emotions well up inside me, and I feel the tears threatening to fall. Taking a deep breath, I let it out slowly and try to concentrate on the task at hand. There are so many choices and decisions with all these markers. Did Papa go to all these places, or had he intended on going? How do I know any of these places will lead me to him or answer any questions?

The last place I went to it had been obvious Papa was there. Tom had even met him, but the only clue was the strange lightning machine Papa made, and it's destroyed now. I don't understand why he made it and what he intended to do with it or whether those creatures in the mine had something to do with it or not. I'm deep in thought when suddenly I realize how quiet it is and look up. I see everyone concentrating on me. Embarrassed, I look down at the map again and point to a spot in West Virginia where there are letters written. "I'm pretty sure that's where Granny's family is and that's why it's marked on the map," I say.

"Are you sure?" asks Tom.

"How do you know?" asks Freckles.

"I said I'm pretty sure. Just before I left for New Joplin, Granny told me that if anything happened I should go to Sugar Creek, which is a town or something in the heart of the mountains. She said that's where her kin folk live and that I should go there and they would take care of me," I say.

"Well then, that's where you should go," says Freckles. "If you have family there then that's where you should be."

"Yea, Abby, you should be with your family," says Charlotte.

"They are only family because they are related to Granny. I don't know those people, and I don't know who they are or if they are, even still there so I'm not going there. At least not until I find Papa," I say exasperated. Freckles' peremptory tone along with Charlotte agreeing with her so readily puts me in a defensive mood.

"Right," says Tom, "so the closest place looks like here in North Carolina."

"Bryson City," I say. I'm thankful Tom steered the conversation away from my possible family ties; I don't want to be talked into going somewhere I might get stuck and delayed further from finding papa.

"There's a place called Rome in Georgia marked too," says Freckles.

"I see that but it has an X over it. I wonder why?" I say.

"What's that word next to Bryson City?" asks Charlotte.

I look closer, so close my eyes hurt, but there's very small writing next to Bryson City, Just one word, Grugen. "Oh, my gosh," I say.

"What?" asks Charlotte.

"That name again," I say. "The name Grugen," I point to the very small word. They all lean in close to the map to see the word better.

"What does that mean?" asks Charlotte.

"Grugen is the mining company that owns the mine we worked in," says Tom.

"It's written on the map next to Marion," I say, pointing to the town on the map. "I also remember seeing the sign," I say. I reach into my pocket, take out a piece of crumpled newspaper, and lay it on the map. The word Grugen is written large and coarse across the print in black as if written with a piece of charred wood.

"Where did you get that?" asks Freckles.

"Remember the German woman from the Hobo Jungle that came to me before we left? She gave me the scarf, and wrapped inside I found a pocket knife, a compass, and a chain bracelet, with this crumpled piece of newspaper," I say.

"Wow, a real clue," breathes Charlotte.

"Yea, but what does it mean?" asks Freckles.

"I have no idea," I say.

"Well at least you know that Grugen is a person," says Tom.

"Yes," I say, looking at him in thought. "You said Grugen owned the mine you worked in."

"What was it that you mined?" asked Charlotte.

"Fluorspar," says Tom.

"What is fluorspar?" asks Charlotte.

"Yes, I would like to know that too," I say.

"I can't say for sure," says Tom.

"I wonder if it has anything to do with what Papa was working on." I ask aloud in thought.

"You know your papa was working on something?" asks Freckles.

"That's what Detective Walker asked me. He said, 'I need to know what your father was working on in his workshop before he disappeared,' and he asked me what I knew. I told him Papa just tinkered and didn't do anything special," I say.

"So whatever your papa was working on, he needed fluorspar, or at least he experimented with it," Tom speculates.

"Maybe, I mean, you helped him, didn't you?" I ask.

"Yes, I told you that, but he told me not to ask questions and I didn't. Nothing he did in front of me made any sense, and I don't know anything about this stuff," says Tom.

"Well we do know it has something to do with lightning because of the lightning machine he had in the mine," I say.

"Yes there is that. I'm sorry, Abby. I wish I could be more help," says Tom.

"It's ok, she knows you're trying," says Freckles, rubbing Tom on the back.

"What about this Grugen guy?" asks Charlotte.

"I'm not sure it's a guy or just the name of the company," I say.

"I thought the System owned all the companies," says Charlotte.

"Not all," says Tom. "The System owns a lot of the companies and a percentage of the rest. At least that is my understanding," he says.

"I thought they just owned everything," says Freckles.

"They might as well for all the good it does the people," he says.

"You don't think the System has anything to do with my papa disappearing do you?" I ask in alarm.

"I don't know Abby, but if it does, you may never find him," says Tom.

"Abby, I've heard stories of people who have questioned the System or done stuff they don't like and then they disappear forever," says Freckles.

"Don't say that, Freckles. You're scaring her," says Charlotte, putting an arm around me.

"Don't be so green, Charlotte. What do you think happened to your dad?" asks Freckles.

"Freckles!" I interject.

"Well, that's how it is," says Freckles. "Nobody just loses everything overnight like that unless the System has something to do with it."

"Ok, let's all just calm down. We all have to stick together, and none of this is helping Abby," says Tom.

"You're right, I'm sorry," says Freckles.

We have a few moments of uncomfortable silence as we all stare down at the map contemplating the words that we know to ring true. Something Papa always told me is that the System is a very bad thing for our country and way of life and somehow, someway America has to break free from this, but it would take the revolt of the citizens to do it.

I take a deep breath. "Ok, so I'm going to Bryson City. It's the closest and maybe Papa will be there, or maybe I will find out more about Grugen," I say.

"Why don't you just head for the spot marked over here," says Charlotte, pointing to a mark in Colorado. "It seems to me these are all the places he has already been and this is the last place."

"No, because he has already been there and back maybe. He gave the map to Jim in New Joplin so there is nothing to say he is there," I say.

"There is nothing to say that he is in any of these places," says Freckles, pointing out the obvious.

"I know, but I have to do something and this is the only hope I have," I say.

"How are we all going to meet up again?" asks Freckles.

"Hot Springs," says Charlotte.

"What?" asks Freckles.

"Hot Springs?" I ask

"Yes," says Charlotte. "It's right there on the map: Hot Springs in Arkansas has a mark by it," she points her finger to the Papa's mark by Hot Springs.

"Yes you're right, but why there?" I ask.

"My parents used to take me there. Of course I never really had any fun because they were always at the spa or the horse races but I had to stay at the hotel with the nanny," her voice trails off for a moment. "Anyway, the town is there and if none of us can meet there we can at least send a wire or letter to the post office, right?" she asks.

"That's a great idea, Charlotte. I can remember the name and if there is a post office there then we can always send word. Even if I find Papa and don't have to go there, I can send word," I say.

"Well that's just stupid, what if none of us go there and we all send word so there is just a bunch of letters sitting there at the post office and no one to get them?" asks Freckles.

"Ok, so we will just have to meet up there no matter what then," I say.

"Right," says Thomas.

"Oh, you're in this too?" I ask, looking at Tom slyly.

"Of course I am," he says. "When I'm not killing trolls, and rescuing children and delivering them back to their families, I am helping young ladies find their papas," he says smiling.

"Ok, we meet in Hot Springs, but when?" I ask.

"By the first of October," says Charlotte.

"Why then?" asks Freckles.

"It's my birthday," says Charlotte smiling.

"I couldn't think of a better reason," I say.

CHAPTER 3

We all head back to the house to find that Calliope has the wagon all loaded up and ready to go. Momma Sampson gave them what food she could spare for the trip and any whatnots she could find that they could use for trade. I find that she has also packed a few things for me in anticipation of my continuing journey in search of Papa.

"I found this old messenger bag, and thought it would be better than the pillowcase you been usin'," says Momma Sampson.

"Wow, thank you," I say, admiring the old canvas bag that has obviously seen better days but still holds strong.

"It belonged to my late husband. I'll never use it so you might as well. I put some supplies in there but there's room for you to put the rest of your belongings and then you tie your bedroll under the bottom there, see?" she says, showing me the tie straps under the bottom. "Then you can either sling it over your shoulder with the one long strap or over your back with these smaller straps," she demonstrates.

"That's way jiggy. Thank you," I say, taking the bag and experimenting with the straps and adjusting them to fit me.

I take the bag into the other room and put the rest of my

stuff in it. The knife the German woman had given me is gone now because I had used that to make a spear to kill the troll in the mine. I still have the compass, though, and the knife Tom gave me to replace the one I used, so I put those in a front pocket where I can to them easily. Papa's spyglass is too long to put in the bag, so I will just have to sling that over my shoulder as usual. I take my blanket and roll the pillow up in it, and then tie it to the bottom of the satchel. I tie my scarf around my waist like a belt and I'm ready to go. The kids are all loaded up in the wagon and ready to go as well. All that is left is to say goodbye.

I see that Tom, Charlotte, Freckles, Calliope, and the kids are all saying their farewells and thanking Momma Sampson. I walk up and give her a big hug as well.

"Thank you so much for everything," I say.

"There is no need, just doing my part," she says, waving off our gestures of gratitude.

"I do have to ask one more thing of you. If our friends Lyza and Julian come through looking for us, please tell them to meet us in Hot Springs Arkansas by October first," I say.

"Sure why not. I've been the inn, the cook, now the messenger," she says, throwing up her hands. But we all know she is kidding, and I give her a big hug because she is a wonderful person and has helped us a lot. I can't tell her how much it means to me just have someplace to stop, even for a short while, and rest a bit. I think she knows this but she is a stubborn woman and for some reason wants to pretend, she doesn't care.

We all hug and say goodbye for now, and they all get up in the wagon, which Tom has fitted with a top over the back to shelter and hide the children. My heart sinks a little as I see them leave. I turn and start walking because I don't want to watch them go.

I know it will be easier for me to leave them. I hear the wagon pulling away north and my heart feels the ache of loneliness already. I can do this, though. I started out alone and I can go this alone again. After all, I can't go north with them. Papa isn't north, and I have to find Papa. Once I find him then we can all get back together again. Maybe we can even all live together somewhere on a farm and be a family. I bet Papa won't mind having a few more daughters.

I have a four-hour walk ahead of me to Paducah from Smithland and my feet already feel heavy against the ground but they are suddenly falling in sync with four soft patters that are barely detectible on the ground. I look over to see Boots walking alongside of me and my heart is lifted and my step lighter. Even a cat is better company than the solitude of one's own somber thoughts.

I wished that Momma Sampson could have given me a ride or something, but I didn't want to ask her. The less she is tangled up in our mess, the better. If Papa is involved with something against or for the System then I don't want anyone else getting hurt. I've already involved too many people but then Lyza, Freckles, Charlotte, and Raine were all mixed up in this mess anyway so there is no helping that. Jim, Julian and Tom too, I guess, are just as much in this, if not more. After all, it was Jim who was entrusted with Papa's spyglass that holds the map, and Julian travels with Jim. As for Tom, I justify him being involved because he would probably be dead otherwise. I kind of hope he finds his family and maybe Freckles and Charlotte will stay up there with him and be safe. It seems to me that being out on the road is a dangerous thing for anyone, especially kids.

Calling me, a kid after all I have been through seems somewhat funny. I don't feel like a kid. I feel old really; I feel old and tired and I just want a safe place to live without all this mess going on around me. I hate having to sneak around and hide from the Crushers. I hate wondering why everything is such a secret about my papa.

After a while, I judge by the sun that it must be noon so we stop and take a break. I look in my satchel to see what Momma Sampson has given me for food and find two cans of peaches, two cans of beans, a can of fish, some hard biscuits, some wrapped cheese, some dried meat wrapped in wax paper and a couple of apples. I break off a piece of dried meat and offer it to Boots who takes it happily and I settle on an apple for myself. Not knowing when or where my next meal may come from, I feel I should ration my food.

After I eat the apple, I relax for a while and enjoy the day. A breeze blows down from the north, cutting the sweltering afternoon and making the heat more bearable. I watch as Boots rolls in the grass, enjoying himself as cats do. I should not linger long though, I know, so I stand and gather my things, throwing my satchel back over my back. "Let's get going, Boots. We should get to town before it gets dark," I say to the cat as if he really understands. Maybe he does, because immediately he is at my side and we continue on.

We are not really on a road but following the river instead. I don't want to draw too much attention to myself so I'll just follow the river to the town. There is a bit of an animal trail along the river so travel is not too difficult as we go. I feel as if I have been walking forever and the cool breeze I felt earlier is gone. The trail starts to veer upwards back to the tree line and I realize it's because the river is cutting into the land and there's a high cliff ahead of me. I see no way to continue on along the river because of sheer cliff walls so I have no choice but to follow the trail back up away from the river.

I find myself walking more into the tree line, farther away from the river. I wonder if this is a smart idea. I don't want to get lost in the woods. It feels hotter here among the trees. It seems to me it should be cooler because of the shade, but the closeness of the trees and shrubbery hold the air in making it impossible for a breeze to flow through. Suddenly I see smoke rising, and it looks like it is coming up from the ground.

"This is very odd," I say, turning to Boots. Boots bounds ahead of me looking very interested. We stop in front of a hole that is as big around as I am with a steady flow of black smoke that smells as if someone is burning and outhouse. I cover my nose with my scarf but the smell does not seem to bother Boots at all. Seeing Boots not afraid of this hole makes me believe that there are no trolls in the hole, at least. I remember when we came to the mine where the trolls lived and Boots acted very strange and wouldn't go anywhere near the entrance. I had to go in there alone. Not that a cat could have helped me any, but it made me realize that I needed to be more in tune with Boots because he appears to be aware of danger before I am.

Just as I'm thinking this, his ears go back and he turns right at the same time I hear the voices coming from the trees. The voices are alarmingly loud, and I look around for the source, trying to figure out where I might hide if someone were to walk out of the trees. I scoop Boots up into my arms and start to run away from the voices. I hope the shrubs and trees will hide me. I run up a small hill and stop short; I find myself at the edge of a camp, but unfortunately, for me I have not gone unnoticed.

"Hey! How'd you git out?" yells a burly man with a scruffy beard.

There are four other men standing near him around a campfire. There are about four or five tents making a semi-circle around a cave entrance where there are two more men standing with guns on either side. I see rail tracks coming out of the cave, which leads off behind the camp. The rails look too small to be for a train though so they must be for mining cars. The man with the scruffy beard keeps yelling at me and I turn my attention back to him.

"I ast' you a question. You better answer me you little pipsqueak. How'd you git outa the cave?" he asks me.

I don't know what he is talking about but I'm not staying to find out so I turn and run back down the hill. I hear the man yelling behind me. "Get her, dagnabit. Don't just stand thar."

I hear scuffling behind me and men hollering in an indecipherable language. Boots has got his claws dug tight in me, and it's very painful, but I can't think about that. All I can do is just keep running. I can't let these men catch me. There is no imagining what they are doing in that camp or cave, and I don't want to know. I turn around to see how far behind me they are, and they're getting closer. I will just have to try to run faster. I turn my head back around and in a split second WHAM! The world goes black.

CHAPTER 4

$\mathcal{I}$ open my eyes, and the world is still black, but I can hear things and I smell the same horrible smell that came up from out of the hole with the smoke. My eyes eventually adjust and I realize there is some dim light here, wherever it is I am. Slowly I sit up and my head starts pounding. Instinctively I reach up, touch my forehead, and feel a crusty lump just above my left eye. Oh why did they have to hit me in the head and so close to my eye? They could have blinded me. Maybe they have; I test my vision by putting a hand over one eye at a time, but despite the dim light, I can still see. Knowing this does not stop my head from hurting.

Boots! Where's Boots? I look around trying to see if Boots is anywhere near me, but I don't see him. Oh, I hope he got away. I hope I didn't hurt him when I fell. I hope they didn't hurt him, or cook him and eat him like a squirrel. Oh Boots, I hope you're ok. I feel tears welling up in my eyes and it stings my left eye even more. I wipe the tears away with my sleeve and reach for my pack to see if I have anything I can put on my wound, and realize my satchel is gone and so is Papa's spyglass with the map.

Oh no! I force myself to stand, clinging to the wall as I do.

The wall is smooth, not like a mine would be. I put my head to the wall to cool my throbbing head. I have to think about what to do next, but my head hurts so bad that I don't know what to do. I don't know where I am or why I am even here. I try to concentrate on my surroundings and not my head. I hear the distant sound of wheels on a rail, and muffled voices that seem to be coming closer to me.

"Looks like the pipsqueak's awake finely," says a nasally voice.

"Boss wants to know who ya are and what ya doin here?" asks another voice.

I turn to see two men I can barely make out in the dim light. They could almost be twins for all I can see. Both are about the same height, both are lanky with no other decided features but their long scruffy hair and beards, and their dirty, tattered clothes. I wonder if I should say anything to these men or keep my silence. They probably work for the system. If I have learned anything in my travels, I have learned that except for the hobos, most adults can't be trusted, Momma Sampson being the exception.

"Where's my cat?" I ask.

"Yer cat?" asks one man.

"Didn't bring no cat, them boys musta ate it," the other man says, laughing.

"They wouldn't eat no cat wit' out us," says Duffus, though I really don't think that is his real name.

"Naw, Numskull, they wouldn't. Cats is fast. It probly got away," says Finus. "I's just funnin ya."

I breathe a sigh of relief. After all, Boots is a clever cat and wouldn't let anyone catch him. He's probably hiding out in the woods somewhere nearby waiting for me. At least that's what I have to believe for now because I can't let myself think anything bad has happened to him. I try to take a more firm stance facing these two pumquats, and move on to the next of my concerns.

"Where's my stuff?" I ask.

"Bossman gots yer stuff. It's his now. You got no need of it down here," says Finus.

"Just where is here? And what gives him or you the right to bring me down here? I have important business to attend to," I say, trying to sound important.

"What kind of importin stuff does a little girl gotta do, huh?" ask Duffas

"Not much, I bet but I'm thinkin she ain't such a little girl at that," says Finus, reaching over and touching a strand of my hair. I pull away and step back but I can't go any further since there is a wall behind me.

"Yeah she look old ee-nuff to me Finus. What'd you say we find out?" asks Duffus, moving in closer to me.

"Later Duffus, we got work to do now but we got all night to find out, don't we?" he says, smiling at me.

My heart is beating in my throat and somehow my head does not feel so bad at the moment. Wherever I am, I need to find a way out of here and quick. There is no way I'm letting these two disgusting men, or any other man, have their way with me. I will find a weapon somewhere and kill them if I have to.

"Come on, you got to earn yer keep fer now. There's work to be done," says Finus.

"Ah Finus does she have ta? She'll smell like the rest of em' if you make her work. Right now she smells so perty," says Duffus.

"Yeah, I know, but we short-handed anyways so it's lucky we got er. Come on girly," says Finus, grabbing me by the arm and shoving me in front of him.

He steers me forward with his hand on my shoulder as we walk through tunnels made by nature centuries ago. The dim light of lanterns placed in various spots only allows a small portion of this miraculous place to be seen. I've never been in a real cave before, but we read about them in school. I thought it would be an incredible thing to see. Of course I had always hoped to visit one, but not under these circumstances. In school, we learned about stalactites, stalagmites, and other formations that actually grow in caves and are formed by drops of water filled with minerals over millions of years. I don't see any of those things here, but I do see large rock formations and strange colors in the walls.

What ruins the natural beauty of this place, other than these two thugs, is the rail track that has been laid down through the walkway. I can guess their mining something out of this cave, and running mining buckets out on the rails. The ground is solid rock. It must have been very hard laying these tracks down, and I have to wonder if these idiots here did it or did they put some poor folk to work on this like at the workinhouse.

"Stop," Finus says, gruffly. Then he puts a piece of cloth over my eyes and starts to tie it around my head. I kick back and pull myself away from him, running ahead as fast as I can. Instead of coming after me as I expect them to, I hear them laughing behind me.

"Yer not gonna get very far when ya hit the dark girly," I hear Finus say.

"Yeah it's dark in there ya ain't got no light," says Duffas, laughing.

"We wasn't try'n to hurt ya, we just gotta put a mask on ya so's you can't see where yer goin, that's all," says Finus.

"Yeah we wasn't try'n to hurt ya," says Duffas.

"Would you quit repeat in' everyth'n I say Duffas," I hear Finus say.

"Yeah quit repeat in', Oh, you mean . . . that ain't nice," says Duffus.

"Come on ya numbskull let's get er," says Duffas.

I keep running. Soon it's getting darker and darker and I realize they're right. I won't be able to see at all. I wish I had my satchel with me; I had candles and matches in it. Even if I had, light to see with they would be able to find me too easily. I can't see anyway of winning this at the moment, and I have to figure something out soon before they catch up to me. I stop to survey my surroundings. It's so dark in here I can hardly see now but I look up and above me appears to be some boulders. If I can climb up maybe I can hide behind them, assuming they're not loose and I don't start a cave in.

I hike up my skirt and tie it off, then carefully I climb, pretending it's just a tree back home and this is nothing, easy peasy. I'm mindful of my footholds, and I make sure they are sturdy before I put my weight into them. As for my hand holds there is not much to hold onto but sheer rock but I search with my hands for cracks and jutting out stones until I find something sturdy. It feels like I've been climbing for a long time before I finally reach the top of a boulder, and there is just enough room for me to slide in over the top, between the boulder and the ceiling it is hangs under. I'm not sure how this boulder is being supported since it's so dark. I only hope it's sturdy enough for me.

Once I'm in position, I have to focus on slowing my breathing down so they won't hear me as they pass by. Everything echoes in a cave. Even my breathing sounds like the wind. I can still hear the two men coming, taking their time, I guess, because they think I will stop once it gets dark and I can't see where I'm going. They might be right about that, it's dangerous to walk in a cave completely in the dark.

I watch as the light slowly invades the darkness and the two men approach walking right under and past me without stopping. As they walk by I hear them grumbling about having to go look for me because the other one let me get away. Now I have to decide. Should I just stay here and wait for them to come back through or should I get down now and go back the way we came? I lay in my spot quietly, barely breathing, trying to decide what to do. I realize that the longer I wait the less of a chance I may have to get away. I guess it would be better to go now because I know there is light back the way we came and if I stay and let them pass back by then they will just be waiting for me.

When I hear their voices far off I cautiously slide back down, feeling for foot holds and hand holds as I go. I'm not very far up but it's still scary coming down and I don't want to break an ankle, leg, or something. I'm relieved when my feet finally touch the ground. I walk swiftly back the way we came, moving toward the light. I'm leery every time I come around a corner because I don't want to run into any more thugs. I come to a split off with one way darker than the other. I reckon maybe I better keep heading to the light when I hear Duffas and Finas talking as they come closer behind me. I have no choice but to duck down the darker path and hope this is not the same way they are planning on going. I go as far as I can before the darkness is just too much for me to bear so I stop and sit on the ground to rest. As I rest I listen intently for any sound of someone coming down the path but I hear nothing, for now.

Well ain't this the stink? Now I'm stuck in a cave in the dark, and I'm lost. Some goober has all my things, including Papa's spyglass and map. Boots is gone and I have no idea where he is and I don't know what to do. I have to think, this can't be the worst I've seen. When they took Granny away in the Crusher Box, and chased me through the cornfields I thought that was the worst. When they caught me and put me in the workinhouse with Ms. Marcs starving me and constantly punishing me, I thought that was the worst of it. When we managed to escape but then the workinhouse exploded with all those children inside, then I thought that was the worst I'd seen. But then Raine fell out of the train from the bridge and that was the worst. Just when I thought nothing could be worse, I had to fight real monsters I never thought existed. I thought that was the worst of it.

Each time something really bad happens, and I feel that nothing could ever get worse than that, something does. I only want my family back. I only want my papa and my granny and our life back in Jasper just the way it was. I hug my knees in close and the tears just start coming. I let them come but I don't make a sound. I cry as quietly as I can because right now I can't help but cry. Maybe I should just let them catch me and be done with it. Maybe all this bad stuff keeps happening because I keep running, and fighting back. Maybe I should just give in and be part of the System.

CHAPTER 5

$\mathcal{I}$ open my eyes to darkness yet again, I must have dozed off while crying. I sit listening to the darkness and it seems to me that there should be silence in this cave but there isn't; I can hear far off sounds of muffled voices and sometimes hammering. I wonder if those pumquats have given up looking for me yet, though I seriously doubt that. However, I can't sit here forever feeling sorry for myself. I've got to find a way out of here without getting caught. I have changed my mind. I don't want to give up, my papa would not want me to give up. I think he would be very disappointed in me if I did.

My head still hurts, but not as bad as before. There's a lump on my forehead where they hit me. I stand up slowly and remember that I came from the right. It's so dark here that I can't see anything at all. I must have run down this tunnel further than I thought. I only meant to go a little ways but still be able to see the light from the other tunnel to get back, but now I can't see anything.

I start walking and suddenly trip over something, stumble, and fall, rolling down some sort of hill that I hope is not a bottomless pit. I finally stop rolling and lie still for a moment trying to catch my breath. "Stupid, stupid, stupid," I whisper to myself. I had forgotten about the rail tracks, which must have been what I tripped on.

I sit up and examine my body parts and I'm thankful nothing feels broken. I feel around where I'm sitting and I think I may be sitting on a ledge next to a drop off. Not good. Carefully I stand, leaning against the ledge I rolled down. The soil feels soft and loose., They must have blasted this part. This could be good and bad; this means the dirt and rocks are lose and unstable, and I could slide right down and over the edge unless I climb it correctly. The good news is that it's not rock climbing like I did before where I had to try and find foot and hand holds which for the most part were nonexistent.

I start ascending the sliding rock, placing my feet sturdily before pressing my weight against the spot. I walk sideways instead of straight up and go steady, fast, and lightly until I finally make my way to the top with hardly a pebble falling, which is good since the less noise I make the better. Now the only problem is I have no idea which way to go because I'm so turned around. I guess it makes no difference one way or the other since it seems to be dark in either direction. After a minute or two of rest and dusting myself off, I pick a direction, and stepping over the rail, I walk the center of the track, aware naturally of the gaps between the ties. At one point I'm curious so I stop and lean down and touch the cold rail; there's no vibration which means they're not running buckets on this line. That's not a completely odd thing, maybe it's break time, or dinner time, or even bed time, who can tell down here?

I keep walking when I start to smell that horrid smell I came across earlier in the forest. It's not as strong but I can smell it faintly on the air. I wonder what could possibly smell that bad. It must have something to do with what they are doing in this cave, I'm sure, but I can't even imagine what could smell so horrid. It reminds me of sour milk mixed with rotten fruit, then throw in a rotting dead animal and that would be the right smell; it almost makes me want to gag. Then I remember what Duffas said to Finas about not wanting me to work with the others because then I would smell like them.

I wonder what Duffas meant by that comment? As I walk I'm not really paying much attention where I'm going, after all I'm walking along a track so there should not be anything in the way but WHAM! Whatever I collided with throws me back so hard I hit the ground in a daze. I sit a moment because maybe it's one of those fellows again but I don't lose consciousness this time. I'm still coherent. I get up gently, and with my hand out, I move forward again until I touch the rock in front of me. Then I start feeling all over and realize that it's not just one rock but also several like a wall only not completely flat. In fact, it feels like maybe it's a cave in. Either way, it's a dead end.

"Drats and Rats!" I say. I can't believe I walked all this way only to a dead end. I'm so tired of this. Why is there always a constant struggle? It's just not fair. I slump down with my back to the wall of rock on the verge of tears again. I'm determined not to cry though, I will hold it back if it makes my face turn blue. I remember Papa used to tell me that when I was upset about something but I wouldn't cry, I would just stay angry. He would say, *Pumpkin, you have to let those tears out or they will fill you up and turn you blue like the ocean.*

Part of me feels sad when I think of Papa because I don't know where he is or if he is in trouble or not, but there is another part of me that feels comforted by remembering things about him. It's as if I can keep him safe and alive just by thinking these happy thoughts about him, and they give me strength to continue on no matter what my circumstance.

I set my hand down by my side as I think of Papa and I notice my hand is cold. Why would only one hand be cold? I lift my hand and touch it to my cheek and indeed, it's colder than the other hand. I put it back down where I had it and feel a breeze coming through the rocks. I lean my face down and feel the air on my face. Unfortunately, I also smell that horrible smell a little stronger here. I feel around the rock and find a sizable hole in the rocks large enough for me to crawl through. The question is, is it that large all the way through and am I willing to take the chance of crawling through there knowing that all those rocks could easily collapse on me and then I would be dead, or worse trapped, and die slowly with no one to know I am here?

I could just walk back the other way I came which is a very long walk as I recall, and stand the chance of being caught. Then those horrible men might have their way with me. No, I would rather die than let those men touch me. I have only ever been kissed by my best friend Joey and that little punk kid in New Joplin, only I don't think a twelve-year-old boy counts. Joey on the other hand is a year older than I am and I think it was a nice kiss, I only wish I could see him and kiss him at least one more time to remember it better.

So that seals the deal, I'm going through the rocks and hope they don't cave in. If they do, then so be it. I skooch down, and inch by inch crawl through trying very hard not to touch any of the rocks on either side of me or especially above me. I crawl very slowly and it seems like I'm doing this for hours though I know that can't be possible. So far, the hole has remained the same size, for the most part. A couple of times it seems like the rocks are closer and I try not to think about the fact that not only do I have all these rocks around me like a tomb, but also the entire mountain is above me. I have no idea how far down they have taken me into the cave but the idea of the earth crushing in around me is a frightening feeling and if I were claustrophobic, I think I would be Crazy Nelly by now.

After what seems like hours but is really probably only minutes, I start to see a dim light. Now this is promising. The dim light becomes brighter as I get closer and closer until I get to the source, which is yet again, a dead end. It appears as though the rockslide has filled this end of the hole I have been crawling through with only a small opening to look through. I peer through the opening and see a vast room filled with the very formations I had expected a cave to have. Large stalactites hang down from the roof of the cave and huge stalagmites bigger around than a large man rise up from the floor, and strange white bubbly looking shapes clinging to the walls. Why can I see this? Where is the light coming from?

Then I discover the lanterns set atop of large boulders around the cavern, causing shadows to dance across the walls and ceiling. Far to my left are women and girls stirring several large elongated pots over coal fires while younger kids are running around stoking or feeding the fires. I see a man pushing a bucket over the rails and stop at one of the pots. He start to shovel something into the pot from the bucket. They all have scarves or some kind of cloth over their mouths and noses, and I can certainly understand why because that horrid smell is definitely come from those pots.

Whatever it is they're cooking, it's not supper, that's for sure. I readjust myself to get more comfortable and feel something cold against my right side. I reach down and find a piece of steel. This must be part of the original rail line for the buckets before it caved in. I turn my head over to look more closely since I have a little room in here and have to cover my hand over my mouth to hold back the scream that wants to come out of me. There is a dead body right next to me and it looks pretty fresh. My heart starts beating frantically and all I want to do is to get out of this death trap.

CHAPTER 6

The body is covered mostly by rocks so I can't see the whole thing, but the head is protruding so I can see the face and hair and the look of horror on her face. Yes, I'm pretty sure it's a girl about my age or a little younger probably It's hard to tell since the skin is covered in dust and looks almost mummified in the light, not gooey like I would expect. There are no worms or bugs either. That's strange, I think. I always thought worms came to eat the remains of dead bodies, but maybe that's just when you bury them in the dirt. There is dirt here, but mostly rock and limestone.

My new found horror is distracted by some familiar voices, and though I don't want to avert my eyes from her cold death stare for fear she may just reach out through the rocks and grab me, I know better; I know dead bodies don't move so I return my attention to the commotion through my peep hole. Every now and again I steal a glance to my right to make sure my friend hasn't moved, just in case. In the cave, I see Finas, Duffas, and another man talking and I turn my ear to the hole to listen while keeping visual out for possible ghostly hands.

"You ain't found dat girl ya lost yet, has you?" asks the other man

"No we ain't found er yet," says Finas.

"She's lost in da caves we ain't never gonna find er," says Duffas.

"Shut up Duffas," says Finas.

"Bossman ain't too pleased whitcha," says the other man.

"Well she cain't go far now, can she?" asks Finas.

"Well you better find er. Bossman says we need new workers; dems not gonna last long, dey mov'in slow, see?" says the other man.

"Naw, dey just sluggish cuz Duffas been given extra food dats all," says Finas.

"Only the tikes, dey still grow' in, dey last longer if you feed them a bit more dats all," says Duffas.

"Quit feeden em' Duffas. They ain't pets. They're workers and dey get fed when it's feeden time," says the other man.

"Fine den," says Duffas.

"Now you two go up top, it's quit'n time anyways. You can look for dat girl tomorrows. Put the workers ta bed first," says the other man.

"Right," says Finas, and I hear some scuffling so I turn to look again and see the other man leave, and Finas and Duffas appear to be rounding up the workers in a line.

Then Duffas goes around turning out the lanterns while Finas instructs a few boys to spread the coals about so as not to start a fire. I see one boy scoop up some of the hot coals into a bucket and pass it off to one of the men who tucks it behind him as if to hide it. I look back at Finas and Duffas and neither of them is paying any attention.

I try to remember where the lanterns are located as Duffas turns them all out but one which he takes with him back to the line of workers. He says something to them but I can't tell what it is because they are too far across the room and his voice just echoes off the walls like a meaningless sound. Finas joins the group behind them and they all march off away from me, the light growing dimmer and dimmer until the only thing I can see is the soft dull glow of a few still burning coals on the cave floor. I think maybe if I wait too long I won't even have that to use for light.

Now my problem is if I try to move these rocks will they just topple more on top of me? Will I even be able to move them at all or will I have to slide myself backwards out of here? I can't sit up. In fact, I'm on my belly and I can barely push up on my elbows, so I don't have much leverage or strength. I lay flat and reach out to the first stone in front, and I find that it does wiggle a little. I work at it listening closely for any sound of shifting in the rock around me. I manage to push the rock through but it's not enough; there is only enough room for me to stick my head through. I feel the rocks around the new hole to see which ones do not seem to be supporting anything and fortunately find that the one next to the first one I moved pushes out even easier. I reach for the third and give it a little push when I feel a little dust fall on my head. That is a sure sign that this is as lucky as I'm going to get.

Now I feel an urgency to get out of here with the possibility that I may have messed with the rocks too much. I'm not comforted by the thought of joining this dead body next to me indefinitely. Maybe I can squeeze my way out of this hole, I have to at least try. I stick my head out and first ease my left shoulder and then I kind of fold my other shoulder into my chest and push with my feet little by little against the ground.

I feel more and more panic because my arms are pinned so

close that I can't move them. The only thing I can do is push myself out with my feet. Suddenly I feel a rock fall and hit my ankle, not very hard and not a very big rock, but enough to shock me into a frenzy and I start scooting and wiggling as fast as I can until I get one arm out. Then I pull the ground with my arm and push with my feet until I get to my hips.

I have always had somewhat larger hips than most girls my age. Granny always told me they were good baby hips. I used to think she meant I would grow out of them until one day she explained to me that baby hips meant that they were good for holding a baby against comfortably and it would make me a good momma. After that, I just felt cursed with my baby hips which is how I feel right now, as I try to get through this small hole. At last after some extreme effort I make it through and I'm so relieved that I just lay on the ground for a moment, panting.

I don't take too much time because I have to get one of those embers before it burns out. I stand up. I'm stiff from being cramped up in that small space for so long. I try to remember how the place looked when I saw it lit up so that I don't trip while I'm walking. I still manage to stumble a few times. I stop at one of the lanterns and feel for where I remembered it to be and thankfully it's still there. I take it with me over to the big pots where the embers are. The smell is so bad I can hardly breathe.

I take the hood off the lantern and lean the wick down to the ember while doing my best not to spill the oil out from the lamp. I get the wick lit and put the hood back on. I feel so much relief to be back in the light. However, this room is so large and the ceiling so high I can't even see it as the darkness swallows me and my little light up. No wonder they had several lanterns lit all over the place. I'm actually wondering if lighting this is such a good idea because if anyone is still down here the light will lead them right to me. Frankly, right now, I just don't care. I'm tired of being in the dark with dead bodies and that stink. I have to get out of this place.

I stand up and start walking in the direction I saw Finas and Duffas march the workers. This must lead to the way out, after all the man said it was quitting time and to put the workers to bed. I follow the tracks and keep my lantern low. Maybe it won't be too noticeable, I hope I can see the light of anyone else's lantern before they see mine if someone comes back in the cave.

Suddenly I'm accosted by some creature at my legs. I jump back and almost trip over the track rail again. I hold the lantern down fearing that I'm going to see some horrible monster about to take a bite out of me when I see a mass of black matted fur and dirty white boots.

"Oh Boots!" I whisper maybe a bit too loud as my voice echoes even here in the tunnel. The cat comes bounding up to me. I sit down and take him in my arms hugging and petting him as he purrs and nuzzles me back.

"I was so worried about you, I had no idea what had happened to you. Oh Boots, I'm so glad you're alive," I say softly to him. His response of affection tells me he feels the same.

"Ok," I say finally setting him back on the ground, "let's get out of this place." I start to walk back along the tracks and look back to see that Boots is not following me but sitting there staring at me.

"Boots, come on. What is the problem? Let's go," I say, waving for him to follow me, but instead he turns and walks the other way. Oh gosh, really? "Are you crazy? That's not the way out," I say.

Boots ignores me and keeps walking, so of course I have to follow him. I'm not going to lose him again and obviously, he is up to something, or, at least I hope he is and not just being a stupid cat. All I want to do is get out of this creepy place.

Boots walks back down the tracks for a little ways then he suddenly darts off to the right so I have to run to catch up with him to see that he has gone down another passageway I never even noticed. I walk through and find myself walking in a narrow twisting path with rock ledges that come up to my waist on either side of me. They are at least four feet deep before they cut back into the wall. It's almost as if a lot of water ran through here at one time and then eventually lessened eating away at the rock then went down to an even smaller trickle cutting the path through. It's really crazy but I can tell this is not manmade because the rock is worn so smooth. No blasting would have left it so smooth.

At last the path ends and opens up to another room not nearly the size of the big room I came from and the ceiling is only about eight feet or so. I raise my lantern to get a better look at the room and find myself staring at gaunt white faces looking up at me from the ground.

CHAPTER 7

$\mathcal{I}$'m startled at first by this sight, until I recognize that these are the workers I saw earlier. They have blankets and makeshift beds arranged around the inner part of the cave wall. They are just as surprised to see me.

"Soxy!" I hear a little voice whisper from across the room, and a small girl runs over to the cat and picks him up protectively.

"His name is actually Boots," I say, unsure of what else to say to her or any of these people.

"Where did you get the light?" asks a man standing up and coming toward me. He is tall, skinny, gaunt, and doesn't look like he has the strength to hurt a fly, but I back away anyway.

"I took it from the big room," I say.

"Who are you?" asks a boy, getting up from his bed.

"Are you from the camp?" asks a woman who looks like she hasn't eaten in days.

"I'm AB'Gale, but you can call me Abby," I say naturally.

"Oh you're that girl they're looking for, the one they lost in the caves," says another man standing in the back of the cave.

"Yea, I guess it's me. I got away. You're not going to tell, are you?" I ask.

"Are you kidding? Why would we? They've been keeping us here for months, always leaving us in the dark so we can't find our way out. Once I tried to steal a light like you did but I got caught and they whipped me," says the man in the back.

"Now they frisk us every time so we can't even smuggle extra food," says the woman closest to me.

"You need to get out of here," I say, mostly in thought.

"Yes but we can't, even with the light. They have the entrance guarded, and we don't have the strength to fight them," says the man who first came close to me.

"Then that cat came in and I don't know how it got past those guards but it got me to thinking maybe there's another way outa here," says another man, sitting in his bed.

"There is, I think. Before they caught me, we came across a hole in the ground where some foul smelling smoke came out, the same smoke that comes from your pots. It might be another way out," I say.

"Well how're we gonna find it?" asks the man on the floor.

"We need a plan. First things first, Stephen go by the door and listen for any footsteps coming," says the man nearest me.

"Yes sir," says a gangly boy from the other side of the room, and rushes past me to get into position.

"Now Miss Abby my name is Mr. Tyler, and this my wife, Mrs. Tyler," says the man nearest me, pointing to a quiet women I hadn't even noticed to my right. She nods to me, and I nod back.

"That boy Stephen is my son and the girl there with your cat is my Lucy," he says. The little girl smiles at me and I feel a stab of pain as I am reminded of the little girl Freckles called Sassy Frassy at the workinhouse.

"Over here is Mr. Penn," continues Mr. Tyler with the

44

introductions, "and his wife Mrs. Penn and their boy Rodger. Mr. Knox over there in bed, and his wife, Mrs. Knox," he says.

They all say hello or nod to me and I note there are about twelve in all of men, women, and children, but I don't hear all the names Mr. Tyler is saying. I'm suddenly aware of how odd it is to have all these families together; at the workinhouse, all the families are separated,.

"Excuse me, but, you're all families?" I ask.

"And neighbors too. It's actually a long story but we all once lived in a town together and owned businesses. One day the System just came in and took over. Anyone who owned a business was taken away, families and all. Some of us ended up here together. We don't know what happened to the town or the people that lived there," says Mr. Tyler.

"We don't have time to get into that right now. We need a plan," says Mr. Knox, coming to the center of the room and motioning both of us over.

"Do you think you can get that cat of yours to lead you to that other exit?" asks Mr. Penn.

"I don't know, but I can try," I say, looking doubtfully at Boots. Cats really do what they want to do when they want to do it. They're not like dogs at all. On the other hand, I have come to realize that Boots is no ordinary cat, so maybe I can reason with him.

I look around now and see that everyone has come to the center of the room and is listening intently or giving out ideas of what to do. One man suggests that we wait another day or two to devise a real plan, but Mr. Tyler shoots him down right away.

"No George, we need to get out of here now. If we wait something is bound to happen to ruin our plans," says Mr. Tyler.

Several people nod in agreement.

"Besides," I say, "I'm certainly not staying another day here."

"Ok, first things first," says Mr. Tyler. "We need to go commandeer some more lanterns."

"If one goes we all go," says Mr. Knox.

"That will make too much noise," says Mrs. Penn.

"We will all be quiet then. I'm not staying here another minute," says Mrs. Knox.

"Ok, we all go to the main room, get the other lanterns, and find another way out, we hope. If we do, then we can sneak around back to the camp," says Mr. Tyler.

"Why in tarnation would we want to do that?" asks another man. I think his name is Mr. Ferris.

"Because we need supplies. We can't just go traipsing off into the woods with our families in such poor condition and not expect to be caught. We need food and other supplies," says Mr. Tyler.

"This whole plan is crazy. We should wait," says Mr. Ferris.

"For what, Tom? What are we waiting for but this little girl here? She has brought us light and hope. She managed to get away in the dark, get light, and find us," says Mr. Tyler.

"Yeah, you're right. Let's get outa here, even if we have to fight our way out," says Mr. Ferris, agreeing.

With me in the lead and Lucy with Boots behind Mr. Tyler, then the rest, we all leave the room as quietly as thirteen people possibly can. We make it down to the main room and the men scatter about, collecting lanterns and tools as quickly as possible. When everyone is ready, I turn to Lucy who has been cradling Boots in her arms the whole time.

"Lucy, you have to put Boots down now so he can lead us out,"

I say. Boots comes over to me and rubs up against my legs and I reach down and pet him.

"Boots, we need to leave this place now. Can you show us another way out?" I ask the cat in all earnest. Boots just sits down and starts primping himself. I'm not going to let this cat make me look stupid or detour me from getting out of this place, though.

I grab a handful of ash and walk around the edge of the walls. As I do, I drop a little ash and watch to see if a breeze hits it. I feel like everyone is just standing there watching me and I look to see that a lot of them are, but some of the men, including Mr. Tyler, have their heads together talking very quietly, probably making up a new plan. I don't blame them. The whole idea that a cat could lead us out of this dark cave is really farfetched. I turn back to what I'm doing when I actually see the ash float away on a slight breeze.

I move closer to the rock wall to inspect when a blur of black fuzz goes darting up the rocks in front of me and through a hidden passage, again. I knew it. Boots knew exactly where to go, and now I do too. I run back for a lantern and climb up the rocks after Boots. It's not a hard climb, only a few feet and then a small tunnel situated behind a boulder in such a way that the entrance is not noticeable from the floor of the cavern.

The space is small, yet big enough to crawl on all fours. It's difficult with a lantern in my hand, but I do the best I can. I hear scuffling behind me and turn to see Stephen, Mr. Tyler's boy behind me.

"My dad said to follow you and see if this is the way out," he explains.

I nod my head in agreement and continue following Boots who has gone so far ahead I can barely see his little white feet.

However, since there doesn't seem to be any other direction to go at the moment, I'm sure I can't get lost. It's a long tedious crawl through the passage, and I have to stop and take a break. Stephen joins me and we both sit there panting for a moment.

"Do you think this is really the way out?" he asks.

"Oh gosh I hope so after all this crawling, but at least no one can find us here," I answer.

No sooner do I say that when we both here a noise in the tunnel behind us. I turn to look for Boots but he has gone so far ahead that I can't see him. I turn back to the other end of the tunnel where the noise is getting louder. I can only assume it's more of the workers coming, at least I hope so. I hold the lantern up so I can see but it's still so dark and the lantern so dim that it doesn't seem to do much good.

CHAPTER 8

"Should we wait and see who that is or continue on?" I ask Stephen.

"Wait, it might be my dad," says Stephen.

"So what were you mining in here anyway?" I ask.

"Bat guano to make saltpeter, you know for gunpowder," he says.

"Does it always smell so bad?" I ask.

"Ah, naw, that's the bat guano we're cooking to get the crystals out of the soil; there's tons of bat guano in the soil, I guess it's like thousands of years of the stuff," he says.

"You mean there's bats in here?" I ask looking around.

"Oh loads of them, they probably use this hole to go in and out of sometimes," he says, unconcerned.

Just then, I feel a breeze wafting down the cave with the smell of pine and cedar. "Smell that?" I ask.

"Yes, I smell it," he says excitedly.

"This must be the way out, how else could we smell pine?" I say.

"Hey kids, you find the exit yet?" asks a voice from the dark. We both turn to see Mr. Tyler crawling toward us.

"Dad, we just felt a breeze and smelled pine trees," says Stephen.

"Why did you stop then? Let's keep going and hope it's a way out," says Mr. Tyler.

"I can take the lantern for a while if you want, Abby," offers Stephen.

"It's ok, I got it. Besides, I have a feeling we are almost there," I say.

I continue moving on but with more zeal this time. I try to go as fast as I can, because being in the lead makes me nervous, and I'm afraid of going too slow. I know we have to get everybody out before we are discovered, but I'm not sure how long that is going to take once we find the way out, then crawl back and get everyone through.

Finally, I see Boots. He comes to me and touches my nose, purring gently. I stop to pet him and feel his cool fur from the night air. I can tell he has been out. I only hope the exit is big enough for a person to fit through. I pick up the lantern and keep going with Boots bounding ahead of me until suddenly he stops and looks up. I hold the lantern up and see that the tunnel continues on but above us is an opening to sky.

"Look," I say, setting the lantern down and standing up. The area is not very big around but by pushing myself against the rocks with my feet on either side, I manage to scale up about eight feet. At the top, I push my body up and through the hole until I'm out in the cool night. I feel so elated. If I never go back in another cave, again it will be too soon.

"Come on," I say, reaching my hand down and helping Stephen up and outside.

"I'll go back for the others. You two stay low and don't get caught," says Mr. Tyler.

We hear him scuffling away quickly and the light below disappears as he takes the lantern with him. We're alone with the night sky and the moon. We both lay back in silence for a moment relieved to be able to see the stars again. Boots settles himself purring on my chest, content that he has saved me I suppose. Then something occurs to me, if this is the same hole I saw earlier today, we are very close to the camp. Gently I set Boots down and roll over on my belly crawly closer to Stephen until I'm close enough to whisper to him.

"Stephen, I'm pretty sure we are very close to the camp," I say.

"Maybe we better make sure where it is so we know where danger will come from," he whispers back.

"How will they know where the hole is if we are not here to help? They may keep going and miss it," I say.

"We should leave something, a sign or mark of some sort," he says.

I think about it for a moment and then remember my scarf is still tied around my waist. I untie it and drop it down the hole then tie it off to a root sticking out. "How's that?" I ask.

"I think that will work," he says, smiling. "Now, which way?"

Looking around, I sniff the air and smell burnt wood. I gaze around, peering through the trees, and I see the ground sloping up a small hill a few feet away from us.

"That way," I say, pointing to the hill. "I remember running up a hill to get away from the men who were coming out of the trees." I turn and look behind me and see a line of trees in the darkness. I wonder for a moment why the men were in the trees and if there could be another camp. The trees give no sign of anything but stand tall and dark against the night sky.

"Come on," I say, making up my mind and cautiously head up the hill, keeping myself low to the ground in case I need to drop and hide. Stephen follows after me until we get near the top of the hill. We both get down on our bellies and crawl the rest of the way up to the top and peer over.

Sure enough, there is a camp just on the other side of the hill. I count five tents in a semicircle. I wasn't sure before because the last time I saw the camp it happened so quickly I hardly had time to register. I lean over to Stephen and whisper, "Look for guards roaming the camp." Stephen nods in understanding and we both study the camp. I don't see anyone standing or walking around. It appears that everyone has gone to bed.

"Wait here, I'm going to get a closer look," I say.

I ease myself over the hill and conceal myself with trees and bushes, as I get closer. I finally see a sentry slumped against a tree, snoring slightly, his gun lying on the ground by his side. I move away from his view and into the camp. I see two men sitting just inside the cave's entrance playing a game of cards by a dimly lit fire, their guns leaning against the wall of the cave. It's clear to me they haven't heard anything going on below or they wouldn't be playing cards right now.

Boots comes over by me and brushes up against my leg then walks casually over to the first tent. Quietly I follow, staying out of the vision of the two guards and the other one asleep by the tree, just in case. When we get to the tent, I see Boots crawl under the bottom and inside. I listen closely and hear snoring inside. Geez this is crazy, but I have to go inside after Boots., He seems to know where he is going. I lift the bottom of the tent and find that it's loose enough for me to crawl under.

Inside the tent is dark, so I wait for my eyes to adjust until I can see just enough not to trip over anything. The snoring man is in a cot on the far right side of the room and sounds like he is in a deep sleep. There's a table in the center of the room and various objects against the walls of the tent. I see Boots jump up on the table so I move over to where he is, my heart is beating so loud that if that man wasn't snoring, I'm sure he would hear it.

A sudden feeling of excitement runs through me as I see Papa's spyglass on the table. I pick it up and examine it. I'm thankful to see that they didn't figure out how to open it and the map is still inside. Relieved, I sling it over my shoulder and notice some other things on the table that are mine. In fact, it appears that the guy just emptied my whole pack out all over the table. I look around for the satchel and find it lying on the floor under the table. I silently gather my belongings, put them back in my satchel, and sling it over my shoulder as well.

The food is all gone but it looks like the rest of my things are here, including my pocketknife and the compass. I scan the room to see if there is anything else I can use. I see the man's gun belt and gun hanging on a trunk. I grab that, throw it over my other shoulder, and pick up the rifle as well. Armed to the teeth and with Boots at my heels, we peek out the tent door. The two guys in the cave are seriously into their game and it looks like they might be drinking from a bottle of something, probably whiskey.

I sneak out and head back to the hill. On my way, I pass the sleeping guard and without a thought, I lean down and grab his gun as well. He doesn't even stir, thankfully. I run as fast and as quiet as I can back over the hill where Stephen is waiting for me.

"Come on, back to the hole. I have an idea," I say to Stephen.

We run back to the hole and find that people are just now coming up through it. "Where's Mr. Tyler?" I ask.

"I'm here," he calls back up.

"I have an idea," I say. Mr. Tyler climbs up through the hole then Stephen continues to help others come up and they move away from the hole and lay low in the grass out of sight.

"It doesn't look like there are very many men here. If we could cause a distraction so loud in the cave that everyone in the camp goes running down, we might have a little time to grab some supplies and leave, but the problem is they will come after us when they discover everyone is gone," I say.

"You found guns?" he asks, pointing to the guns in my hands.

"Yes. Here," I say, handing over the guns. "I wouldn't know how to use them anyway."

Mr. Tyler motions the other men over and the four men crawl up to the hill to observe the camp. Stephen and I wait patiently along with the rest. After what seems like ages the men return and everyone gathers to hear what they have decided.

"Abby has something with her idea of a diversion," says Mr. Tyler. "Tom here will go back down and create an explosion which should cause a cave in," continues Mr. Tyler. "They have a pumper car over on the other tracks which is how they must have taken the supplies in and out of the camp to the main tracks. We will wait until the explosion lures the men into the cave, then as quick as we can the women and children will get to the pumper car while the rest of us locate supplies and get to the pumper car ourselves. Tom, we probably won't be able to wait long for you, I know it took about twenty minutes or so to crawl through that tunnel but you're going to have to make it quicker than that," says Mr. Tyler, turning to Mr. Ferris.

"Don't you worry about me, if I'm not there by the time you're ready, you go on without me, you hear?" says Mr. Ferris.

"Don't go looking for her. Tom. She's been gone too long. You know she's not alive," says Mr. Tyler, grabbing Mr. Ferris by the arm.

"Yeah, I know," Mr. Ferris says, nodding his head. Then he turns and goes back down the hole.

"Who are they talking about?" I ask Stephen quietly so no one else will hear me.

"Mr. Ferris's daughter, Janie. There was a cave in a few weeks ago. She was in the tunnel when it happened. For a while, after that we thought we could hear her crying as if she was still alive but trapped. Those men wouldn't let us try to find her or even help her. They said they would kill us all if we tried. It drove Mr. Ferris mad, I think. After two days we stopped hearing her. It was horrible," says Stephen.

"Oh jeepers. I saw a girl buried in the rubble not far from the main room where you were all working, she was dead," I say.

"It must have been Janie. She was my age. We went to school together in town," he says sadly.

I think about the girl, her face covered in dust and buried in rocks, buried alive and no one to help her as she calls out. I shiver at the thought. My mind wanders to the workinhouse and the explosion and horrors that must have occurred in there that night and I just want scream and cry. I concentrate on Granny at the oldies home and hope that she holds out until I find Papa and we can get her out. I just have to make sure I stay alive.

CHAPTER 9

"Come on," I hear Stephen whisper, snapping me out of my thoughts.

I follow the rest of them up to the hill and see everyone lying in the grass waiting. The only one missing from our group is Mr. Ferris. Even Boots has joined us along the hill line. I wonder, as I'm looking at all these people if they will have the strength to get away. They all look so pale and weak. Stephen comes up beside me.

"Hey, here's your scarf. I thought you might want it back," he whispers.

"Thanks," I whisper back and tie it back around my waist.

With so many of us here I hope the sentry doesn't hear us whispering and rustling around and wake up before Mr. Ferris has time to cause the explosion. So we wait for so long that I'm afraid it will be daylight before anything happens when suddenly I hear it and feel it: a loud thunderous sound shakes the ground beneath us, and we all hold our breath and watch to see what will happen next. The men in the camp come running out of their tents shouting at each other. The man by the tree jumps up and runs into the camp, so stunned, or maybe even afraid, that he forgets to grab for his gun, which of course is not there.

We can hear the men shouting protests as a large man, who must be the man they all referred to as Bossman, orders the men to go into the cave to find out what has happened. Even the two men who were playing cards at the entrance run back out as dust and smoke come billowing out of the mouth of the cave. Suddenly we hear a gunfire off and the shouting stops.

"Get yer lily-liver gizzards in that cave and find out what's go's on or I'll kill the lot of ya," shouts the bossman.

All the men go running in the cave, choking and coughing as they do. The bossman reloads his weapon, grabs a lit lantern, and strides in after them. Mr. Tyler puts his hand up to us to wait, just to be sure they have all gone in the cave. It will take them a while I guess to get down to the main room, assuming they can even get to the main room anymore, but we wait just a little while longer until he gives the ok. Then we all get up and run as fast as we can to the pumper car on the other side of the camp.

I run through the camp past the first tent I'd already been in without stopping. As I get to the next tent, I decide to chance it and run inside, even though Mr. Tyler said all the women and children should go to the pumper car. I understand he is trying to take care of everyone but I have to look out for myself as well. It's dark inside the tent, I listen for any sounds to be sure no one is in the tent, we saw a bunch of men run to the cave, but that doesn't mean that everyone left. I reach over and flip the tent flap back so some of the light from the night sky and the campfire comes in. The tent appears to be empty thank goodness, but I don't know what I should take or what will be useful.

I see a pair of boots on the floor and some clothes thrown over a chair. I grab those and throw them onto the blanket on the cot. Then I grab a can of lamp oil and add it to the pile. On a table there's a box of fresh made bullets. I grab those as well. I'm about to wrap all this up into the blanket when I see I a small wooden box on the floor by the bed. I look inside and find a cigar box and hunting knife, adding this to the pile I wrap it up and head out the tent with Boots running with me.

I'm disappointed there's no food in the tent but maybe the others have had better luck than I did. Whatever we don't use we can always trade. It seems to me that this is what it has come to for me: finding whatever I can along my travels to use for trade. This is an odd concept for me coming from a life where I never needed anything because I always had what I needed. I don't consider this stealing though I guess it kind of is, but these people work for the System, and they are just as cruel if sometimes not more so.

I make it to the pumper car, which turns out to be a platform of wood on top of some rail wheels very similar to a train's but a bit smaller. On the top in the middle of the platform is a double-sided handle where a person can stand one on each side and pump the rail up and down which keeps the vehicle moving. In front of the pumper car is a push car which is just another platform with wheels underneath but no pumper handles. My guess is that the men in the camp put barrels of saltpeter on the push car and then use the pumper car to push it to the main tracks and meet up with the train for loading.

The night sky is clear with stars and a bright half moon that trickles brilliant light down through the trees making it fairly easy to see. I notice that there are tools and toolboxes all over the pumper car but the push car is empty except for a couple of barrels, one on each end opposite each other. The women and children have climbed aboard the push car so I throw my blanket of stuff up on the deck and climb on too. Boots jumps up and settles himself with Lucy who, though obviously frightened, is elated to have Boots to cuddle with. In a matter of moments Mr. Tyler, Mr. Knox, Mr. Penn, and Stephen join us throwing what items they have managed to obtain onto the push car as well and then with all their strength together push until both cars start to move on their own, then they jump on and start pumping the handle. Apparently, no matter how you pump it, the direction the car goes is the direction you push it in the first place.

I look around but I don't see Mr. Ferris anywhere. I see Mr. Tyler look back behind us as well, looking for Mr. Ferris too. I catch the men all looking at each other with some sort of odd knowing look and I fear this may mean that they believe Mr. Ferris has either been caught, or killed. My heart feels a little tug even though I didn't know the man If it weren't for him, we wouldn't be getting away right now. The men pump the handles feverishly in an effort to get some distance between us and the camp as fast as possible. I'm not sure how fast this thing goes but I see the trees pass by me faster and faster until we come out into an open area briefly and around a bend. As we come around the corner, I see someone up on the hill above us running down toward us.

"Look," I cry out.

Everyone turns to see where I'm pointing. I'm afraid at first that it's one of the men from the camp, but as we get closer, I realize that it's Mr. Ferris running as fast as he can down the hill. I think the others realize that it is him too because they slow their pumping though they don't apply the brake.

"Come on Tom!" Mr. Tyler calls out.

Mr. Ferris puts more speed into his run until he makes the

tracks but is now behind us. Mr. Tyler shakes his head slightly, and applies the brakes to the pumper car slowing it down for Mr. Ferris to catch up. The push car however, still has momentum and keeps going. It occurs to me that we have no control over this thing in case something happens. I look around but all I see is a long metal bar which I have no idea what it's for.

I'm not too concerned really about how fast we're going right now because the pumper car will catch up to us. I watch as Mr. Ferris board and the men continue their pumping, but suddenly they are so very far behind us and we're going downhill now. Not sure of what else to do we all huddle close into the middle and hang onto each other, trusting we won't jump the tracks as we increase speed.

I look behind us and see the pumper car is really far behind us. They appear to be picking up speed as well, but they have more control over their speed because of the brake pedal built into the car at the base of the pumper bars. Sparks fly off their wheels as they descend the grade. There must be some sort of braking mechanism for this contraption. I look down along the deck for some sort of pedal or something I might have missed and see the metal bar again. I grab it and study it a moment.

"Everyone, look for some sort of hole or something this rod might stick down into," I say.

Everyone starts looking around and carefully moving the bags and boxes appropriated from the camp. They move slow and careful so they won't fall off as we speed dangerously down the rails.

"Here!" Mrs. Knox shouts.

I crawl to her where she is fixed near the back of the push car but in the middle looking down at the deck. I follow her gaze to an elongated hole about the length of a pencil and four inches wide. I peek through the hole and see that in the middle is a metal piece that looks like the bar fits into. I need to stand but with the speed, it's hard to balance myself. I untie my scarf partially from around my waist and hand both ends to Mrs. Knox.

"Hold onto me please and don't let me fall off," I say.

She nods at me and grabs the ends of the scarf, handing one end to Mrs. Penn so that they are in front of me on either side. Carefully I stand up using the metal rod to help me up and keep my knees bent to adjust my weight as needed, like being on a boat in bad weather. Then I stick the rod down into the fixture and pull back slowly. I remember Papa telling me stories about trains that derailed because the brakeman applied the brakes too quickly and too hard causing the wheels to jump off the tracks.

I hear the screeching of metal on metal and see sparks fly on both sides of us so I ease up a bit. I get so I alternate pressure and easing up until I feel the cart slowing gradually. Thank goodness, this is working because up ahead I see we're coming to a curve which at a high rate of speed would surely cause us to derail. If that were to happen it could be deadly as I note a landscape change and a sudden cliff drop on the left side of the tracks.

CHAPTER 10

$\mathcal{I}$ hear something behind me and I want to look back to see what it is but don't dare or I may lose control of the car. I'm pretty sure it's the pumper car. I'm not sure I have very good control of the push car as it is, but we're going a lot slower than before and I keep alternating.

All of a sudden, I feel a slight bump and nearly lose my balance. I look down at Mrs. Knox who is smiling up at me but not at me, behind me. I feel a shift in the boards beneath my feet as someone jumps onto the deck beside me, and for a brief moment I turn and see Mr. Knox next to me. Comforted by this, I turn my attention back to my job of alternating the brakes.

"Have you got this, Miss Abby?" he asks.

"I guess so," I say, unsure.

"Just hang on a bit longer and keep doing what you're doing. We are going to tie the push car to the pumper car," he says. I nod in understanding.

There is another shift in the deck and Mr. Ferris is standing beside me. He scrambles over to where Mrs. Knox and Mrs. Penn are still holding my scarf and sits down. I'm confused about what is going on as out of the corner of my eye I see Mr. Knox lay down on the deck and Mr. Ferris grab his feet. Then I understand ; this is a flat deck with nothing to tie on to so Mr. Knox is going to have to tie the rope up underneath the push car somewhere while it's moving.

Mr. Knox is bent over the edge of the push car for a very long time and I am wondering if he is having problems finding some place to tie the rope when I hear him yell, "Pull me up!"

"Pull him up!" I repeat, in case no one heard him.

Mr. Ferris pulls at Mr. Knox's legs until Mr. Knox is back on the deck and sitting next to him. Then I see him give a thumbs-up. Shortly after that, I feel another bump from the pumper car and Mr. Ferris gets to his feet and comes over to me.

"I'll take it from here, girl," he says.

Thankfully, I relinquish the brake iron to him and sit down on the deck and not a moment too soon as we come to the bend and the drop off. I close my eyes. I don't want to see if we go off it. I open my eyes to see that we have already gone around the bend but we're still traveling very close to a drop off to our left. At least the rails are straight now and we're slowing down considerably to a fairly normal pace.

After a while, the rails turn away from the cliff and back in toward the hills and the trees until we reach what appears to be the main train line. Here the tracks stop at a small wooden platform and a water tower. There's nothing else around, not even a ticket office or waiting station. My guess is this is a water stop where someone decide to make it a pickup location for the mined saltpeter. The cars come to a not-so-smooth stop, and without a word everyone gets off.

"This is a short stop so if anyone needs to do anything, now is the time," says Mr. Tyler, nodding over to a small clump of trees.

As one, all of us females get his meaning and run behind the trees to relieve ourselves since there are no outhouses anywhere. My guess is the men are doing the same somewhere else. Men have it so easy when it comes to having to go to the bathroom. It's really very unfair, I think.

After we attend to our needs, we head back to the tracks where we find the men attempting to remove the cars from the tracks and put them on the main line. Once that is done, they secure them together again, only this time putting the push car in the back of the pumper car. The women and smaller children settle back onto the push car and the men, Stephen, and myself all put our backs into pushing the cars forward until we have them at a good roll before jumping on ourselves.

Mrs. Tyler and Mrs. Knox work the pumpers as we head southeast on the steel rails at a comfortable pace. We continue this all through the night and part of the morning with everyone taking turns, including little Lucy who insists she must help too. At times when we see a curve coming on ahead, Stephen or one of the other boys will jump off and run ahead or up a hill to check the tracks for any oncoming train. Our luck holds out though and we continue until midmorning when we come to a very tall and long rail bridge over a rushing river.

The bridge reminds me of the one that Raine fell off. I wonder how Lyza and Julian are doing and if they found Raine. I look at the bridge. It looks pretty high above the water. If Raine fell of a bridge that high, the water below would have to be very deep for her to have survived. I have no idea how high this one is or how deep the water is here. I just don't want to think about all this. I don't want to think about any of this. So many people around me have died since I left home.

I realize that we are slowing down now, and I turn to see that Mr. Tyler has stopped pumping the pumper car and is applying the brake while Mr. Penn applies the hand brake to the push car as well.

"What are we doing?" I ask.

"We're stopping and getting off the tracks. Mr. Tyler has an idea," says Mr. Knox. Once the cars stop, we all get off and gather around close to Mr. Tyler to hear what he has to say.

"It's about mid-afternoon, about the time a train usually comes over this bridge. We're not sure when, but it wouldn't be good to be caught on the bridge when the train comes across," says Mr. Tyler. "Besides, I've got an idea."

"It better be a good one because you're right, we can't stay on these tracks for too much longer, and if we try going on foot they will only catch up with us," says Mr. Penn.

"Assuming they will be looking for us," says Mr. Ferris.

"Don't you think they will be?" asks Mr. Knox.

"Well the way I rigged that explosion it caused a pretty good cave-in, or at least I believe it did. I'm pretty sure they will either think we're trapped or dead in the cave," says Mr. Ferris.

"They'll be looking for someone when they see their camp ransacked though," says Mr. Tyler looking at me.

"Where did you come from anyway? Why were they looking for you?" asks Mr. Penn looking at me as well.

"It's kind of a long story really, but I don't think they know who I am. I just stumbled onto their camp. They thought I already belonged in the cave because one of them yelled at me, asking how I got out," I say.

"What do you mean who you really are?" asks Mrs. Tyler suspiciously.

"I'm no one really, I'm just looking for my papa who used to work for the railroad. When I tried to ask the railroad people about him they acted like he never worked for them. The next thing I know my granny was taken away to an oldies home and they took me to a workinhouse. The Holder of our farm got everything we owned," I say.

"Oh, I'm so sorry dear, I didn't mean to sound accusing. It sounds like your luck is as bad as ours," says Mrs. Tyler.

"Or worse," says Mrs. Penn, sympathetically putting her arm around me.

"I'm sorry to hear that, girl. Seems the System has its hands on everyone these days," says Mr. Ferris.

"What we got to do right now is get out of this area, and I have a plan," says Mr. Tyler.

"Let's hear it then," says Mr. Knox.

CHAPTER 11

"We ditch the pumper car and drag this push car down to the water. We can strip off all the metal from the frame here, fortify the deck with logs, and make raft. I reckon there should be plenty of debris caught up on the trestles down there. We can get down river faster than anything and out of this area," says Mr. Tyler.

"It's worth a try anyways," says Mr. Penn.

"If you're not going to use the pumper car, I would rather take that myself down the track to get as far as I can to Calvert. The river is not the path I need to take," I say.

"That's the Tennessee River and it goes south, but if you feel you need to take the train route then no, the river would not be your best choice at the moment," says Mr. Ferris.

"Oh dear you can't go it alone. You need to stay with us and let us take care of you," says Mrs. Knox.

"I appreciate that ma'am, but I have to find my papa. Besides I've been on my own for a while now," I say.

"Ok, understood. We will get the pumper car off the tracks for now and hide it until the train goes by. You have to wait at least until the afternoon train goes by," says Mr. Tyler.

"Ok. I can help until then," I say.

We all help remove the cars from the tracks. The men grab everything they feel useful from the pumper car and put it on the push car. Then they lay the thing on its side and cover it up with brambles and bushes to hide it from view. All the supplies are piled on the push car and we all do our best to push the car over the ground and down to the water under the bridge.

"Stephen, you and the boys run back up and do your best to cover up those grooves and tracks we made," orders Mr. Tyler.

"Yes sir," says Stephen, and he and the other two boys run up the hill.

"Ladies, if you would please get everything off the car and take inventory while the men and I strip the metal from this deck and make it into a proper raft," orders Mr. Tyler.

I help the women gather the bags and blankets of stuff off the car and begin sorting clothes, shoes, food, knives, guns and gunpowder, and various other items including the cigar box I procured myself. I start to say that the box is mine and I want to keep it when Mrs. Knox lets out a small squeal and grabs the box hugging it to her chest.

"George look!" she exclaims, holding the box up. Mr. Knox comes over to his wife and takes the box from her examining the outside very carefully. Then he opens it to reveal empty contents. Of course, the box is empty, what did they expect?. I find myself very lucky that I found all my belongings still on the table, but then the men in the camp hardly had the time to go through it all. These people have been held in captivity for I don't know how long. I guess nothing they hold dear is left except for each other, and some of them don't even have that anymore.

Mr. Knox surprises me though by flipping the box over and holding the corners and pinching. In doing this, he releases and lifts another lid and pulls out an envelope. I watch in amazement as he opens the envelope and takes out a handful of paper money and looks at it amazed himself.

"We are going to be alright, do you see that everyone? We're going to be alright," he says, kissing the wad of money and shoving it in his pocket.

"Oh not there dear, it may get wet or lost," says Mrs. Knox. "I'll put it in something where it won't get wet," she says, holding out her hand.

"Good idea," he says, taking the money back out and putting it in her hand.

"Oh George, don't you know better than to trust the women with the money?" says Mr. Tyler, jokingly. They all laugh heartily and I marvel at this.

Despite all that these people have been through, they still manage to find a little humor in life and latch onto it with a good hearty laugh. Papa told me once that everyone deals with stress differently, that some people deal with it by going into hysterical laughter. I don't think this is what he meant though. Papa said to try to find something to smile or laugh about on a daily basis to keep your heart young and your brain fresh. I'm not very sure what he meant, but I can see that laughing, even in your darkest hour, can make things seem a little lighter.

After the men strip the metal from the platform, Mr. Tyler and Mr. Penn wade out into the water while Mr. Ferris and Mr. Knox hold ropes tied around their waste. Carefully the two men wade through the water until they can't walk anymore and then they swim and pull themselves through until they get to the logs and debris caught on the bridge trestles. They then tie rope to the bigger pieces and give the signal for Mr. Ferris and Mr. Knox to pull the logs to shore. They do this a few times until they are satisfied they have enough logs for the raft.

Once back on shore the men secure four logs along the bottom of the platform deck using the holes left from the bolts they took out removing the wheel hardware. Then they secured two more logs one on each side and then slipped in any pieces of wood they can find laying around to make it all snug. Stephen finds the antlers of a deer and with some tree bark tied in, branches, and strips of cloth, Mr. Knox creates a piece to help steer the raft.

The women and I organize and put together food, clothing, blankets, and such in the two barrels that are left on the push car and then put the lids on so that nothing will fall out or get wet. I'm just amazed at what these people have accomplished on so little, relying on each other for ideas and help to make it all work.

"Here dear, you take these for yourself," says Mrs. Tyler, handing me three cans of food.

"Thank you," I say, putting the cans in my satchel.

"You will need a blanket too, since you managed to take this one yourself, it's only fair you should have it," says Mrs. Penn, handing me the blanket I had stashed everything in from the tent.

"Thank you, I had one, but I guess those men at the camp took it," I say.

"Since you were the one to find the box too I think it only fair that you should be rewarded, not to mention that it was you who saved us from that place. So here's twenty dollars," says Mrs. Knox, handing me some money.

"Oh no ma'am, I couldn't take that much, you're going to need that," I say.

"You have no idea how much was in that box, besides really, if it weren't for you, who knows how long we would have been down there?" says Mrs. Tyler.

"Thank you," I say, and turn my head because I don't want them to see me cry. I don't know why I feel this way but suddenly I feel like showing my emotions to anyone is a sign of weakness and I don't want to be weak. If they see I'm weak, maybe they won't let me go and I have to go. I can't go with these people, as nice as they are. I have to find Papa and get my family back.

In the distance, I hear that sound, the sound that haunts me and sooths me at the same time always. The sound of a train whistle as it releases its steam pressure and nears the bridge. We all duck under the bridge, throwing branches and leaves over our stuff so that no one will notice it. I'm not really sure how much attention anyone from a train pays to what is below or at the bottom of a bridge, or if they can even see that far down but it is better to be safe than sorry, so we hide and wait for the train to cross over.

CHAPTER 12

The sound of a train as it goes over the tracks is usually a soothing comforting sound, clickety-clack, clickety-clack. When you're inside the train like in a boxcar, add that sound with a sort of whooshing as the wind blows across. However, under a bridge listening to the train cross overhead is a horrible loud and frightening sound that just makes me want to scream. After what feels like an eternity, the train is finally gone and we can get on with our travels, only this is where we must part ways.

I like these people just fine but they're not my family and they have their own worries to think about. I've lost too much time already, and I have to get back on my way to Calvert. Then on to the Nashville train station to take a train through Knoxville and Maryville, which will take me to Bryson City, my destination and, I hope, answers. It's a long journey but better than walking the whole way.

As I say goodbye to everyone, I feel an obligation to fulfill and give closure to someone who desperately needs it. If I don't do this, Mr. Ferris will always wonder and fret over it. I go up to Mr. Ferris and with a knot in my stomach I take his hand.

"Mr. Ferris, I should have told you sooner but I didn't know until Stephen told me about your daughter, and there just wasn't time. I saw her in the cave, but she wasn't alive," I say.

"I think I knew that deep down," he says.

"But she did look peaceful," I lie. I don't know why I lie to him. I guess because no one wants to hear that their loved one is covered in rocks and dirt with a look of agony on their face. I know I wouldn't.

"Thank you, thank you so much for letting me know," he says with tears in his eyes.

I say my goodbyes to everyone and Mr. Tyler and Mr. Knox walk up the hill with me to the pumper car to help me get it back on the tracks. It's a little heavy and awkward and they want to be sure I get it on the tracks right before crossing the bridge, which is something I'm very nervous about doing.

Crossing a railroad bridge in a train can be scary enough in itself. Even walking across them is very intimidating because if you miss your footing you can break a leg or fall. However, taking this pumper car across is a completely different matter, although Mr. Tyler says it's a lot safer than it looks. I maybe if I just don't look down and concentrate on the other side I should be ok.

"Now remember, just push, pull, push, pull. Got it?" asks Mr. Tyler after we have the car on the rails.

"Yes sir, I got it thank you," I answer.

"I still don't like letting you go off by yourself, a young lady all alone," says Mr. Knox.

"She'll be fine, remember she's the one wandering around in the dark cave while those bumbling idiots couldn't find her. I think you got some smarts, Miss Abby, mind you keep to them and be wary of strangers," says Mr. Tyler.

"Have you got some sort of weapon for protection?" asks Mr.

Knox.

"I've got a pocket knife," I say, taking out the knife I had retrieved from the tent the night before and showing them.

"That's a good knife and you could do some damage with it if you stabbed someone in the eye or throat, but you're too close to danger if you're doing that," says Mr. Knox.

"Mr. Knox is right, you should have some sort of weapon to protect yourself," agrees Mr. Tyler.

"I picked up this Derringer in one of the tents, I'm not sure where its twin is, since they usually come in pairs, but anyway, this is a good weapon for protection, and I think you should take it," says Mr. Knox.

"Oh no, I couldn't. I've never shot a gun before," I say.

"It's not hard, these guns were made for women really. To load this you need to first half-cock the gun on the first notch, then pour about 15 to 20 grains of powder in the barrel, then take this little patch of material and place it around the ball and put it in the barrel," says Mr. Knox, showing me as he does this.

"Then take this rod off the side here and ram it down in the barrel, this makes sure you have a tight fit with no air. If there is any air inside it will misfire and you could get hurt. Then you take these little copper caps and put one here on this tube, and the gun is loaded and ready to fire. Keep it half-cocked to prevent the hammer from falling if the trigger were bumped accidentally. All you have to do to fire the gun is pull the hammer all the way back, aim, and squeeze the trigger," he says, showing me without actually firing the gun.

"Thank you, but I'm sure I won't need to use it," I say.

"Just the same, we will feel more comfortable knowing that you have it with you," says Mr. Tyler.

"And don't go putting it in your bag where you have to dig it out, that's no good, and it could cost you your life," says Mr. Knox.

"Keep it in your boot or pocket where you can get to it easy," says Mr. Tyler.

"Ok, I will," I say, putting the gun in my boot.

"You will need these too," says Mr. Knox, handing me a little tin and a small bag.

"Thank you," I say, taking the items. I look in the tin and see several brass caps and some small lead balls and pieces of round cotton, and the bag containing gunpowder. I put these in my satchel and sling it over my shoulder along with Papa's spyglass. Boots jumps up onto the pumper car and settles himself down on the blanket Mrs. Penn gave me.

"You be careful on those tracks young Miss, if you hear a train you ditch the pumper car straight away," says Mr. Tyler.

"I will. You be careful on that river. It looks dangerously fast," I say, looking down at the water and thinking of Raine.

"Don't you worry about us, we'll be fine. Now off with you. It's getting late in the day," says Mr. Tyler.

"Right then, goodbye," I say. They both give me a hard push while I pump the handle on the pumper car down the tracks and start over the bridge.

At first, I feel ok, a little scared to be on my own again, but maybe it's just loneliness. I try and think about other things as I make my way over the bridge; I think about how they are going to be and if it will be safe for them to travel down the Tennessee river in that makeshift raft they made. I think Mr. Tyler and Mr. Penn may have over done the whole log thing and tied too many sticks and logs to the deck. At least it will float, though. I truly believe that.

I have a pretty good rhythm going with this pumper car and I think I'm halfway across the bridge now when I make the big mistake of looking down. Suddenly I feel a sickening panic spread throughout my body. I know this makes no sense because I'm safe as long as I stay on the pumper car which shouldn't come off the tracks unless I make it. But what if I lean too much one way, or if there is something on the tracks like a rock, and then the pumper car will jump the tracks and I will go off the bridge.

I just have to think about something else to get my mind off my fear. The first thing that pops into my mind is Joey and the time I crossed the giant tree trunk over Willow's Stream. It seemed so far up, and the water had been going so fast below us. Joey kept hold of my hand as we walked across, talking about funny things like the different sounds the birds make and where we can find a beehive for some honey. I figured it out later that he was just trying to keep my mind off the idea of falling until we were all the way across.

I almost kissed him that day except for the fact that I was only eight, he was nine, and boys didn't like to be kissed by girls then. Funny how that changes when you get older. I wonder what Joey is doing now, and if he misses me at all. Sometimes I wish he were here with me. What if he had been home that day I went to his house, the day his mom turned me in to the Crushers? If he had been home she wouldn't have done that. He would have stopped her, or he would have helped me get away. Maybe he would have run away with me to help me find Papa.

"Oh Joey, I miss you so much," I say aloud. I feel the tears streaming down my face. I look down and realize that I'm on the other side of the bridge. I didn't even remember getting here because I was thinking of Joey. Even if he is not here with me, he is still helping through my memories of him. Who knows, maybe someday after I find Papa and we get Granny, we can go back for Joey too, if he hasn't already found himself another girl.

I press on through the rest of the day, only stopping to take a drink of water from the canteen Momma Sampson had given me. The pumper car has good momentum so it just keeps rolling for a while on its own. I pour some water in my hand for Boots to drink too and then get back to work keeping the thing going.

I notice I'm getting blisters on my hands but I can't let that stop me. Twilight has set in and it will be dark soon. I thought I'd be in Calvert by now. I don't want to be walking in the dark, but on the other hand, I don't want to sleep here in the wilderness alone. I have Boots with me but he is hardly a match for a bear or a panther, and I'm not sure about using this gun.

Papa never had a gun, or least I never knew of him having one. It's not as if he was against them I don't think. I guess he just never thought to show me how to use one if I ever needed to. He showed me how to make things and to use my wits but I don't think Papa ever realized how much I would have to rely on every little thing I know to stay alive. But that's what I'm going to do, stay alive just like I know Papa is doing wherever he is.

CHAPTER 13

As the night sky sets in I can see there are lights on the horizon, which means I'm close to Calvert. I put a little more effort into pumping even though my arms ache, but if I can just get into the city then I can get some rest. Maybe I can even take some of this money and get a bed at an inn.

I'm almost into town when I hear the train whistle so soft and pretty and I hang on its every note until I suddenly realize this means danger. That train whistle means there's a train coming down the tracks and I'm on the tracks. I stop pumping and apply my foot to the brake pedal, slowly at first, then with a bit more urgency when I hear the train whistle coming closer.

I could just jump off with Boots but I don't want to leave the pumper car on the tracks. I have to stop the pumper car and get it off the tracks. If I don't the train might derail, and people would get hurt if it's a passenger car, and it would be my fault.

I see sparks flying at either side of me as the brakes dig into the steel rails until at last the pumper car comes to a stop. Boots is already jumping off as I throw the blanket aside and drop my satchel and Papa's spyglass on the ground by the blanket. Then I go back to the pumper car and try to move it from the tracks but it's too heavy for me to move.

I sit down, brace myself, and push hard with my legs until I manage to rock the pumper car off the tracks. I jump up with a struggle and pull it away from the tracks and into a clump of bushes so it's not easily seen. My heart is thumping and I'm sweating and panting but I manage to grab my stuff and Boots and jump behind some trees so no one from the train can see me as it passes by.

I wait for the train to pass and to catch my breath before I start out in the dark with Boots following at my heels. We walk the rest of the way into Calvert. The only thing on my mind is where to sleep tonight. My stomach makes a growling sound. Maybe I need to think about eating something too.

Calvert is nothing like I expected; I guess I didn't really know what to expect, but Calvert is by no means a big city. In fact, Calvert is probably the same size as Jasper. I keep to the shadows even though it's night time, just to avoid attention, but then a young girl with a cat following her into town really does scream attention.

I'm fortunate that I go unnoticed through the town; I guess it must be suppertime as there are very few people out in the street. I hear some noises from a building that turns out to be a diner filled with people, laughing, drinking, and eating. I stop and watch them for a moment through the window, reminiscing. I don't stay long but leave before someone sees me; I don't want someone thinking I'm some kind of beggar.

I pass a couple of shops that are closed and see a livery across the street. The thought of going into a livery now gives me the shivers; I can still see the face of the dead girl lying by the well when the wind blew the tarp back. It scares me to think that I could have been that crazy man's next victim. I feel dizzy and stop to steady myself against the building for a moment. I must be hungry. I can't recall the last time I actually ate.

I survey the street ahead of me and see the train depot. I look around to make sure no one is watching me and quickly make my way to the depot. I'm not surprised to find the ticket booth closed. Papa told me that small towns don't keep their depot manned all the time unless they are expecting a train. This means they're not expecting a train anytime soon, which is not good for me since I need to get on going south. I really don't want to hang around a small town.

"Need to catch a train, dear?" asks a female voice startling me.

"I turn to see a young woman, maybe only five or six years older than me standing on the other side of the street at the post office.

"Yes ma'am," I say politely.

"Well they closed the office for the night. The northbound train just left about half an hour ago and the southbound train won't come through until morning," she says as she turns and locks the door behind her.

"Oh, ok, thank you," I say. I look around wondering what to do with myself that doesn't look suspicious.

"There is an inn over on the next street behind the post office. Mrs. Drear is very nice and doesn't charge too much for her rooms," says the woman.

"Thank you, that sounds very nice," I say, thinking that a nice comfortable bed would be great.

"It's the big blue house, you can't miss it," the woman says smiling.

"Thank you again. Have a good evening," I say.

"Likewise," she says, as she heads into town.

I walk over to the next street and find a row of houses that all look the same except for one. A big blue house with white ornate trim dominating the center of the right side of the street. I go up the walkway lit by oil lamps on poles and lined with various flowers and plants some of which are giving off a delightful aroma. I step up the three wide stairs to the porch, and smooth my skirt down, adjust my jacket, and try to fix my hair so I look somewhat presentable.

"Boots, go hide yourself somewhere and I will get you in a little later," I say, turning to the cat.

He stops walking and sits down on the walkway for a moment looking at me as if trying to read my mind or something, I'm not really sure what goes on in a cat's mind, but I would love to know what he is thinking. Somehow, he understands me, I think, because he takes off into the bushes acting as if he is chasing something.

I pull a cord hanging by the door and hear the sound of bells chiming in the house. It's not long before an older woman, about Granny's age, comes to the door and opens it.

"Yes, can I help you?" asks the lady.

"The woman at the post office said you might have a room for rent? I need to catch the train but it doesn't come through until tomorrow," I quickly explain.

"Of course dear, I have a room, come on," she says, opening the door wide.

I enter the house and gaze admiringly at the beautiful wallpaper with painted flowers in multiple colors that makes me feel like I'm walking through a garden. A small table stands in the center with a tall vase filled with lavender. Sconces with fanned glass are mounted by each door of which I count three, not including the front door. I'm thinking this house is too fancy to be an inn, anyone who has the kind of money it takes to decorate just the entrance to their house like this must have a fair bit of money.

"I have a room in the attic I can rent the room to you for fifty cents a night, another ten cents if you want breakfast. If you want a hot bath that's another ten cents and clothes laundered will be twenty cents," says the lady.

"Yes ma'am, I'll take it all and some supper, if you have any," I say.

"So a dollar even then. Up front, if you please," she says.

"Sounds fair. Will I have my clothes in time to make it to the train station tomorrow?" I ask.

"I can have them washed tonight and they may be a bit damp tomorrow but they will at least be clean," she says.

"Thank you very much," I say, as I dig out a dollar from my bag, careful not to show her how much money I really have.

"I'm Mrs. Drear. Come with me and we will find you something to wear while I get your clothes washed," she says.

I follow Mrs. Drear through the door to the right, which appears to be a sitting room in the front part of the house with the most beautiful red velvet couch and two matching chairs facing a large wood mantle fireplace with carved animal heads. Above the fireplace hangs one of the biggest mirrors I've ever seen, but I'm not sure why anyone would hang a mirror so high you can't even look in it. The walls are covered with more wallpaper but this time there are little pictures of hunting parties on horseback. On the floor are red and black braided rugs a large rug in the middle of the room and one smaller version under each chair.

Small wood tables with marble tops dot the room some having little oil lamps with glass covers set in the middle of the tables.

The back part of the room is dominated by a wide staircase, with dark wood railings and polished stairs. Mrs. Drear walks up the stairs and I follow behind, running my hand along the smooth banister as we go up. Abruptly a young girl who looks to be only eight years old or so hurries down the stairs and stops suddenly at seeing us ascending. She has beautiful blond curls that dangle haphazardly to her shoulders and she is dressed in a tight gingham dress to her ankle boots with a full white apron over her dress.

"Adie! I've told you not to run down these stairs, and you're to use the kitchen stairs anyway," says Mrs. Drear.

"Yes'm," says the girl Adie.

"Now finish whatever it is you're doing and then go make a hot bath in the back bathroom. We have a guest who is in need of a bath right away," Mrs. Drear says, turning to me feigning a faint smile. The little girl nods and continues down the stairs.

"And take the kitchen stairs next time!" yells Mrs. Drear. "I declare it's difficult to find a good helper with manners," she adds and then continues up the stairs.

I don't comment but continue up the stairs after her until we reach the landing where a table is set with two small oil lamps but only one is used to light the hallway. Mrs. Drear carefully removes the lamp covers of both and lights the other lamp with the one already lit. Then she places the covers back on, and picks up the lamp and continues walking to her right. We walk down a hallway past four doors to the end of the hall and a smaller door with glass panes, centered in the wall. Mrs. Drear opens the door and goes up another flight of stairs only much narrower than the other stairs and not as ornate or polished but simple wooden stairs between two walls.

I follow and as we reach the top, she offers me her hand and pulls me up to the floor level of the attic. The attic is dark and the oil lamp casts unearthly shadows along the walls. We walk past boxes, old furniture and several trunks until she gets to one large trunk in particular and hands me the lamp.

"Would you hold this, please?" she asks. I reach out wordlessly and take the lamp from her as she flips open the latches and lifts the lid to the trunk revealing piles of clothing inside.

"These clothes belonged to my daughters when they were growing up, I only use them for the help now so feel free to rummage through for whatever you need," she says.

"Thank you ma'am," I say looking down at my clothes. I hadn't noticed before, but now even in the dark I can see they are covered in dirt and mud from crawling and climbing through the caves. What a sight I must be., I look at Mrs. Drear who I know can only be wondering what I have been doing.

CHAPTER 14

"I had to do a bit of traveling on foot," I say. "I'm not much used to that so I must have fallen a few times." This is not in any way a lie, so I don't feel bad in telling her any of this. I don't know this lady, so I have no idea if she can be trusted.,

To my relief Mrs. Drear just nods at me in what I think is an understanding look and then walks to the front of the attic where there is a door open to a room. I follow her inside the room where she lights another lamp. The room is small and tucked into the eaves of the roof but still large enough to stand upright in. Two single beds with a small table between them line the wall on the right. The table only holds a candle and a small decorative dish. On the left is a wash table with a slender mounted mirror and little shelves on each side for toiletries, and a small hook with a towel. In the center of the table is the washbasin and pitcher that sit empty.

"I'll get Adie to bring you some fresh water," says Mrs. Drear motioning to the washbasin. "The bed sheets are clean and fresh, and though I don't think you will need it on a warm night like this, there are extra blankets in the trunk under the window."

She points to a dormer window at the front of the house that at the moment has dark curtains drawn across it. Up here, the walls are not ornately covered but simply painted white with a couple of scenery paintings hung on each side of the window. The other two walls are slanted so I imagine nothing can be hung properly from them. The floor is bare unpolished wood with several dark braided rugs to cover as much of the wood as possible; the rugs on the floor I suppose so no one will get splinters in their bare feet.

"There is no water closet up here but there is a chamber pot under the bed if you need to go in the middle of the night and don't feel like maneuvering the stairs," says Mrs. Drear.

"This will be great, thank you ma'am I'm sure I will be very comfortable here," I say.

"Good then, find yourself some clothes and I will check on your bath and my other guests. Your bath will be down these stairs and the first door on your left. I will make sure Adie is there to see if you need anything else," says Mrs. Drear, and then she turns and leaves.

She seems like a nice lady but there is something about her that is not necessarily cold but not altogether warm either. She just seems kind of, matter-of-fact like and to the point. I get another feeling from her as well that I can't put my finger on. It worries me a little that she doesn't ask any questions, though that's a good thing, but curiosity is natural and she hasn't even asked me where I'm from. It's almost as if she already knows and that kind of creeps me out a bit. As usual, I will just have to be on guard.

I go to the trunk and start rummaging through the clothes looking for something to wear after my bath. The thought of a nice hot path is so wonderful to me since I have not had one in a while. It'll be nice to be clean again. Being on the road, I don't have much of a chance to get cleaned up as often as I would like, maybe that doesn't bother some people but it sure bothers me.

I find a long white nightgown that looks to be about my size which should do nicely after my bath and I set that aside. I inspect the contents further and find a brown plaid skirt I think will fit and a matching top coat. Together these would look more like traveling clothes, and though they would be hotter this time of year to wear, they would be good for when it gets cold. I set them aside as well, and I keep looking through finding several underpinnings that look like they will fit me including a chemise, pantaloons, and stays, which I hated when Granny made me wear mine. Now I'm thinking I could use one on occasion. I also find a petticoat, which only comes to my ankles but flares a bit so if I wore it with the skirt it would give it a nice full look. I add a pair of stocking to my pile and then look through in the hopes of finding some shoes my size. On the very bottom of the trunk is about five or six pairs of shoes but only one pair catches my eye.

A dainty pair of pointed ankle boots that lace up. So pretty and so much more ladylike than the boy boots I've been wearing since I left the workinhouse. I sit down and take off one of my boots to try on the new ones. I'm delighted to find they fit beautifully. I take the boots off and set the pair by my pile. I close the trunk, and gather all the items and place them on the bed. It seems like I have a lot of things on the bed from that trunk, and I wonder if I've taken too much. She did say 'take what you need,' didn't she? I don't think I will be able to fit all this in my bag but I will work out something I'm sure. I head downstairs in anticipation of a hot bath.

I find Adie waiting for me in the bathroom that is a small

room with a sink, a toilet and a deep bathtub with feet on the end of it that look like animal claws. The tub is filled full of water and I can tell it's hot by the steam rising off the top of it. Adie is holding some towels in her arms and smiles sweetly at me.

"Hello Adie, thank you," I say.

"You're welcome Miss," says Adie. "Do you need anything else?" she asks.

"No, not right now, I think I have what I need," I say.

"Ok. There's soap in a basket on the table there and that blue bottle has special perfume soap for your hair. The Mrs. has that for her guests, she don't let none of use that," she says, handing me the towels.

"Who else works here?" I ask.

"There's Ms. Mary who cooks and does the laundry and clean' in' of the house, and I help her. Then there's Mr. Joe who does all the yard work and the house fixing and then there's the boy who Mrs. Drear just calls boy. He helps Mr. Joe, he's only six though, but he gets to ride with Mr. Joe when he takes the guests in the steam carriage on picnics or wherever they want to go. He has to be the step boy, where he puts the step down for the people to get out of the car," says Adie.

"Wow, that sounds like a big job, I wonder why Boy doesn't have a name though? Does he get paid like the rest of you?" I ask.

"Paid? Ain't none of us get paid Miss, we all from the System. Mrs. Drear got a deal work'n so she has a lot of big railroad people come through here and stay so the System let her have people to work here to help," says Adie.

"Oh," is all I can say to this at the moment.

"We got it better than some I guess though because we have a little house we got in the back to stay in and it's warm. Mrs. Drear makes sure we get food, and after everybody else has had supper we get the leftovers, and she got trunks of clothes in her attic we can have clothes from. It's not bad, she don't beat us or nuth'n'. I just miss my family, and I think Boy does too cause he cries at night," says Adie.

"Adie, are you supposed to be telling me all this?" I ask.

"No, ma'am," says Adie, looking down at her shoes.

"Don't worry, I won't say anything, but you should remember to be careful what you say and to who," I say. "If you make Mrs. Drear mad she may send you away and this does look like a good place to be instead of a workinhouse," I say.

"Yes, ma'am, your right," says Adie brightening.

"Ok, well I'm going to take my bath now, maybe we can talk later," I say smiling at her reassuringly.

"Ok. I'm supposed to take your clothes downstairs to wash right now," says Adie.

"Right, just a minute," I say setting the towels down on a stool and going behind a changing screen standing at the corner of the bathtub. I hand Adie everything, even my undergarments and she leaves, closing the door behind her. Now I have nothing but the nightgown and undergarments and towels. I do still have the satchel with my personals and Papa's spyglass that I keep with me always, but a quick get away in a nightgown would not be desirable to me. However, I feel comfortable that I'm safe here so I turn my attention to the enticing bath.

CHAPTER 15

$\mathcal{G}$ingerly I step into the hot bath and immerse myself head and all into the water, enjoying every tingly sensation the heat creates on my skin. Hot water to me equals clean and that is what I want to be, clean. The first thing I do is reach for the hair soap and uncork the bottle. The smell of roses blooms forth from the container. I lather up a good amount in my hair and rinse it several times. Then I get the soap from the basket and smell it; it's not lye soap but lavender and honey smelling perfumed soap that lathers up soft bubbles. After I clean every inch of my body I lie back in the water to relax, smelling the flowery soaps permeate the room.

I reflect on the things Adie said now that I have time to think on them. So Mrs. Drear makes money from her boarding house and doesn't have to pay anyone wages because these are all System workers. It seems to me that there is something wrong with this; she could be helping honest people who need to work to keep their families together and their homes by paying wages, yet she chooses to profit off their hard luck instead.

Despite the fact that they're no longer with their families, I have to believe that Adie and Boy and the other workers here really don't have it so bad as I did or thousands of other people for that matter. Despite how I think Mrs. Drear is wrong, she is at least being kind in some way. On the other hand, I now understand why I have a strange feeling about her. I don't feel safe here now even though I paid, she might know who I am. After all didn't Adie say she works with the railroad and a lot of big railroad people come through here. Maybe this is a chance to ask someone about Papa? But then maybe this is not a good situation, as I recall what happened in New Joplin when those railroad men found out I was Bishop Steel's daughter. They almost had me taken away right then.

I'm not sure what to do and I have to think things through more carefully but not on an empty stomach. I reluctantly get out of the bath, dry off, and wrap my hair. I put on the nightgown which falls all the way down to the floor so far I almost trip on it. Mrs. Drear's daughters must be awfully tall if I'm stepping on the nightgown and half to hold it up when I walk. I'm five feet and six inches last time Papa checked my height but whoever wore this nightgown must have been at least six feet tall. I thought Mrs. Drear said her daughters grew out of these clothes. If they did, they must be really tall now.

In the hallway, I hear voices downstairs of men talking and laughing. I can't make out what they are saying but I'm guessing these are some of Mrs. Drear's other guests. The smell of cigar smoke floats lightly on the air and I can just imagine a group of railroad suits sitting in the parlor smoking cigars and drinking Brandi while they tell stories of how they make their millions to each other. Well I don't want to be part of that, besides I'm in a nightgown, not appropriate to be seen by strangers in my nightclothes so I don't have to be polite and go downstairs to meet anyone.

I'm about to go up to my room when I hear a noise and see Adie coming up the stairs with a tray of food. She stops at the landing as if unsure for a moment and then walks over to me. "Mrs., Drear said you would want your food in your room since we was washing your clothes," she says.

"Yes of course, I can take the tray from here," I say.

"It's ok, I supposed to do it," she says.

"Ok, then let's go," I say, leading the way to the attic stairs.

When I get to the landing, I hold the tray of food while Adie climbs up and then she dutifully takes it again. We walk through the maze of trunks and boxes to the room and Adie puts the tray down on the table next to the bed. She looks over at the pile of clothes I found in the trunk and smiles.

"I told you she gots lots of clothes in trunks," she says.

"Oh, well she told me I could rummage through to find what I needed since my clothes are being washed," I said. "I wasn't sure if I needed to get fully dressed or not or when my clothes would be clean and dry," I quickly add.

"It don't matter she gots so many trunks of clothes here she won't miss nuth'n if you keep it anyway," says Adie.

"Oh I wasn't going to take anything without offering to pay but then she did say to take what I needed. She said she didn't need them anyway since her daughters grew out of them," I say, a little defensively.

"Daughters? Mrs. Drear don't have no daughters. She only gots a son and he works for the railroad. He comes by every now and then to see if she needs anything, she's a widow but she don't want everyone to know it so she says her husband is away on business a lot," says Adie.

"Oh, I must have misunderstood what she said then," I say. "I thought she said she had some daughters, my mistake."

"Do you need anything else tonight?" asks Adie.

I look at the tray of food and think a moment. "Can I have a cup of warm milk? It helps me sleep when I'm in strange places," I say.

"Ms. Mary is all done cookin' for the night but I can get that for you," she says. She hurries out the door and down the stairs and I'm hoping I don't get her into trouble by asking for warm milk. But, I am a paying guest, so why should that be trouble?

Before I even consider eating, I go to the window and open it up. The cool night air comes through with the scent of flowers. Softly I whisper because I know cats have good ears, "Boots, kitty, kitty, up here Boots."

I hope it is not too hard for him to find his way up onto this roof but I don't think it will be, after all he managed to get up to my window somehow when I was at the workinhouse so this should be a lot easier. I sit down on the bed next to the table and investigate what Adie brought me; my meal that consists of meatloaf, potatoes, green beans, three rolls, some butter, and a tall glass of lemonade. I eat everything except two of the rolls that I put in my bag and some of the meatloaf which I set aside for Boots on the windowsill. Maybe the smell of meatloaf will help him find his way to the window since he hasn't made it to me by the time I've finished my meal.

I hear someone coming up the stairs and its Adie carrying a teacup and saucer, which she hands to me triumphantly. "I didn't spill a drop," she says. "But it took a while because I had to clean up after I was done making it so Mrs. Drear and Ms. Mary wouldn't be mad at me."

"That's fine, thank you so much for your trouble," I say.

"You're very welcome. You know, you are a lot nicer than other people who come here who just order me around," says Adie.

"Just because you have to work here doesn't mean people shouldn't be nice to you, but don't expect it Adie. I'm sorry to say there are a lot of mean people in the world, but you are in a better place than you could be," I say.

Just then, my attention is drawn to a sound at the window. I get up from the bed and cautiously go to the window and pull the curtain back. Boots is sitting there priming himself and the meatloaf I left on the sill is gone. I scoop him up in my arms and carry him over to the bed.

"Adie, I would like you to meet my friend Boots. Boots, this is my friend Adie," I say, setting Boots down on the bed. Then I take the teacup and saucer from Addie's hands and put it down on the table, because I know what comes next.

"Oh my, he's beautiful. May I pet him?" she asks excitedly.

"If he allows you, which I'm sure he will," I say, with a slight laugh.

She sits down on the bed and reaches out to him. Boots is immediately in her lap and purring while Adie pets him, oohing and awing as she does. Boots has such a way with children. It's as if he knows he is the most favorite thing in the world to them and he allows them to hold and hug and pet him as long as they are not too rough with him. Something about cats sooths and relaxes people and brings joy to children, almost like a tonic.

"You know Mrs. Drear would have a fit if she knew he was in here," she says.

"I kind of figured that, so I just didn't mention him to her," I say.

"Oh, that's why you wanted the milk," Adie suddenly realizes.

"Oh, yes the milk, I almost forgot," I say, taking the cup and carefully pouring some into the saucer and setting it on the floor for Boots. Boots, seeing another chance for a meal leaves Adie and jumps to the floor to lap the milk up. Adie and I watch him as he cleans the plate and then looks at me as if asking for more. So I pour the rest of the milk from the cup into the saucer and he continues to drink that up as well and then sits to clean himself.

"Well, I guess he is finally full," I say.

"I'll bring him some more in the morning and maybe I can find some scraps of meat for him too," says Adie.

"That's very kind of you Addie, I'm sure he will appreciate that. Thank you," I say.

"You're welcome. Anyway, I got to take your tray and then I'm supposed to go to bed. I always got to get up early with Ms. Mary before anyone else gets up so we can make breakfast," says Adie picking my tray up and adding the cup and saucer.

"Adie, would you mind waking me up when you get up, but don't tell anyone that you're waking me up early ok?" I ask.

"Ok, sure, I can do that, but you're going to stay for pancakes right?" she asks.

"If I can I will. I don't want to miss my train, and besides, I like to wake up early and there does not seem to be an alarm clock up here," I say, looking around.

"Ok, but it will be five in the morning," she says.

"That's ok. Thank you," I say.

"Goodnight," says Adie.

"Goodnight Adie." I say.

I hear her leave and close the door behind her. I get up and close the door to the attic from the bedroom. Even though I'm the only one up here, it kind of gives me the creeps having an open door to a dark attic. I take a chair and wedge it up against the door and under the doorknob since there is no way to lock the door. This is my only means of protection against anyone in the middle of the night. I feel at least that this is safer than sleeping out in the open alone, where I thought I might end up.

I leave the window open incase Boots feels the need to go outside in the middle of the night. I'm sure no one will be climbing on the roof to come in my room. As an added precaution I take out my pocketknife, the one Tom gave me, and put it in the open position on the table by my bed. I think about Tom, Freckles, Charlotte, and their journey north to take the children home. I hope that they are safe and that their trip is uneventful unlike mine.

I crawl in between the sheets of the bed, and am suddenly overcome by exhaustion. I can't remember when I've actually had a good sleep. It's not long before I feel myself drifting off, and as I do, I feel Boots jump onto the bed and snuggle up next to me; his soft purring lulling me further into sleep.

I'm standing before the oak tree in front of my house. The wind blows through my hair and through the leaves of the tree bending the branches back and forth. Suddenly there is a loud crack and a sizzle in the air and the tree lights up bright like the sun. It's so bright I have to shade my eyes. Then the light dims and flows down the tree to one of the roots. I watch as the lighted root grows and twists across the ground and up toward a mountain in the distance and turns to gold.

Then the world around me shifts and I'm in a dark room with a girl's voice speaking to me. *It don't matter. She gots so many trunks of clothes here she won't miss nuth'n if you keep it anyway.*

Daughters? Mrs. Drear don't have no daughters. She only gots a son and he works for the railroad. My eyes fly open and I'm suddenly wide-awake.

CHAPTER 16

Sitting up in bed, I look over to the window and see that it's still dark outside but I have no idea what time it is. I'm not even sure if I've slept, though I must have since the dream is still heavy in my mind. I can still hear those words echoing through my head over and over again; *Mrs. Drear don't have no daughters. She only gots a son and he works for the railroad.*

I have to use the bathroom so I get up. Boots seems a little put out by my disturbing him as I get out of bed, but he gets over it quickly and curls back up into the blankets. I feel like lighting the lantern will make it too bright, so I reach for the candle on the table and light that instead. I try to walk as quietly as I can to the stairs and then down them, keeping in mind that I'm above everybody and the slightest bit of noise can be heard if it wakes them.

When I finally get to the door to the hall, I find it shut tight and locked. My heart skips a beat and I can't believe it's really locked. Maybe I just didn't try hard enough so I set the candle down behind me and I try with both hands, but sure enough, the door is completely locked. I try to feel for a release around the knob but there is none and all I can feel is the key hole, which means this door, can only be locked and unlocked with a key. I turn around and grab the candle, searching the wall beside the door thinking maybe there is a key hanging somewhere near. Finding none, I walk back up the stairs trying to figure out in my head why the door is locked.

Maybe Mrs. Drear is protecting me from the other guests by locking the door. However, I can't shake the thought that she locked the door to be sure I didn't leave. Why would she do that? The words from my dream echo again; *Mrs. Drear don't have no daughters. She only gots a son and he works for the railroad.* They know I'm here, somehow they know I'm here. She sent word through her son and they are coming for me. Could this really be true?

I use the chamber pot under the bed because I have no choice. Then I go back into the attic with the candle and look at the trunks. I hold the candle up high over my head to light up as much of the room as it can. Adie was right; the attic walls are lined with trunks of various sizes, some stacked on each other and two or three rows deep. I go to one wall for a closer inspection and find tags on some of the trunks that have different names on them. None of them have the last name of Drear on them.

So, Mrs. Drear's son works for the railroad and brings his mother the lost trunks no one claims, I rationalize. What else is he going to do with them? But then why doesn't she sell the items? Why do they stay hidden up here in her attic?

Something on one of the trunks catches my eye and I move the light to get a closer look. It's almost hard to read, but stamped on the side of the trunk are the letters SST, System Storage Transport. I start to inspect some of the other trunks and sure enough every one that I inspect has SST stamped somewhere on it, and my heart just drops down into my stomach. I really don't know what this means, except that Mrs. Drear lied to me about having daughters, I'm locked up in this attic, and I'm in a very dangerous position.

I have to sit for a minute to try and work out what to do. I find myself sitting down on the floorboards of the attic looking at all the trunks around me. These are not lost items from the train. People don't lose or forget their trunk of clothes or books or personal items. If they did, I doubt it would be this many people anyway. These trunks must have been filled with the belongings of people who are now in workinhouses or worse maybe even dead. I suddenly get a chill as if feeling their ghosts around me.

I spy a small travel bag made out of carpet and crawl to it. I unlatch it and find inside a man's shaving kit and two shirts. I take them out and discard the shirts, but I think I might keep the shaving kit, who knows, maybe I can trade it for something. I notice as I'm about to put the kit back in that there are more latches. I inspect closer and see that these latches allow the entire bag to open up and lay flat on the floor like a small carpet.

"Well that's pretty jiggy," I whisper to no one but myself. I put the bag back together. I decide to peruse some of the other trunks close by to see if there is anything else I can use. I have come to the decision that if it belongs to the System, I have a right to take what I need to survive, considering the System has taken everything from me.

I find quite a few of the trunks are locked. However, I manage to find myself another pair of breeches, a jacket, a flat cap, and some gloves. I go back to the room, hoping I haven't made too much noise up here. I get dressed in the travel outfit I first picked out and shove as much stuff as I can into the carpetbag.

I think about taking my old boots but I hate them so much, and their so heavy, and they'll take up too much room in the bag I decide to leave them. There is still a lot of room inside the bag so I go through my satchel and put what I can into the other bag making my satchel lighter on my shoulders. I still carry the most important things on me like Papa's spyglass with the map and matches and pocketknife and the Derringer in the satchel. I look around the room and decide that since there is nothing more for me here, I just have to find a way out of this house.

I pick Boots up off the bed and go to the window. I put him down on the ledge and lift the window up as far as it will go. I realize this is not going to be easy. I get the chair and put it under the window, then set my bags outside the window and climb up onto the chair out the window. I grab the bag and while keeping my knees bent to balance myself I climb and crawl to the top of the house, which is not very far, to get my bearing.

It's dark still but I can see pretty well with the moonlight. Close to the house is a tree and I watch as Boots heads for the tree, easily prancing across the roof on his paws. Oh, I wish I had cat feet right now. I will just have to pretend I'm a cat and maybe that will make me more agile and quiet. Slowly I go to the tree by walking sideways and holding onto the top of the roof, almost like scaling a cliff, I suppose.

I make it to the tree and see why Boots was so keen to go this way. There is a large limb hanging very close to the house; the limb is close enough for me to reach and climb on to. I look down to be sure no one is around and then toss the carpetbag down near the base of the tree and sling my satchel around both my shoulders. Back home I used to climb trees all the time so climbing into this one is cake to me and I'm down on the ground in no time.

I don't stop to pat myself on the back though, because time is my worst enemy and so is sound. I don't know if I've been quiet enough or if I've woken anyone from the house so I grab the travel bag and run as fast as I can with Boots fast pacing beside me. I head over to the train yard because I don't really know where else to go but I know that if alerted to my absence that will be the first place anyone will look. When I get to the train station, I follow the tracks to the southeast away from Calvert. Once I'm safely on the outskirts of town, I find a cluster of trees and bushes where I can rest. I hope this is a safe spot. Now I just waited for the train.

I'm not sure how long I will have to sit here and wait but it's not even daylight yet. I hope I'm not just paranoid, I mean what if I didn't have to leave the house, what if everything is fine and Mrs. Drear just locked the door for my own protection? But then why did she lie about having daughters. What about Adie, she will be so sad that I left without saying goodbye. I really hate to leave her too but I do think she has it ok where she's at. It's not as if I can save everybody from the System.

I take my blanket and lay it over me as I lean against a tree. Boots climbs on top of my lap and helps to warm me up. I reach over and pet him listening to the crickets in the night blending in with his low purr. I must have fallen asleep because I open my eyes to daylight suddenly and the not-so-distant sound of a train whistle.

I look around, alarmed that I may have missed the train. I don't see Boots anywhere, and I feel a bit confused. I fold the blanket shoving it in my bag and stand up. Peering through the bushes at the train rails, I don't see the train anywhere. I'm not sure how far away from town I walked but I know I rounded some kind of a bend in the rails so that the train would have to slow when it goes around making it be easier to jump on when it slows.

The train whistles again and I'm relieved to hear it come from the north of me which means it has just gotten into town. This means I have at least twenty minutes to an hour to wait for the train to come around the bend. I hope within that time Boots manages to make it back to me wherever he's gone. I go and relive myself in the bushes, something I have grown accustom to doing now that I'm on the road, and then make my way toward the best vantage point to catch the train.

"Boots! Here kitty, kitty," I call, as I walk. I'm so very anxious about where he might be. I don't want to leave him, in fact, I have made up my mind. If he does not show up by the time the train gets here, I will just wait for him. No man gets left behind. But just as I think this, I feel that familiar rub against my legs and look down. Boots greets me pleasantly and I'm happy to see him too.

"Oh dear, how am I going to get you on a moving train?" I ask the feline.

Of course, he doesn't answer me but sits down and begins to clean himself. I think hard. How am I going to do this? I have the carpetbag and my satchel and I have to grab onto the train, how am I going to carry Boots too? The train will be going way too fast for him to jump on himself. I look down at my stuff loathed to leave anything behind when it comes to me.

"Boots, you're going in the bag!" I say triumphantly. I hear the train whistle again which tells me the train is moving out of town. That didn't take them very long. They must've just filled up with water and no passengers or cargo. I unlatch the bag, pick Boots up, and gently put him in the bag.

"It may get a little bumpy, Boots, but this is the best way," I say. Before he can jump out or protest, I latch the bag and pick it up. I hear the train coming and I ready myself.

Trains start out slowly when they come out of a yard or station; trains take a while to build up speed, especially when it has a lot of cars. This supposedly makes it easy to run and hop on the train as it's coming out of town. Going around corners and up steep grades also are supposed slow a train down. But I'm very nervous and afraid I won't be able to do this. I wait until the engine passes and goes on the turn so the engineer can't see me, then I get real close to the tracks and watched for an open car or a place that would be ok for me to sit safely. When I do this, I looked down the train and I'm surprised to see I'm not the only one out here as several people run from out of nowhere and jump onto various places on the train.

Seeing other people hop on the train gives me more confidence, but I still feel nervous about it and I'm not sure how or what to do. The first time I hopped a train it was from the yard and it wasn't moving. Papa taught me a lot of things about trains, but he never taught me this.

I see an open door open and I start running alongside. I reach up and get a hold of the grab iron and step up this is good. I can do this. I set the carpetbag with Boots in it in the car and give it a little push out of my way. Then I step up to climb in when my foot slips and I fall. Suddenly it feels as if the train is going faster and I'm just hanging from the grab iron. I struggle to get my feet up onto something but the train is picking up speed and it's harder to do get my feet up because the wind is pushing me back. I could let go but if I do this, I have to make sure I push myself away or I will get pulled under the train into the churning wheels. I'll also lose Boots since he is already on the train and I have no way of reaching the bag. Determined, I finally get my feet up but not in a good spot, and I feel like I'm falling backwards and holding on for my life when I feel hands grabbing me and pull me in. The next thing I know I'm in the boxcar and the door is sliding shut.

CHAPTER 17

$\mathcal{I}$ hear a match strike and a candle is lit. I look around to see several people, including my savior, who appears to be an old woman. She smiles at me from a sooty face and says, "You'll get the hang of it, love, after a while."

"Thank you," I say.

"Is this your bag?" asks another woman from the other side of the car. "It seems to be making strange noises."

"Yes, it's my bag and I think Boots wants out, I don't think he liked me putting him in the bag very much," I say, taking the bag and unlatching it. An indignant Boots jumps out of the bag and sits down glaring at me.

"Sorry Boots, it was the only way," I say again. I find an empty spot in the car and sit down waiting to see if he will forgive me and join me. After a moment or two, he walks up to me and plops down on my lap. Relieved I pet him and look around at the faces all looking at me.

There are three women, and one older gentleman riding in the boxcar. They're all kind of quiet. I guess they're sizing me up or something. I suppose that's normal but I don't know since I haven't been doing this for very long. I wonder if I should introduce myself or just sit here and keep quiet. They all seem to keep to themselves so maybe that is what I'm supposed to do. The woman who helped me comes over and sits next to me.

"Where you headed, sweetie?" she asks.

"Nashville," I say, hoping that's not too much information I'm giving out.

"You got any food in that bag of yours?" asks another woman with a toothy grin.

"I might," I say, taking my bag in hand and rummaging through it. I can't remember exactly what I have as far as food but I know it's not a whole lot. I pull out the three cans of food and set them down. One of the women grabs the cans and pulls them to her.

"Ester, remember we share," says the woman next to me. Ester puts two cans back down and hugs the other one.

"Ester, we will share it all," says the woman sternly. Ester puts the other can down and scoots back against the wall, pouting.

"You don't mind sharing with us, do you dear?, We haven't eaten in days. As you can see, it makes Ester a little cranky," says the third woman, coming closer to me.

"Of course I don't mind sharing, especially if you haven't eaten in so long," I say. I'm about to offer them the two biscuits in my satchel when the man moves closer to us.

"That's very kind of you young lady to offer us your food, I certainly hope you've kept a little for yourself and your friend. The road is long and hard and you never know when you'll get your next meal," says the man.

"I'll be fine," I say.

I realize again the dangers of traveling alone. These people may seem very nice and gentle but who is to say they don't try and overpower me and take everything I have. I remember the Hobo Jungle and the speech I made. I don't want to live in fear. I want to have friends. I want to trust people, and I want them to trust me.

"Besides, we have to stick together. It's the System we need to watch out for," I say. Oh maybe I should not have said that, maybe that means nothing.

"Yes, yes, the System it consumes us all," says Ester, coming closer to me seemingly more friendly now.

The man takes out his pocketknife and begins to open the cans. It appears one is pears, one is green beans and one is creamed corn. Ugh, I really hate creamed corn, but food is food. When I see that there is really not that much for five people I stand up and move out of the circle they have created suddenly around the food.

"I had a big meal last night so I'm not really hungry. You can have it all. In fact I have a couple of biscuits here you can have too," I say, grabbing my bags and taking the biscuits out. I had them over to the woman closest to me and then casually walk over to the other side of the car to let them eat. Boots is disinterested in them and comes over by me curling back up on my lap.

"Are you sure, sweetie?" asks the woman holding the biscuits as if I had just handed her a treasure.

"Yes, I'm sure. You go ahead and eat," I say.

I tried not to watch while they consumed the food. I'm not sure how they divided it all up, especially the creamed corn but somehow they managed, and there is nothing left but three empty cans which Ester takes and puts in her bag.

"Thank you again dear for your kindness," says the man.

"You're welcome. I'm sorry it's not more," I say.

"It was plenty. I'm Nita by the way," says the women who helped me get on the train.

"Hi Nita, I'm Abby," I say.

"That's Lois and Ester of course, and Joe," says Nita.

"Nice to meet you all," I say. "Oh this here is Boots," I say, gesturing to the cat sleeping on my lap.

Nita and Lois look like they could be sisters. They look to be about fifty years old or more and probably within a few years of each other. They both have similar facial features including the weatherworn skin and hardened look about them. Their clothes are dark skirts tied up like pantalets and their tops are men's faded grey button up shirts with wool overcoats. Though their clothes look a bit tattered, their faces are clean and their brown hair up and tidy.

Ester on the other hand looks the opposite. She looks almost ancient, her face and hands covered in soot and wrinkles. She wears a long black dress that is torn and dirty, with a shawl pulled over. Her gray hair though pulled back up, spills out all over the place making her look like a madwoman. Joe kind of reminds me of Jim in his worn-out suit and black shoes with obvious holes in parts of the soles. He has a fancy dress shirt on as if he had been to an evening party and then suddenly found himself on a train. What makes the story picture perfect is his scrunched top hat that he wears askew on his head.

"So you're going to Nashville? That's a nice place. I think I've been there," says Ester.

"You have, and we are going there too," says Lois.

"Do you have friends or family in Nashville?" asks Nita.

"No, ma'am, I'm looking for my papa, Bishop Steel. He works for the railroad only he disappeared and I'm trying to find him.

Have you heard of him?" I ask hopefully.

"No, sorry dear, I haven't," says Nita.

"Bishop Steel, I know'd that man. He gave me a job once. Paid me real money for it too. Wasn't a very long job, just clean'n out some of the gunk in the oil pans and putt'n new oil in. He was short some people at the time I think. Nice feller, bought me and some of the guys supper too," says Joe.

"Really? You know my papa?" I ask, delighted to hear such an amazing and happy story about him.

"So yor' his lil' girl, the red haired one. He talked about you at supper," says Joe.

"How long ago was that? Do you remember?" I ask.

"Oh, tha'd be about a year or so I guess, I been convoless'n. Hurt my back, been laid up at a friends for a while," says Joe.

"Oh that was a while ago," I say.

"How long he been missing?" asks Joe.

"It's been four or five months now I guess," I say.

"Geez I'm sorry to hear that, he's a good feller he is," says Joe.

"They got him they did, got him hid away so's you can't find him," says Ester.

"Don't listen to her. She's crazy," says Lois.

"It's very dangerous to be traveling on your own. You never know who you're going to meet," says Nita.

"I know, but so far other than trolls, the scariest people are those who work for the System," I say.

"Trolls?" asks Ester. "You say I'm crazy."

"Don't pay her any mind. We understand what you mean," says Lois.

I don't really think they do though, and I'm not about to launch into a story telling them how I found a mine full of children being eaten by trolls. Then they would think I was just as crazy, if not more so, than Ester. I think there are just some things better left unsaid. Besides, we are nowhere near any mines so I don't think we are in danger from those things at the moment.

"It's a bit of a ride to Nashville, dear. Rest easy now, you're among friends," says Nita, taking out a blanket from her bag and covering herself and Lois with it.

Ester smiles at me and nods then she too pulls out a blanket wrapping herself in it and rolls over facing the wall. I look over at Joe who has already placed his bag behind his head and laid his hat across his eyes. I'm not really tired but I am a little cold so I slide into the corner and pull my blanket out throwing it over both myself and Boots who continues to lay in my lap undisturbed by the motion. I keep my satchel and Papa's spyglass around my shoulder and the carpetbag between me and the wall with my arm linked through it.

I guess these people don't really mean me any harm but I would rather be safe than sorry. I casually slide the Derringer out of my satchel and into the top of my boot where I can get to it easy enough. Just in case and it does give me a little peace of mind. I wish things hadn't gone so badly at the boarding house, I could have woken up like a normal guest and had breakfast. After breakfast, they'd drive me to the train station and with the money I had I could've actually bought a train ticket all the way to Bryson City and road the train in style and comfort.

I lie back and listen to the rhythm of the train and let my mind wander to happier days on the farm, when I see Joe get up and go to the door. I pretend I'm asleep and watch him through the slits of my eyes as he slides the door open. The candle blows out instantly but sunlight streams in taking its place. After a while, my eyes adjust and I can see that Joe is still just standing there by the open door and I suddenly realize he is urinating out the door. I almost start to laugh because for some reason I find this amusing. However, my humorous mood is cut short when Joe suddenly shuts the door and shouts, "Oi!" Engineer's on deck."

The women rouse from their slumber and calmly but quickly put their blankets away and gather up their gear. Not knowing what is going on I get up, careful to move Boots politely off my lap, and do the same. I push the Derringer down my boot a little more to where no one can see it and it won't slip out. I don't dare put it away since I have no idea what is going on or if there is a dangerous situation arising.

"What's going on?" I ask.

"The engineer is on the deck which means he is heading to one of the cars for some reason or another. He could come in here, and if he does we have to be ready to either bail, go with him quietly, or do whatever the situations requires," says Nita.

"I'm not sure I like the sound of that," I say.

"None of us do," says Lois.

"It just so happened that this engineer ain't one of those nice fellers like yor papa, and he is liable to just throw us off the train at top speed if he so feels like it," says Joe.

"Yea, a real System man," says Nita.

"They're all System. Don't you see they got them brainwashed into thinking their way," says Ester.

We all move over to the far corner of the boxcar where we would not be seen right away if the door should be opened. The darkness envelops us and we wait. Suddenly I hear a soft thump as someone lands on the roof from the other car and walks across the top. I can hear the crunching of his boots across the top and

I cringe. I reach down and pick Boots up, afraid of what will happen next.

CHAPTER 18

We wait and listen as the footsteps walk across the top of the boxcar and then are gone. A sigh of relief comes from all of us, but I'm not sure what to make of all this. Maybe the engineer is gone on to the next car or maybe he is still waiting up on the roof for us to make noise.

"Are you sure it's safe?" I whisper.

"Safe enough, but I suggest we keep quiet for a while," says Joe.

"But we were being quiet," I say. I walk back over to my corner with Boots and sit down.

"What else you got in that bag, dearie?" asks Lois.

"My personal belongings," I say.

"Let's have a look maybe?" asks Lois, looking at her comrades.

I stand back up and in the dark boxcar, I can't make out their faces but I can see menacing shapes and I'm suddenly afraid.

"I thought we were all friends here?" I say.

"We are dear. But when we travel together we all share," says Nita.

"Yes, we all share," says Ester.

"Well I'm not traveling with you, I just happen to be on the same boxcar with you and going the same way at the moment. Besides I'm out of food, there's nothing in here you would be interested in," I say.

"Be that as it may dear, you are just a child and need looking after. You shouldn't be traveling alone. It's too dangerous for you. We will look after you," says Nita, coming closer.

"Oh leave her be, Nita," says Joe.

"Mind yor trap Joe or you'll get what for," says Ester.

Suddenly a shadow runs toward the door and slides it open letting the sunlight stream in. I see Joe standing there in the door. The world is passing us by at about fifty miles an hour; trees and shrubs clinging to hillsides of dirt and rocks and occasional jagged bits of white quarts protrudes out like dragon's teeth.

"Come on girl, git your stuff together," hollers Joe over the sound of the wind.

I sling my satchel over my shoulder along with Papa's spyglass. I pick up Boots and apologetically put him in the carpetbag and slide it up my arm as far as it will go. I'm afraid about what will happen next. Nita and Lois's demeanor has abruptly changed, and they don't seem so friendly anymore, well except for Ester who appeared crazy from the start. I realize now looking closer at them that these women are hardened and may not have the goodwill nature I expected, and I suddenly feel threatened. I look at Joe who doesn't look afraid of them at all. In fact right now he reminds me a lot of Jim.

"You need to get out of here now. Climb on out, girl," says Joe.

"I can't climb out. The train is going too fast," I say.

"Come back here child. Don't be stupid. You'll get yourself killed climbing out there," says Lois.

"We're not going to hurt you dear. We only want to take care of you," says Nita, coming closer to me.

"Nita!," yells Jim. "You let this girl go her way and leave her be. I know'd her father and he was kind to me, there's no need for you to go make'n more trouble for her."

"I don't know who her father is, I never met him, but it's clear she's someone's daughter and needs caring for. She can't be out on the road alone, there's dangerous people and she might get hurt. We can look after you child," say Nita, turning to me.

"I know'd how you look after folk Nita, you ain't foolin' no one. I ain't gonna let her fall prey to your dupery," says Joe, moving closer to Nita putting himself between us. Without warning Nita strikes out and punches Joe in the head, knocking him to the floor.

"Joe! Are you alright?" I scream. I want to run to him but he is too close to Nita and I don't want to be within her grasp. I back slowly to the door.

"It's ok, I'm ok, just get out, get away," says Joe. He sits up and wipes away some blood from his lip.

"Nowhere to go, nowhere to run. The train is too fast girl. You're gonna die," Ester cackles.

"Reach out for the hand-iron, grab tight and swing yourself over to the ladder that goes up the boxcar," says Joe.

"No need for that," says Lois, coming over with her hand out to grab me.

All of a sudden, the train lurches, shakes, and slows down so abruptly that we can hear and feel the boxcars bumping each other violently. We all fall to the floor and struggle to stand and regain our balance. I take this chance and reach out grabbing the hand-iron like Joe said to do and swing myself around to the ladder, thankful the train is not traveling as fast as it was.

I don't know why the train is stopping and I don't care right now, I just want to get away from these women. I climb up the ladder and peer over the edge of the roof and see a pair of boots coming at me so I duck back down quickly. Whoever is running on top of the car is in a hurry because they jump right over to the next car and keep on running. I hear voices all around me but I don't know what they are saying or where the voices are coming from. I climb back down the ladder to the hitch and jump down to the ground.

I see a line of trees and I run for them as fast as I can, and I don't stop or look back until I get to the trees where I collapse. I turn to see if I'm being followed and see all kinds of people around the train and one of the boxcars has caught on fire. Men are lined up from the train engine to the boxcar passing fire buckets between each other. I see other men disconnecting the other boxcars from the back and watch as the train engine moves forward pulling away from the last line of cars. Then they unhitch the burning car from the other side while flames of fire are licking out at the men. The engine pulls forward again separating the cars until the flaming boxcar stands alone on the tracks. The fire brigade stops, and it looks to me like they have given up and just stand there watching it burn.

I look around for any sign of Nita, Lois, Ester, or Joe but I don't see them or anyone else who might have been hitching a ride. I guess they either hunkered down where they were or ran the other way when I ran. I just sit here and watch for a while catching my breath and wonder what I should do now. Should I wait until the train continues on? How long will it be before it moves on? I don't know how far I am from Nashville but it might be better if I just start walking.

I hear a noise from my bag. Oh Boots, poor baby. I forgot him in the bag. I open the latch and let him out. "Sorry Boots, but I had to make a quick get away," I apologize. Boots looks around a moment and sniffs the air. He looks at me and then comes over nuzzling me as if he is telling me he understands.

"Alright, so let's go, buddy, we're hoofing it for a while," I say, reminiscent of something Papa used to say to me. Papa would say, "No need for the steamer, you can hoof it down to the school yard." Thinking about Papa makes me feel very lonely. I'm also extremely frustrated. Every time I think I catch a break or let my guard down something goes wrong. People just aren't right and there's a cause for it. I can't help but feel that if the System wasn't messing up people's lives maybe they would be a lot nicer to each other, maybe.

I start walking in the same direction the train had been traveling following the tracks but staying within the tree line and out of sight. Of course, I tried that before and ended up in a cave. This time I have my eyes and ears open to all sounds and movements around me. I look everywhere I even look over my shoulder to make sure I'm not being followed. I try to make as little noise as possible so that if there is anyone around maybe they won't hear me. I think about what it is I did wrong back on the train, and I guess the only thing is I should have traveled alone. But I had no way of knowing those women were going to be the way they are.

How can I trust anyone now? I suppose I could've taken out the Derringer but I don't want to shoot anyone. Maybe I don't have to. Maybe if they just see the gun, it will scare them enough to leave me alone. I stop and take the gun out of my boot. I look at it and check to see if it's halfcocked like the man showed me, but that seems more dangerous to me so I set it back and stick it back in my boot where no one can see but where I can grab it quick if I have to.

It's still morning and not too hot, though I've been gone from home for so long I'm not sure what month it is anymore. At home, it was easy to tell because we calendared the days but out on the road, unless I find a calendar or ask someone I can only judge by trying to keep track of the days since I left or the weather. I've lost count of the days since I've left so all I have now is nature around me.

I remember the first day I went out to look for Papa it was so hot and mid-summer so that was the end of June. By my figuring it must be sometime in September. It's still pretty hot, but I'm going south which according to Papa, the south stays pretty hot on up until the end of November. In any case, the day isn't too bad right now and I need to walk my frustration off anyway so I just keep putting one foot in front of the other.

I come up over a hill and am elated to find a city spread before in the valley below. I sit down on the hill and get Papa's spyglass; I can still use it since the map opens up inside the tube unnoticed by anyone who would look through it. Boots comes up beside me while I take in this marvelous sight.

CHAPTER 19

The city of Nashville sits in a lush valley surrounded on three sides by hills and skirting a large long river. In the distance, I see magnificent sculpted buildings rise from the center where I presume all the excitement of a city takes place. I imagine downtown is where all the businesses are and maybe even shops, just like New Joplin only bigger. Around the city, smaller buildings and houses crowd together as if they're afraid of being left out. On the river's edge, I see steamships all along the docks where they load and unload cargo from other cities; there are probably even passenger ships for travelers going to other river cities.

To the south of the city center smoke rises from several factories and workinhouses, no doubt worked by the poor, homeless, and children. I can tell by the houses even from this distance that the west side of town is where the wealthy live, far from the industrial prisons. What do the rich people do anyway? How do they make their money? If the System runs everything how is it that anyone can make a profit I wonder.

I can't worry about that sort of thing. There's nothing I can do about the way things are anyway. I just want to find Papa so we can get Granny and find a home. Maybe we will go to West

Virginia where Granny said her kin are and we can live there in the mountains away from everybody.

I hear a train whistle and look to my left to see the very train I rode on coming over the hill. Or at least I'm pretty sure it's the same train. It would have to be, but I don't see the flaming boxcar. I suppose they pushed it off the tracks somehow. Typical, after all that walking I just did the train would arrive here right about the same time. I should've just waited and found another boxcar to ride in. Of course, I might've had more trouble with those women. I wonder if they're still on the train.

I let out a deep heavy sigh because my situation hasn't improved much since I can see through the spyglass that I still have a long walk ahead of me and a river to cross. I watch as the train loops around the hills and out to a bridge and over the river. I wish it were that easy for me. I could take the train bridge and hope another train doesn't come along while I'm on it. Or there must be another bridge somewhere for carriages and steam carriages . People don't just take trains.

I scan the river and see a partial bridge over the river so I guess they're building one. Further scanning more closely to the shore finds my answer as I spy a ferryboat just coming ashore. Ok so I'll have to take a ferry across the river. That will cost money but not that much. I wonder if it will be a problem for me to cross alone. Maybe there'll be other people and it'll be ok.

"Time to move, Boots., We got a river to cross," I say. I get up and walk carefully down the hill and across a field. I come to a road and realize I will be coming in contact with people again and I probably look a mess. I decide to try to clean myself up.

I stop and comb my hair back and twist it up into a bun. Then I wipe my face real good with water from my canteen and my scarf. I don't have a mirror so I just hope I've done a good job. After I clean my face and hands, I wash my boots off so it doesn't look like I've been traveling for a long time. I straighten my clothes and dust them off wondering if maybe I should change clothes but there is no place to do that so this will just have to do. I look down and see Boots primping himself too, and it makes me smile.

"What should I do with you, Boots?" I ask. "Should I put you in the bag?" I ask him. I'm not sure what to do because I don't know what I'm going to do. I know I need to catch the train to Knoxville from here. I suppose I could buy a ticket. I think I have enough money, but then if I spend all my money on a train ticket I may need it for food later. I can only just go into town and see what happens. I should check at the station and see if any of them have heard of my papa or know where he is. Doing that kind of scares me though, because of what happened last time and I don't want to get caught.

I think I'll let Boots follow me for a while, at least until we get closer to the ferry. After walking for another twenty minutes I come to a road that leads off away from the train tracks but obviously toward the city and the ferry.

I walk along the road happy that the ground is somewhat level instead of rocky and up and down hills but I'm very tired of walking all together. I can't wait to get back on the train but I will be more careful this time and try to find a place where I can be alone.

At last, I see the river flowing by like a blue ribbon before me. Beside it sits a small shack and a dock stretching from the land to the edge of the ribbon. The ferry tied to the dock looks more like a miniature steamship with a little roof over it for the passengers and an open part on either end, I suppose for carriages. There is already a steam carriage on the ferry and several people meandering under the roof waiting for the shove off. I pick Boots up, put him in the bag, and hurry to the dock where I find a burly man leaning against the railing chewing tobacco and spitting in the river.

"How much for the ride across," I ask.

"Fifty cents," says the man, barely looking up at me from under the rim of his hat.

"Fifty cents? Are you kidding? That's highway robbery. I don't even have a carriage," I say.

"You want across? It's fifty cents, and I'm leaving in about three minutes so make up your mind quick," says the man. He spits again and then walks over to some ropes, untying them.

I rummage in my satchel and find a dollar. I hope the man at least has change.

"Here," I say shoving dollar at him. "You got change I hope."

"Yep," he says. He digs in his pocket, pulls out some coins, and counts them out to me. I'm a bit miffed right now but I need across this river and I need to sit down for a while. I find a seat as far away from anyone as I can and sit. True to his word, the man has the ferry off and running across the water in about three minutes.

I watch as he uses the current and rudder to push the ferry along instead of using an actual steam engine or rope pull like they did in the old days. I sit back and try to relax and enjoy the ride. I open my bag a little so Boots can see out and breathe better but he can't get out. The man running the ferry may not like cats on his boat. It's hot and mosquitos buzz about me like its dinnertime and I'm the feast. I watch the other passengers, three gentlemen and two ladies, laughing and enjoying themselves as if it were an adventure.

I unfortunately know what a real adventure is and it's not fun at all. I would rather be home up in my tree or helping Granny with the chores. I sigh and take a few deep breaths to hold back the tears. I don't want to cry, if I start crying now I just might not stop.

The trip across the river only takes thirty minutes but it has been enough of a rest for me and I'm more than ready to move on by the time we reach the shore. I reach inside my bag and give Boots a reassuring pet before I close the bag up again and debark from the ferry. Once on land again I walk past the ferryman without bothering to thank him. I would have had he not charged so much to bring me across, but I just think he is taking advantage of people. I hurry along the road and nearly get run over by the steam carriage of the other passengers as they ride past me laughing away like looneys. I don't even think they saw me.

I let Boots out of the bag, and we continue walking toward the city. I look back to the train bridge and try to figure out which way the rails are going so I can find the station but they seem to twist around into the mountains and trees again. This place is funny; one minute you're on top looking down and you have your bearings and the next you're lost in a valley with no clue where you are.

I hear the train whistle and it's not far off and to my left, but that hardly tells me exactly where it is or how to get there from where I am. For now, I just keep to the road and eventually I start to see houses popping up on either side of me. I try not to look at them for fear they will make me homesick. I'm also afraid I may look like a hobo walking down the road with my carpetbag in hand and my cat following after me.

I keep to one side of the road near the tree line the best I can and am glad of it as another steam carriage goes whizzing by me honking their horn and scaring me out of my wits. I look back behind me to another sound of horse hoofs and see a wagon coming up the road. The wagon is driven by an older man and filled with several barrels. When he gets closer to me he slows down.

"You can hop on back if you've a mind too, I'm goin' into town," he says politely, with a smile.

I look at the man for a moment and I decide it should be safe if I'm sitting all the way in the back and he is in the front. I can always jump off at the first sign of trouble. Besides I'm tired and I keep thinking at every step that I will be there and at every corner I take there is just more road.

"Thank you, that's very kind of you," I say. I stop to pick up Boots then run to catch up. I put Boots on the wagon and then jump on and bang on the side of the wagon to let the man know I'm on. At this signal he picks up speed again and I have a ride.

There was a time not long ago in my life when a trip to the city excited me. All the beautiful dresses and hats in shop windows; the vast amount of eateries and the smell of fresh baked pastries; vendors on every street corner with knick knacks and baubles to tempt the ladies out of their money; and a bustle of people everywhere all doing something different. Papa and I loved to people watch while Granny shopped. So many interesting faces all holding thoughts and conversations we could only imagine.

Now the luster of it all is wasted on me as I ride through the outer circle of Nashville. Only the smell of food grabs my interest mainly because I haven't eaten since dinner last night. I wish I could be happy and cheerful about being here in a place I've never been, but I'm so homesick and lost that my heart just hurts. Even if I could just have Lyza, Charlotte, Freckles, and Raine by my side, maybe I wouldn't feel so sad. Without my friends by my side I feel so alone that it's almost hard for me to keep going.

Boots snuggles up to me and I realize that I at least have him by my side, and that is something. I just have to keep positive about everything and not think about the bad parts. But if bad things keep happening to me it's hard to be positive. Jeepers, a person can only take so much.

CHAPTER 20

$\mathcal{L}$ost in thought, I didn't realize the wagon had slowed nearly to a stop. I look around to see where we are and I'm surprised to see we're in front of the train station. The wagon stops and I jump off the back, grab my bag and Boots and walk around to the front of the wagon to thank the man.

"Thank you for the ride sir, but how did you know I needed to come to the train station?" I ask.

"Maybe it was your bag you're carrying or maybe it's because I got a wife who sees things sometimes in dreams," he says.

"Really?" I ask.

"This morning my wife tells me she has a dream about a girl with a cat who needed a ride to the train station. Sometimes I don't pay too much mind to her dreams, especially something as silly as that but when I saw you walking down the road with your travel bag and that cat following you, I had to ask myself, 'now what are the chances of that?' so I decide to give you a ride to the train station," he says.

"Wow, mister. Your wife has an interesting talent," I say.

"Tell me about it," he says, laughing as if to a private joke.

"Well tell her thank you and I thank you. I can't tell you how much this has helped me," I say.

"You're welcome, Miss, just stay safe," he says, and tips his hat and rides on.

I watch him leave, in awe of what has transpired. Imagine dreaming the future. I wish I could dream about where Papa is and save myself some time but all I ever dream about is the old oak tree in front of the house we used to have. Another sign of being homesick, I assume.

I turn and face the train station and am amazed at the lavish building with ornate designs incorporated in the building. Big cities always have to outdo themselves with big elaborate buildings. Small towns just have a little building or shack with a bench outside to wait for the train. I suppose it's a matter of money and big cities seem to have more of it. I think I will scope out the train and the yard from a different perspective this time and just go into the station through the front door.

I pick Boots up and put him in my bag, he seems to be getting used to this now because he curls up as if to take a nap and doesn't try to get out. I walk through the door and by the big mirror on the wall by the entrance. I think someone must have figured out that ladies appreciate having a mirror at the entrance before they go further into the building to assure they look ok, maybe even men too because I noticed in the other big train station I've been to there was a mirror at the entrance there too. I straighten my hair and wipe my face with my scarf to get the road dirt off. I look a little road worn but it will just have to do.

I wish I had a fancy hat to put on and make myself look more presentable. I remember Granny always says that a hat can make all the difference in how one looks. I must try to find myself a hat to keep handy for occasions such as this. It might make my travels a little better. I should have grabbed one when I was in Marion. Of course having money would make things a lot easier, but I don't have much of that either, at least not enough for a train ride and food.

I walk through the station trying not to make eye contact with any strangers and come out to the landing where the passengers board the train. There just so happens to be a train waiting at this moment. I nonchalantly look down the end of the train. Too many train workers and I suddenly see an abundance of Crushers meandering around the station. Without thinking or even looking, I board the train and find an empty seat in the passenger car.

I know I shouldn't be here in the passenger car because I'm sure to get caught, but I have no idea where I should go. I should just run back through the station and out the door and never look back. Maybe I'm being paranoid or something, but every time I see a Crusher now I get scared like they are after me. That was so many towns ago there is no possible way these Crushers even know who I am. Sure, they are looking for hobos and System dodgers but I'm just a kid, a girl at that, so they wouldn't be looking for me.

The passenger car is very nice with velvet curtains on the windows pulled back. The seats are benches with backs covered with the same type of red velvet. The rest of the car is polished wood floor to ceiling with oil lamp fixtures at each bench on the wall. I don't think I've ever been in a passenger car before. Papa would describe things about the trains and stations to Granny and me and he always told us how some of the trains had very elegant passenger cars.

"All aboard!" I hear the conductor shout, and the train whistle blows.

Oh no! I've got to get off. I don't have a ticket. I get up and turn to head for the door but I see another Crusher through the window so I sit down in another seat opposite a gentleman engrossed in the newspaper. He has the paper pulled up high I can't even see his face which is just as well since he can't see my face either or he might see how concerned I am about my situation.

Suddenly the train lurches forward and starts to move so I know there is no getting off it now. It probably won't be long before the conductor goes through the car verifying tickets. I set my bag on the floor by my feet and adjust my satchel to my left and settle back in the seat while I try and figure out how I'm going to get out of this.

I look out the window and watch as the city slowly goes by as the train winds around the outer edge of city center. I guess I will just wait until we get outside the city and jump off like we did outside of Paducah. The train will go slow through the city and will start to pick up speed as it leaves. I will jump off there before any conductor can catch me. Assuming they don't go through checking for tickets before then. For now, I sit and watch out the window and wait.

"You look a little worried. Is it me that concerns you?" I hear a deep strong voice with an odd accent ask me.

I turn to the man across from me who has put down his paper and is looking at me with genuine concern in his eyes. I don't know how to respond or at least my mouth does not or maybe it's my brain but one them is being rude. It's not his question that has stunned me but his appearance; I have never seen a man like him in my life. He is a big man, just barely fitting into his pinstripe suit, and his bowler hat sits slightly cocked on his head to offset the fact that it doesn't fit his head properly. His eyes are as dark as coal but bright and his smile is wide and sincere but what strikes me most about this man is the fact that his skin is almost as dark as his eyes.

"I'm sorry sir? I don't understand." The words manage to stumble out of my mouth. I find myself staring at him even though I know it's impolite.

"I can see by the look in your eyes that you have never seen a black man before," he says, laughing. His laugh is loud but jovial and it sets me at ease at once.

"No sir," I say, smiling shyly. "I haven't, but we read about Africa in school." Again, his laughter rings out through the passenger car.

"I'm pleased to hear that, so I'm not so much a stranger in your land as you would be in mine," he says, a broad smile on his face.

"I guess not," I say. Just then, I notice the conductor coming slowly down the aisle asking to see tickets.

"Oh dear me. Is it something I said?" asks the black man.

"No sir I just, um," I let my words trail as the conductor approaches us.

"Tickets please," he says, rather than asks.

"Here you are, my good man," says the black man as he hands his ticket over. "I'm afraid I have forgotten to purchase one for the young miss here, she is my guide you see. Would it be possible to purchase that with you?"

"No problem sir, just remember to get her ticket at the next town. I'm sure it will be no problem," the conductor says handing him his ticket back. "You enjoy your stay here, sir." The conductor continues past us and I breathe a sigh of relief and bewilderment.

"Why did you do that?" I ask in a whisper.

"Because I can see you are in, how is it that you say? A bit of pickle. I think. Yes, yes, that is right, and you could use some help," he says.

"Thank you, and yes, you're right. I'm in a bit of a pickle," I say.

"How about some food then," he says, clapping his hands and rubbing them together as if he were about to perform a magic trick.

"Yes, thank you. Food would be nice. Do you have some?" I ask, looking down at his bag on the floor.

"Alas, no, I do not, but I hear they have an excellent dining car," he says.

"Oh," I say shaking my head. "I don't . . ."

"My treat of course," he interrupts.

"Ok, then sure, I could join you," I say. There is an inner voice telling me to be very careful because if I have learned anything so far, and that is you cannot trust strangers even if they seem to have good intentions, especially when they offer you food.

CHAPTER 21

"Come, then. I believe it is this way," he says, standing up and walking toward the front of the train, his satchel in hand.

I grab my bag and satchel and follow after the gentleman as we walk through the passenger car through another passenger car and into the dining car. There are bench seats with tables next to each of the windows. We sit ourselves down at one of these tables across from each other. A man dressed in a blue and white Southern Railroad suit comes to our table. He almost looks like a bellhop from a hotel with a funny hat except that he is much older than a bellhop would be, has a towel draped across his left arm, and bows to us respectfully before speaking.

"Today we are serving fried chicken or fried pork chops with side servings of mashed potatoes and gravy, pole beans, and Johnny cakes.

"What would you have, Miss?" the black man asks me.

"The fried chicken sounds good," I say.

"Very good, and I shall have the pork chops, and two tall glasses of lemonade" he says to the waiter.

The waiter leaves only to return quickly with the lemonade and then leave again. I take a long drink of the lemonade and it is so good I can hardly stop myself from drinking the whole glass, but out of politeness, I set my glass down.

"I think it would be proper if I introduce myself first," says the black gentleman. "I am called Boipuso Mbeki but you can call me Mr. Bo like my friends do," says Mr. Bo.

"Hello Mr. Bo, my name is AB'Gale Steel," I say. I think about how Granny always told me not to talk to strangers and how it wasn't polite to be in the company of a gentleman without a chaperone if you did not know him. But, I wonder if this counts if the gentleman is old enough to be your papa and if he is from another country.

"I'm very pleased to meet you Miss Steel," says Mr. Bo, extending his hand to me to shake. I take his very large hand and shake it politely.

"Good, good, now we can talk since we are properly introduced," he says.

"Yes, I suppose we can," I say, laughing.

"So it would be impolite of me to ask what you are doing or where you are going, so I will tell you about me," he says.

"All right then," I say. The man is paying for my train ticket and is buying me a meal right now so I guess the least I can do is sit here and listen to him tell me his life story if he wants to.

"I come from Africa as you guessed, South Africa to be more precise. I won't bother you with details of my village since you won't even know where it is anyway. It is a small village though, and one day a man came from America with a hunting party looking for guides through the bush."

"The bush?" I ask.

"It's what they call the wilderness, most of it is really open desert but there is a lot of big game out there. So I volunteered to go along with the hunting party and became good friends with one of the men there. He took me back to Boston and sent me to school, and then the university."

The waiter comes and brings our plates, mine piled high with crispy fried chicken and mashed potatoes smothered in gravy and his with two huge pork fried steaks. The waiter leaves for a minute only to return with a plate full of Johnnycakes and butter and a pitcher of lemonade to refill our glasses. I wait to see if Mr. Bo is going eat or if maybe I should wait until he's done talking, though my stomach is gurgling at the smell of the food.

"Please, go ahead and eat," says Mr. Bo, after seeing my hesitation.

I dig into the mashed potatoes first. They are so good and creamy, maybe a little too creamy. Granny always has some lumps in her potatoes. Papa said they gave the potatoes character. The gravy is ok too, but again I find myself comparing this to Granny's cooking when instead I should be thankful for something to eat at all. I try the chicken and it's real good and crispy, no complaints here on that. I break off a couple of small pieces, and when Mr. Bo is not looking, I open my carpetbag I set on the floor just a crack and slip in the piece of chicken. I feel Boots take it gently from my fingers. I only hope he doesn't purr right now, that would really give him away.

"So after I leave the university," continues Mr. Bo, "I decide that I want to stay in America and mine for gold."

"Mine for gold? Really? Where?" I ask, finally interested in what Mr. Bo has to say.

"Well I hear that there is gold in the hills of Georgia,. That is where I am going first," Mr. Bo says taking a bite of a Johnnycake.

I'm about to tell him that I'm on my way to Georgia, too, but

I stop myself. I don't think it would be wise to tell anyone where I'm heading unless I truly trust them and I don't know this Mr. Bo very well.

"So you bought a mine or land or something?" I ask.

"Yes, yes we have land. You see I have several supporters in my endeavor so they are helping me purchase the land and I will build a place for the workers and we will have everything we need to mine the gold."

"How do you know there's gold on the land you bought?"

"We had it inspected. Everything is already taken care of and I coming to set up shop, I think is how you say it." he says, and takes a bite of food.

"Where do the workers come from? Will you hire local people to help you mine?" I ask.

"Oh no, that is already taken care of. The System has given me workers in exchange for a percentage of profit; that is how it works right?" he says.

I set my fork down and push my plate back suddenly I'm not very hungry anymore.

"So you will have slave labor working your mine?" I ask quietly, but loud enough for him to hear.

"Oh no, it is not like that," he says, putting down his half-eaten pork chop and licking his fingers. "I will have a nice place for the workers to live and food to eat, the System helps with that as well. See it's no problem, the people will be well cared for," he says, returning to his meal.

"I see. So you don't think that taking away everything from someone because it's not enough according to someone else's rules and putting that someone in a place to work for a hard bed and a pathetic meal, you think that is ok?" I ask.

"I'm sorry, I don't follow you," he says, shoveling mashed potatoes in his mouth.

"Those people the System send you used to have homes and families but because they didn't have enough money to pay their rent that the holder probably raised anyway, they were separated and sent to workinhouses and mines like yours to work so that people like you and the System can make money," I say, a little flushed.

"I see what you mean, but it is not slavery, not like that. I will take care of these people and give them a home. Their families can stay with them," he says confidently.

"No," I say, shaking my head. "By the time they come to you they will have lost everything already, including their families. It's nice that you will be kind to them and take care of them, but it's no different really." I finish my lemonade, set the glass down quietly, and look at all the food on my plate that I didn't finish. I'm too full to eat anymore, or maybe I'm too upset, but there is still a leg of chicken and at least a half a cup of potatoes and I haven't even touched the pole beans yet. About five Johnnycakes still sit on the plate too.

"Well that was a very fine meal. I'm sorry I have upset you but you are young yet and there are many things for you to learn about the world. It is not all as bad as you think it may be," Mr. Bo says, smiling his broad cheery smile at me.

"I suppose so," I say.

"Now you finish up your meal. I'm going out to the caboose deck to have a smoke. We can finish our conversation when I get back," he says, standing up, and heads down to the end of the train.

I look around and I don't see the waiter or anyone else about so I take the napkin and wrap up the rest of my chicken and the Johnnycakes and shove it in my satchel. I have no way of saving the mashed potatoes or pole beans so I at least take a bite of the beans so I know what I'm missing. Not much, I gather. Granny made them better.

I look down and see the newspaper Mr. Bo was reading. I decide he won't mind and I flip through it to see what is going on in the world around me while I'm out running around trying to find Papa. Suddenly I stop and almost lose everything I just ate as I see two sketches above an article entitled *System Fugitives at Large.* The sketches are of a girl that looks very much like me, and a man that almost looks exactly like Papa. I scan the words in the article and find both our names, Bishop Steel, and Abigail Steel, wanted for questioning by the law. Of course they spelled my name wrong.

CHAPTER 22

$\mathcal{I}$ don't have time to waste reading the article right now, the way I see it if Mr. Bo has this paper, so do other folks on this train and they more than likely have read this and have seen this picture of me. I shove the newspaper in my satchel as well and sling it over my shoulder, grab my bag and head toward the back of the train. If I were to guess, the easiest way off the train, and the least painful at this speed, will be jumping off the back. The only problem is that is where Mr. Bo went to go smoke.

I walk to the back of the train into the cab and expect to see the conductor but he isn't in the cab. I hear voice just outside and I know Mr. Bo and the conductor are out on the deck. I look around the room, which is a lot bigger than I expected. I see a couple of cots against one side of the cab, a desk on the other side and stove in the center. There's a ladder going up to a dome with windows and bench seat. I remember Papa telling me that it's called the cupola where the conductor sit's and watches over the train. That's not going to be much help to me.

I survey the room further and see two small doors across from each other by the deck door. Quietly I inspect to find one to be a water closet and the other a coat closet. Quickly I step inside the coat closet and close the door enough to be able to peek through it. Just in time too as Mr. Bo and the conductor come in from the deck.

"We will be sure to take care of that business for you, Mr. Bo as soon as we get to our next stop. Nothing to worry about, and you will be rewarded I'm sure, for your troubles," says the conductor.

They walk past me through the cab and into the next car. I don't think I have much time because it sounds to me like that dirty scoundrel has turned me into the conductor and they are probably on their way to the dining car for me right now. I slip out of the closet and through the door to the deck. I adjust the satchel across my shoulders and tie the strap around my waist then put my arms through the carpetbag handles and push it up as far as I can.

I look at the tracks coming out from under the train. The train is going a lot faster than I thought. I look to either side of the tracks at the landscape and all I see is the mound of rocks built up around the tracks, which I'll hit before I even get to the grass and brambles along the track and then the line of trees. Maybe this is not such a good idea after all. I turn around to go back inside and see Mr. Bo and the conductor coming back into the cab. They don't see me, at least not yet.

I see a ladder to the roof and climb up it as fast as I can, struggling with the bag as I go.. At the top I carefully I stand up, keeping my knees slightly bent for balance. Maybe this isn't as bad as I thought it would be. In front of me I can see the entire line of the train. I look down and see the cupola. If the conductor gets up into that, he'll be able to see me. I've got to get somewhere safe and quick.

I get back down on my knees and look through the window of the cupola in time to see Mr. Bo and the conductor going back toward the passenger cars. Maybe I have some time if the conductor stays below. I guess I'll have to get past the passenger cars to the boxcars beyond and hope I can get into one. The train goes around a bend enabling me to catch a glimpse of cars and I think I see a cattle car. I remember Papa telling me that cattle cars have a top door in case they have to go inside the car for some reason like if a cow is sick or something. I count the cars ahead remembering also in my head where I've been; there's the dining car, three passenger cars, and two boxcars I have to get over until I get to the cattle car.

I stand up and go to the front of the caboose, jumping across to the dining car. The passenger cars will be no problem since they are so close together for people to be able to pass through safely. It's not easy walking on top of the train while it's winding through hills. The wind doesn't help either as it keeps trying to blow me back, but I won't give up and I can't fall off. I just keep moving slowly forward keeping to the middle of the deck.

From the dining car I jump across to the first passenger car, here I walk extra careful to the next car until I'm at the last one passenger car near the end. I have to get back on my knees and hold on until the train evens out before I can get back up again. While I'm down on my knees, I chance a look behind me but I don't see anyone. It's pretty far away now but I don't think I see anyone in the cupola either. Now I have to decide if I should try to jump over to the next car or climb down.

I go to the edge to judge the distance and I think it's pretty close. I can do it if I just don't think about it. I get up and step back a few paces, check to see that the train is going in a straight line which it is, and then run and jump, landing low. I'm very careful not to let the bag hit the roof either. I don't want to hurt poor Boots. I'm lucky the roof of the boxcar is flat instead of rounded like the passenger cars are; the passenger cars are more difficult to walk on having a narrow deck.

I have one more car to go but the train is starting to round a corner, I don't want to stay up here and wait so I make a run for it, not thinking, just going, and I make it to the next boxcar without a hitch. I'm so thankful I'm right about the next car being the cattle car. I only hope I'm right about the door on top. Once more I make a run and jump. This time I almost slide off but manage to catch myself and lie flat and wait for a moment until I stop shaking so much. The part of the train is turning now so I crawl rather than stand to the other end of the car where I find a square door right on top just like Papa said. I look behind me again but there is still no one there, thank goodness.

I lift the lid, which almost gets away from me, when the wind catches it, but I stop it in time and let it down easy. The smell of cows has already been present but when I open the hatch it's overwhelming. Oh well. I'll get used to it. The hole is very small, only big enough for someone to just fit through. I look down in and see that there is no one in there but several cows. There are no stalls separating the cows, but there is a boxed area in the front of the car. I guess they store hay and tack for long trips in this box. There's no ladder down into the car so somehow I have to get in there and close the door here on the roof.

"Hello pretty cow," I say, so the cows won't be disturbed by my sudden appearance. The last thing I want is to be trampled.

I get my scarf, run it through a slat of wood on the door, and drop it down into the car. It seems long enough to where I will be able to reach it. I position myself down the doorway and jump. I'm thrown off balance because of the bag I carry but I get up fast before any cow has time to step on me.

"Nice cows, everything is ok," I say, soothingly.

I reach up and can barely grab it but manage to get a hold of my scarf blowing in the wind. I pull as hard as I can and the door finally comes down. Fortunately, it does not slam since I'm fighting the wind. I get it pulled down and in place. Then I pull my scarf down and tie it around my waste. I have no idea how I will get back out but I'm here now.

I walk between the cows slow and deliberate, cooing softly as I go so I won't startle them until I get to the bin in front. The cows seem a little nervous but not on the verge of trampling, so I think I'll be alright. There is some hay in the bin already which makes a nice cushion. It's not long enough to lie down but I can stretch my legs out.

I set the carpetbag down next to me and open it so Boots can stretch his legs too. He sniffs the air cautiously then jumps up on the ledge to assess his surroundings. I watch him and after a long look he jumps back down and begins to bathe himself at my feet. I reach into my satchel, pull out the newspaper article about Papa and me, and read it:

Bishop Steel, former employee of Southern Railway Incorporated is being sought out for questioning under the authority of the System Regulatory Unit. Mr. Steel is under suspicion of treason, bailiwick foolery, and violation of scientific ethics. I can't believe this. *Papa wanted for treason?* I know Papa grumbled now and again about the System but I didn't think he would ever do anything against it. I can't even imagine what he would have done. I don't even know what bailiwick foolery and scientific ethics is.

I continue to read the article about me now; Abigail Steel is *sought out for questioning under the authority of the System Immoderate Conduct Unit. Miss Steel is under suspicion of radical acts against the System including the deliberate destruction of System property and loss of financial prospects. She is guilty of encouraging inappropriate unionizing and piracy. She is deemed dangerous.* I'm flabbergasted. What does all this mean? I have no idea what they are talking about or what any of these accusations are.

I put the paper down, hug my knees in tight and lay my head on them. I can't stop the tears now they just come out. I cry silently so no one can hear, not that anyone could over the roar of the train. I just don't know what to do anymore. Why has all this happened? What has Papa done to us? "No!" I say aloud. I look around making sure there isn't anyone around who heard me or I haven't startled the cows. I know my papa didn't do anything just as sure as I know I didn't do anything.

Maybe they think I have something to with that workinhouse explosion. But how would they even know I made it out of there alive? How would they be able to even put that accusation on me unless, Ms. Marcs is alive? No, that can't even be possible. We all barely made it out of there ourselves it just could not be possible she survived. Even if she did, how could she blame that on me? I answer my own question, because she hated me that's why and if she is still alive, I sure bet she would do something like this.

I stop crying because now I'm just angry. Even if it's not even possible she is alive I'm going to believe she is because it keeps me angry, and angry is better than being sad and crying all the time. I'm not going to let the System get me down. They're not going to pin this on me and get away with it. I wonder how many times this has happened to other people and we never knew about it? We just trusted the source of the news that of course comes from the System. What if everything they say about the world is wrong? What if it's a lie that we're at war with other countries and have to keep our borders closed? Didn't that man come from Africa? I don't remember Africa being on the list of dominant countries so maybe that doesn't count. In any case, I realize now that the System can just be feeding the whole country their bill of goods and no one is the wiser.

CHAPTER 23

$\mathcal{I}$'m going to find Papa, get Granny, and then we'll hide away or go to another country or something. The first thing I need to do now is disguise myself. The clothes I took from Mrs. Drear's trunks in the attic, they might do well for a disguise. I think I managed to find some boy breeches too. I look through the carpetbag and find the breeches, coat, and flat cap. I'll just have to dress like a boy.

I change my clothes and shove everything back into the carpetbag, including the newspaper. I will have to figure something out about the carpetbag. I don't want to get rid of it because it's very useful, especially when I have to hide Boots, but it doesn't look right for a boy to be carrying. I also need to find some boy shoes, the ones I have on are a dead giveaway that I'm a girl. Oh, why did I leave my other boots?

I don't know how long the ride is to Knoxville. But all that running across the train and with my belly full again, and the emotional stress combined makes me sleepy. I pull out my blanket and cover myself. I think I'm pretty safe here; who would think to look in the cattle for me anyway. They probably think I jumped off. Content that I'm safe, I let the rhythm of the rails lull me to sleep.

It's the slowing of the train and the sound of the whistle blowing that wakes me. This has become my constant alarm. I sit up and look around to see where we are. The cattle car is built with large long slats for walls, with space between each slat so it's easy to look out. I wonder how the cows feel about that. I see that we are getting into the city and the train has slowed to a crawl.

It's dark out now, which is good for me, but I'm sure they will be looking for me getting off the train if they think I'm still on it. I gather my things together and call softly to Boots. He comes to me easily and I open the bag for him to jump into. I look at all the walls of the cattle car trying to see how I'm going to get out of here. So far, my only idea is to wait until they unload the cows and then try to sneak out. I don't like that much, but maybe that's my only choice. Perhaps that's best, then I can wait until everyone is gone from the train including the Crushers inspecting.

But what if they inspect in here? Oh I don't want to get caught I just can't have that happen. I look at the slats that make up the walls of the car, would it be possible for me to slide through the side of the cattle car near the bottom. It seems kind of wide, maybe so it's easy to reach in with a broom and sweep out the manure. I climb out of the bin and walk through the crowded cows over to the side of the car facing away from the city.

"Nice cow, pretty cow, everything is ok," I repeatedly say quietly to the cows as I push past them until I'm at the wall.

I drop down to the floor and see this is going to be tricky but I can do it. We are pulling into the train yard so it's now or never. I set my bag down, carefully slide my upper half out, and climb up onto the car side holding on to the wall of the car. The train is moving so slow that I can easily drop down now, walk alongside the train, and pull my bag out. I duck down low to the ground, take a careful look around, and try to work out where to go next. There's another boxcar next to me and I scurry under that and wait in the dark.

I feel the track the car is sitting on, and it's cold and quiet which means this train is sleeping so I'm safe for the moment. I crawl out on the other side and climb up to the door of the boxcar. The door is shut but it's not locked. I steady myself and push the door finding it opens easier than I thought. When I climb inside it's dark so I call into the darkness.

"Is there anyone in here?" I whisper. No response, but I'm not taking any chances.

I set my bag down, reach in my satchel for the Derringer, and feel around for a candle and the matches. I light the candle and look around. I've got the Derringer cocked and ready but the car is completely empty. Thanks goodness. I close the door and let Boots out of my bag. Poor thing is probably hungry. I remember the chicken I saved from dinner in my satchel and take it out ripping the meat off the bones for him.

I sit down now and take out Papa's map so I can figure out what I'm doing. The plan is to go to Bryson City but to get there by train I will have to catch a train here to Maryville, assuming I'm in Knoxville which I'm not even sure of. If I am, how am I to know which train is going to Maryville? I guess I'll do what I always do and just follow the tracks south until I'm away from town but close enough to where the train is still slow and easy to hop on.

"Are you done eating, Boots?" I ask, giving him a fond pet. He purrs a little and rubs against me letting me know he is pleased with his meal.

"Alright then, let's be off. Do you want to ride or walk?" I ask, opening the bag. He immediately jumps in the bag and settles down. I believe I'm being duped here. I thought perhaps he would be upset having to ride in the bag, but now I think he requires me to carry him. Well I guess it's best at the moment, at least I won't worry if he is getting lost in the dark.

I blow out the candle and carefully open the boxcar door listening to all the sounds around me. There aren't as many as I expected, but then I guess Knoxville is not as big as Nashville. I walk through the train yard keeping close to the shadows and hiding behind barrels and bins and under trains to avoid being seen. I hear laughter and talking coming from the roundhouse and the smell of cooking on the air tells me it's supper time. Good, everyone will be too busy to notice me, I hope.

I follow the tracks going south from the back end of the train yard. I see a train on the southbound tracks but it's not moving. I hear the engine snorting and steam swooshing out of it, which means it should be moving soon. Maybe I've caught a break. I don't see any Crushers around, but they might be waiting for me. I hear a sound and see a man come out of the caboose and walk to the roundhouse. I wonder if there is anyone else in the caboose, I'll have to keep a close eye on that. I notice as I walk the length of the train from the backside, that there is no passenger car on this train which means it's strictly cargo.

There's no way I can get on the train from this side. I'm going to have to risk it and get on the other side where the doors are. I crawl under the train, which really is a dangerous thing to do when it's running. I look down both ends of the train but I still don't see anyone. I run the length of the train looking for an unlocked boxcar or open one. I see one, two, three cars from the caboose that appears to be open a crack. I look around once more, and then grab the hand iron pulling myself up and set my bag inside while I climb in.

"Anyone here?" I whisper. No answer. I move away from the door a little and light my candle to get a good look. I almost drop the candle when I see rows of coffins before me. I know dead people can't hurt me only the live ones, but I just can't stand the thought of sharing space with a dead person again. I blow out the candle, grab my bag, and jump back out in search of another likely spot. I see another car two up that's still open. It looks like maybe they are still in the process of loading or unloading it. I'm going to just hope that they are loading. Again, I set the bag up inside, grab the hand iron and stepping onto the hitch, I manage to pull myself in.

"Anyone in here?" I whisper loudly. No answer. I look around the boxcar filled with crates and barrels. The door is open wide enough for me to see all around but the car is pretty packed. I am able to squeeze to the back corner and find an open space with just enough room for me to lie down if I want. With all the boxes and crates packed in, I don't think anyone will be able to see me.

The only problem is I will be locked in until the train gets to the next station, which I'm hoping is where I want to be. I don't really care at this point, I feel kind of numb inside right now, and there's a haze all around me. I settle down in my little hidey-hole and wait which is all I can do at the moment. I try not to think about things but it's hard not to. It's not long before I hear some men outside the boxcar talking.

"Hey we gotta finish loading this car, Bart," says one man.

"On it," says another.

"Hey Len, come help Bart load this car so we can get a move on. The galloper's hot. I gotta go to the gashouse to see if the general is ready to ride," says the first man.

"Yeah boss," says a third voice. "How many more we got?"

"This is the last," says the second man, answering the third.

I hear someone jump up in the car and I make myself as small as I possibly can. I hear them load the boxes, the thump as they drop them down on the floorboards that shake with the weight. The men grunt and grown and small talk, I don't pay any mind to them I just pretend I'm invisible until at last they finish and I hear them leave and the door close. Enclosed in darkness, I breathe a sigh of relief because they didn't see me or hear me. I keep still a little longer until I feel the train tugging on the boxcar and we start to roll.

"Ok Boots, I think it's safe now," I whisper while opening the bag. Boots takes a big long stretch before jumping out. I look at the bag a bit longer and remember when I first found it I noticed that it opened all the way up to a flat position. I go through the items inside and rearrange putting some things in the satchel instead so that the only thing left is the blanket and the clothes I took. I open up the bag all the way and lay it out on the floor.

"Wow, Boots, it's just like sitting on a carpet. Pretty jiggy," I roll the clothes up into a pillow, lie down, and cover myself up with the blanket. It's not home but it will do for now. I'm not really tired but it's easier to lie down then be scrunched up against the boxes. I only hope none of them falls on me. I just lie here in the dark thinking about what I should do. It will be harder to travel being on a wanted list. It really makes sense now why Mrs. Drear locked me in, she planned on turning me in, I suppose, in the morning.

I'm not asleep, just kind of resting when I think I hear a loud thump on the roof. Startled, I sit up, I definitely hear someone walking around on top of the boxcar. I strain to listen but just as soon as the sound came it's gone. Maybe the conductor is walking around checking on things. I start to relax when I think I smell smoke. It isn't good to smell smoke when I'm trapped in here; if this boxcar catches on fire I'm likely to die. I stand up, I'm seriously concerned now because the smell of smoke is really strong.

"Boots!" I call out in a frantic whisper. I don't hear or feel him anywhere. He's probably hiding which is what he usually does when there is real danger. This isn't a good time for him to be hiding. I may have to try to break the door down or something to get out of here in a hurry.

Suddenly I hear walking on the roof again. I feel a little relief, maybe someone is here to put the fire out. No, they're not just walking they're hammering on the roof. It's loud and almost sounds like the wood is splintering; the sound is as if someone is chopping through the roof. I pull the Derringer out of my boot and press myself against the wall. At first, I can't see anything because it's dark and I don't dare light a candle. After a while, though, I can see a faint glow of embers in the roof at the far end of the boxcar.

I hear another loud crack of wood then the embers fall into the car and moonlight streams in from the roof. I feel myself start to shake, remembering the men who came onto the train before and attacked us, causing Raine to fall out of the train. I don't know what I'll do if it's those men or someone like them come through that hole. Maybe if I just stay quiet they won't know I'm here.

I watch a shadow drops down onto one of the boxes from the roof and climbs down. Something about the way the shadow moved makes me think it's not a man. It moves almost cat-like.

I keep very still and quiet as I peer through the boxes trying to get a better view of the person to see what they are doing, but there are too many boxes and crates in my way. I still smell smoke heavily in the air and wonder if some of the embers that fell in from the roof have caught fire inside the boxcar now. I hear a clinging sound that makes me think that somehow the shadow inside is maneuvering the door lock mechanism.

"Ah ha!" proclaims a female voice and the door slides open allowing the full glow of moonlight to splash into the boxcar.

A cool wind blows into the car and something tickles my nose. I try very hard not to sneeze but I just can't hold it back. I sneeze as quietly as I can into my sleeve but it's no use I've been found out.

CHAPTER 24

"Whose there?" demands the female voice.

"No one," I say quietly.

"No one? I hear someone. You get out here where I can see you or I'll come find you and tear you out," says the voice.

"Ok, no need to get uppity. I'm coming," I say. I tuck the Derringer into my pants waist behind me so I can grab it fast if I need to. I wind my way through the maze of crates and boxes until I'm where we can both see each other. The moon gives out a brilliant light revealing a young girl about my age or maybe a year or two younger. She has long dark hair pulled to one side and a scarf tied over and around her head with the two ends blowing behind her with her ponytail.

She's wearing breeches with high black boots, a black waist corset over a dark long sleeved blouse and long black coat the flaps in the wind. In her right hand she holds a hatchet. Strapped low around her waist is a gun belt with a long barrel pistol, so much for my little shooter. For all appearances, I would say she looks very much like a pirate and would even say she was one if we were on a ship and not a train.

"Why is there a hobo on my train?" she asks me.

"I'm not a hobo," I say. "Is it really your train? If so why have you set fire to it?" I ask.

"Do you have a home?" she asks me, ignoring my question.

"No," I say, "not anymore."

"Do you have a job?" she asks.

"No," I say.

"Do you go to school?" she asks.

"Not right now," I say.

"Then you're a hobo! A vagabond! A tramp!" she yells defiantly.

"I'm no such thing. I'm a traveler searching for my father. What are you?" I ask.

"I'm a pirate!" she says, triumphantly.

"We're not on a ship. This is a train, and you've set fire to it," I say. I look behind me and the wind has caught hold of the embers just as I suspected, and a fire has started to burn a couple of the boxes in the corner.

"I'm an air pirate," she says. "Mandy Moon the Airship Pirate. Haven't you heard of me?" she asks.

"No, I haven't," I say.

"Well, you will. What is your name?" she demands.

"Abby, just Abby the Traveler," I say.

"That's a funny name for a boy," she says.

"I'm not a boy," I say, taking off my hat for a second and then putting back on.

"Well you're not supposed to be on this train, Abby the Traveler who's not a boy. We put word out no hobos on this train tonight because it's our mark. We ain't got time for you get'n in our way so I'll have to throw you off," she says, and hangs her hatchet in a loop on her belt.

"I told you I'm not a hobo and I never heard anything about not being on this train. I happen to be going in this direction so I need to take this train so stuff it. You aren't throwing me off this train," I say.

Frankly, I'm a bit irritated with this little girl playing pirate and I really don't want to be bothered with her. Who does she think she is saying she's going to throw me off this train.

"I will, I got orders to throw all hobos off the train," she says, reaching for her weapon. I reach back, grab the Derringer from my waist, and point it at her.

"Stop right now you little pumquat. Don't make another move or I'm throwing you off the train," I say.

"You don't have to be such a sourpuss. I wasn't gonna shoot ya. It ain't even loaded. They won't let me have a loaded one. Anyway I got work to do so just do me a favor and stay outa my way," she says. She has her hands out away from her weapon.

"What work are you doing besides chopping holes in a perfectly good train and setting it on fire?" I ask. She gives me a dirty look for that remark, and turns around and looks at the fire behind us which is starting to get bigger.

"Yep, we don't have much time," she says.

"Time for what? Now I have to jump off the train again, so I guess it wouldn't matter if you throw me off or not," I say.

"Right, ok so here's the scoop, toots. I gotta job to do, and that's to throw these crates and boxes off the train," she says.

"What? Why? Those don't belong to you. They belong to someone else," I say.

"You mean the System," she says, stiffly.

"So you're not a hobo, but you're against the System?" I ask.

"Yeah, you got it hobo girl, the System's putt'n the hurt on us, so we found a way to hurt back. We got a system of our own. In a few minute here we're gonna take some of this back to our people," she says gesturing to the crates and boxes.

"Really? And how are you going to do that?" I ask.

"Take a look," she says gesturing out the side of the train.

"Oh no, I'm not falling for that," I say, stepping back from the door.

"No really. Here, I will go way over here," she says, moving away from me and the door.

Hesitantly I walk over to the door and hang onto the side while peering out down the train. I can see several of the boxcars with smoldering roofs are open and I remember them being closed when we left the yard. I back away from the door still cautious.

"Aren't you afraid you'll get caught?" I ask.

"No, there's only one eagle eye drive'n along with the fire boy, the rest of the grease monkeys are in the doghouse snoozing. We put a little green tea in their fire pit so they'll be out for a while," she says.

"I didn't understand that but it sounds like you got it all under control, so what happens next," I ask. She sighs heavily and rolls her eyes.

"There's only one engineer drive'n with the fireman and the rest of the crew are sleep'n in the caboose. Now, I ain't got time to give you anymore lessons. We spin by a drop spot, which is coming up any minute and push the cargo out as we go," she says.

"Who gets it after you push it out?" I ask.

"Geez what are ya a suit? It gets collected and taken to the hideys," she says.

"The hideys?" I ask.

"Look I don't got all night to explain it all. Our people got places outa the System's sight, where they live in secret. Not everyone knows where they all are. But the stuff gets distributed to them," she says.

"You mean other pirates?" I ask.

"No, just people, the pirates, as we call ourselves, just do the work," she says.

"It seems we have a common enemy. I wouldn't be riding in a boxcar in the middle of the night, if I was friendly to the System, but I'm no hobo either, though I do have some hobo friends," I say.

"You wanna help?" she asks.

"Why not, I'm already being accused of piracy. I might as well be guilty of it," I say. She looks at me hard for a moment then shrugs.

"Ok, why not? When we get to the bridge, Just start chucking it off as fast as you can right?" she says.

"I hope that's soon because that fire is getting bigger. Wait, I have to find my cat. Don't throw him out," I say.

"You gotta a cat?" she asks. "That's jiggy."

"Boots! Where are you?" I call out. I begin to search frantically through the boxes and crates making my way back to my makeshift bed. I quickly gather my stuff together all the while calling for him. I hear a noise opposite in the other corner and call to him in that direction.

"Kitty, kitty. Boots, come on it's fine! I'll take care of you," I say. Suddenly he comes out from behind the boxes and I'm relieved. I open the bag I had put back together and he jumps in. I go back to the door where Mandy Moon has pushed some boxes to the door in readiness.

"Don't throw this bag out, you hear me? My cat is in it," I say.

I set the bag to the far left of the door so it can't fall out but to where I can grab it in a hurry. Mandy nods in understanding but is in a stance ready to throw boxes. I push my satchel and Papa's spyglass around to my back and get ready myself.

"Now!" Mandy yells. Suddenly we're over a bridge and Mandy is pushing boxes out of the train and so I do the same.

Some of the boxes and crates are really heavy, so Mandy and I help each other move them to the door and push them out. I don't know how long the bridge is but we move as fast as we can to get as many out as we can except for the ones that have caught on fire. The fire is progressively spreading and I'm choking on the smoke as it swirls around inside before escaping out the door.

We are abruptly faced with earth instead of the bridge, so we stop pushing boxes out and turn to see what damage we have done. We have managed to throw almost half the car's contents out. The fire is now out of control and dangerous. I wonder if Mandy has a plan to get out or if she was supposed to jump off the bridge too. I grab my bag with Boots inside; I'm sure the poor guy is just frantic.

"Now what?" I ask

"Grab a rope and hold on," she says.

"What rope?" I ask. No sooner do the words come out of my mouth then several ropes trail across the door from above. Mandy runs and jumps grabbing a rope as she does. I'm not so bold but I can't stay in here so I grab a rope quickly before their gone. I wrap it around my arm and wrap my leg around the tail end as I see Mandy do and hold tight with both hands with the bag hanging on my arm.

Suddenly I'm in the sky above the train. I feel tugging on the rope as though someone is pulling me up. I'm very confused right now because I don't know how I can be in the sky unless someone has a balloon. I try not to look down but that doesn't seem to help since I'm staring at the night sky all around me. It's as if I'm floating in the sky, but if I let go or someone cuts the rope, that's it for me. I close my eyes against this fear; I try to pretend I'm in a very tall tree but this is nothing like a tree. Oh my, what have I gotten myself into now? What is going to happen to me?

CHAPTER 25

"Grab the bag, her cat is in there," I hear Mandy Moon's voice. I feel hands grab my arms pulling me over the edge of something. Someone grabs the bag but I won't release it. I feel my feet finally land on a semi solid surface and I open my eyes.

"I'll keep my bag," I say.

"Ok, just didn't want you to drop your cat," says Mandy.

"Where are we?" I say, looking at several faces around me.

"Take a look," says Mandy, moving away so I can see.

I recognize the fact that I'm in some type of flying machine. From what I can see we are in a very large basket and above me is the biggest balloon I have ever seen. I remember seeing one at a carnival that came through town once but it couldn't compare to the size of this one. The basket is not as big as a boxcar but very close to that size and square. I'm not sure what it's made of but it's not wood. I think maybe more like some sort of reed or grass material woven very tightly together.

I walk over to look over the edge and see the train so far down traveling across the tracks with about seven or eight of its cars on fire. Farther back, I can see flat rafts in the water below the bridge and people gathering the goods thrown from the train. On the shore are horses and wagons, some already being loaded with the goods. Some of the rafts are already floating down the river with boxes on them. I'm amazed at the entire set up and the number of people involved in the heist.

"How long have you been doing this?" I ask Mandy.

"We've been pirating trains for a while, but this, tonight, was the big one. We've not done a haul like this big before," she says, excitedly.

"It's very dangerous if you ask me. My fire nearly burned me," says one the boys in the balloon with us. He is a tall lean lad dressed similar to Mandy, minus the corset.

In fact I notice there are about ten people all together, all dressed very similar with dark shirts, breeches, high boots and scarves on their heads and some around their waists. Honest to goodness pirates but they're all young some my age and some a few years older than me.

"You weren't supposed to let it keep burning," says another boy much older.

"You know, it just didn't work out the way we planned," says a girl with long blond pigtails.

"How do you mean? We got lots of stuff off that train," says the same stalky boy.

"Yeah, but I could've got more if I didn't have to worry so much about the fire and if I had someone to help me," says the girl.

"I agree, this should have been a partner job, I think we were bee'n a bit greedy try'n to have one person per load," says another boy. The others nod in agreement.

"Abby here and I nearly got half out together. I think Tweety is right, it's a two person job," says Mandy.

"Yeah you haven't introduced us to your hobo friend here, Mandy," says the tall boy.

"No time for introduction, goofs, we gotta blow outa here, man your posts like the others. We'll talk about this later," growls a gruff looking man I hadn't noticed join our group. "You, new girl, sit down and stay outa the way till we get to our destination," he says, pointing at me.

"Here Abby, you can sit over by me," says Mandy.

I follow her over to a spot near the side of the basket where there is a cluster of ropes and handles. I look around and see that everyone has a spot similar with a set of ropes and handles that go up to somewhere on the outside of the balloon. In the center, two people stand on either side of two large knobs. The gruff looking man walks around the deck and every now and again blows on a whistle. The whistle doesn't always have the same tone and I notice that certain sounds cause different people to tug and pull on their set of ropes, and one or both of the boys in the center will turn a knob allowing a hiss of air to sound off.

As all this occurs, we are flying through the air at great speed, almost, if not faster, than a train. The gruff man is obviously flying the balloon and keeping it on course by commands through the whistle. I can't see what the ropes are doing when they are pulled or even where they are attached because I can't see further than the underbelly of the balloon.

This is absolutely amazing. I never thought I would ever be flying through the air in a balloon. The air is chilly up here but I'm too excited to care. I'm almost tempted to let Boots out to see what he thinks of this but maybe it's not such a good idea. I don't think the gruff man will like it very much. I get the impression he's not very happy that I'm here.

Oh, if Papa and Granny could see me or even be here with me now they would be so happy too. I suddenly remember myself, and my mission. I'm anxious about what direction we are heading. I certainly don't want to back track after all I have gone through to get this far. I stand up and look over the edge again, trying to determine where we are but it's no use since I've never been here before. I look up trying to find the North Star and after turning around a bit I finally find it.

Papa showed me once that if I can locate the North Star than I can tell what direction I'm going. By the looks of it, we are heading south which relieves me a great deal and I relax a bit. Now I only hope we don't go too far south or southwest since North Carolina is southeast from where I am or at least where I was when on the train.

"Mandy, where are we going?" I ask in a whisper.

"Shh, don't talk. Mr. Henry will get mad and you're already in danger being here," she says.

Oh great, I'm in danger again. Well when am I not? At least they're not the System so whatever the problem or the danger they might at least be easier to reason with, I hope. I want to sit down because I'm tired of standing, but I need to see where I am, or at least try to memorize some landmarks for reference later. All I can see though are mountains and hills and they all look pretty much the same to me from here.

"You need to sit down now, hobo girl," I hear a voice say behind me.

I turn round and see the gruff man standing there looking rather mean. I sit down right away and pull my bag to me, holding it in my lap. He turns to Mandy.

"Keep that hobo girl sitting down while we land, she's your

responsibility since you brought her on board," he says, then walks away.

"Stay down and stay quiet if you know what's good for you," Mandy says to me.

I feel a surge of defiance in me but since I'm hundreds of feet from the ground I keep my temper in check. It's not my fault she got me into this. I don't understand why everyone is getting upset at me and calling me a hobo girl. I'm not a hobo!

All at once I feel the balloon descending. Not slow or gradually but a sudden drop and then stop and then drop again. My stomach churns, I think I'm going to toss my cookies if this keeps up. To keep my mind off this I open my bag just a bit and reach in to feel a soft tuft of warm fur that responds to my touch with a little purr and a lick on the hand. At least none of this seems to be bothering Boots. Of course, he can't see how high up in the sky he is. He might not be so loving if he knew the predicament we are in.

I feel the basket touch down on the ground with a jolt, then it slides a little and bounces a couple of times before lighting down again. I hear some shouts outside and I'm guessing there are people out there tying the balloon down.

"All out!" I hear a voice shout.

"Come on hobo girl," says Mandy, helping me to my feet and then over the edge of the basket. "It's the end of the ride for you."

Oh great, just what does she mean by that? Shakily I land on my feet and survey my surroundings only to find that I'm in the middle of nowhere. Now what am I going to do? How am I supposed to find my way to Papa from here?

We're on a hilltop in the mountains surrounded by a deciduous forest near as I can tell. That could be anywhere as far as I know.

I follow along behind everyone as we trudge through the dark trees guided by lanterns along a hardly noticeable animal trail. I look back behind me to see the men who had tied us down are now deflating the balloon and disassembling the rigging. I wonder where they hide such a large contraption.

Mandy has been way ahead of me talking with the gruff man for a while, and I see her coming back toward me now with something in her hand. She stops and holds her hand out to me revealing a piece of cloth.

"You need to put this on so you can't see the way to the hidey," she says.

"Are you serious? Who am I going to tell?" I ask.

"I don't know. It doesn't matter. You have to do it, or else," she says.

"Or else what?" I ask.

"You don't want to know, he'll make you one way or the other," she says, looking down at my bag where Boots is.

"You wouldn't," I say.

"No I wouldn't, but someone else might, so just do it ok?" asks Mandy.

"I don't have a choice, I guess," I say rather than ask.

"No, not really. They're very serious around here," she says.

"Ok," I say as I pull the bag close to me and nod my head.

CHAPTER 26

$\mathcal{M}$andy ties the cloth around my eyes and then leads me the rest of the way through the trail. I feel us make several turns and go down some hills and up hills until at last I feel a change in the air. My other senses are more acute without my eyesight and I can smell things that don't seem like they belong in a forest. Like I detect the scent of clay and brick as well as cotton, coffee, baking bread, and animals. Not forest animals but livestock such as a cow or horse or goats, something of that nature. I feel closeness about me unlike trees but something larger such as buildings. I also don't feel the crunching of leaves beneath my feet as much as before but hard packed earth that has been well worn. I get the impression we are in some sort of village.

My impression is correct as I'm ushered through a doorway and into a room, then Mandy removes the cloth from my eyes. We are in a small room with dirt floors that meet walls of log and chinking. There's a closed door on either side of the room and a hearth set into the back wall with a friendly fire crackling in it. The fire is the only thing that feels friendly about this room for there is nothing else but a table and four chairs set in the center of the room. Bad memories flood my mind of the room at the workinhouse where they first took me, the horrible shower, and the haircut. I catch myself touching my head and bring my hand down.

"Abby, you'll have to wait here until Cinder gets here," says Mandy.

"Cinder? Who's Cinder, and why do I have to wait for him?" I ask.

"He is kind of our leader and you're really not supposed to be here so he has to be the one to say what to do with you. I'm real sorry you got mixed up in this but you shouldn't have been on that train," says Mandy.

"What do you mean what to do with me? Let me go on my way is what you will do with me," I say angrily.

"I'm sorry we can't just do that without you talking to Cinder first. It'll be ok I'm sure when I tell him you helped us," she says, as she leaves and closes the door behind her.

I go to the door and try the handle but it's locked already. I go to the door to the left but it's locked as well. I run to the other side of the room and try the other door and that door is locked too. Totally trapped like a rabbit. Oh, this is dreadful! There must be some way out of here. I look around the room but there's not even a window, only the fireplace. Well that's stupid. What if there's a fire?

"Hey!," I yell very loud. "What if there's a fire? I'd die in here!" No response from anyone outside the room.

I slump down on the floor and open my bag. A very miffed Boots jumps out and starts pacing the room. He sniffs the ground and all around the doors but even he can't find a way out for us to get out. I just sit and watch the fire. Boots comes over to me as if to ask me what the heck is going on?

"I don't know, Boots," I say.

Suddenly the door opens and a tall man steps in closing the door behind him. He's wearing dark clothes that sort of resemble a Crusher uniform but it's a little different. There are no shiny buttons or tassels. He wears a flat cap like mine only the same color as his uniform and sandy colored tuffs of hair stick out from under the cap. He looks at me from a rugged face and smiles.

"Wouldn't you rather sit at the table?" he asks, gesturing to the table and chairs in the middle of the room.

"Sort of looks like a Crusher interrogation table to me," I say.

"It does but it's not and I'm not a Crusher even though my uniform is similar to theirs. We do that on purpose, it helps us get around better in places we need to go," he says.

"I don't really care either way. You are holding me and my cat prisoner and we wish to be released," I say. He looks down at Boots a moment.

"Here kitty, kitty, kitty," he calls to Boots. Boots runs over to him and sniffs his hand as he reaches down to him. The man pets him and Boots begins to purr, the traitor.

"What do you want?" I ask, standing up and glaring at Boots who totally ignores me.

"Come sit down and we will have a little talk," he says, pulling a chair out for me. I reluctantly go to the chair and sit.

"Ok, let's talk," I say, trying to hurry things along. He sits down and folds his hands in front of him on the table, kind of a weird thing to do I think but at least I know where his hands are.

"Well, little hobo girl you kind of got mixed up where you shouldn't didn't you?" he asks.

"First of all, I'm not a hobo so please stop calling me that. Not that I have anything against hobos most of them are very nice though some are not I've found of late, but I'm not one. I'm AB'Gale Steel and I'm looking for my papa who has gone missing. It's not my fault your people decided to rob the train I was on and set it on fire. Since I had to get off the train because your people set it on fire I agreed to help Mandy so that I had a way out of there," I say.

"I know who you are Miss Steel," he says, pulling a newspaper from his coat pocket and laying it on the table with the article about Papa and me face up.

"I'm in disguise, how did you figure it out?" I ask.

"It wasn't hard, when Mandy described you as a redheaded girl dressed as a boy, traveling like a hobo, and going by the name of Abby, it was very easy to figure out Miss Abby," he says.

"I suppose you're going to turn me in now in hopes of collecting some sort of reward then?" I ask.

"No, not at all, that would be very dangerous for me since I too am just as much a wanted man as you are if not more so," he says, laughing.

"I don't think it's funny at all. Who are you anyway?" I ask.

"I go by the name of Cinder here, and we can just leave it at that. What I want to know is just what you did to be put on the wanted list anyway?" he asks.

"I have no idea. I told you I'm just looking for my papa," I say.

"Where are you heading?" he asks.

I don't think I should tell him about the map. In fact, I don't think I want to give any information at all. On the other hand, what if he knows something that might help me? I'm confused, I don't think I should trust him. But, I have to tell him something or maybe he won't let me go.

"Bryson City," I say at last.

"Why Bryson City?" he asks.

"Because I heard word from someone that my papa might be or may have been there so I'm going there to find out," I say.

"Hmmm," he says in thought. "Ever hear of the name Grugen?" he asks.

"No," I lie. I don't know why I just lied, that's the name all over the map what if he knows something about Grugen? "Who's Grugen?" I ask, in as an uninterested voice as I can.

"Grugen owns most of Bryson City along with a lot of other mining towns and a good part of the railroad, if I'm not mistaken. You need to be careful not to cross paths with him. His pockets are deep and his ties with the System even deeper," he says.

"My only interest is to find my papa. Please just let me go on my way," I beg.

"You said you're friends with hobos. Not a good sort to be mixed up with," he says, ignoring my plea.

"Not all hobos are bad. A lot of them are just like you and your people. They're just trying to survive without getting caught by the System," I say.

"They are nothing but a bunch of thieving bums and you will do best to stay clear of them," he says.

"No they're not! I just told you they are people who have lost everything, escaped from the System, and are just trying to stay alive. Everyday those people try not to get caught. Some even work for meals and clothes when they can. You are certainly one to talk about thieving, you and your people just robbed and burned a train, what was that?" I ask.

"That's different, we're helping people. We only take from the System. Your hobos rob anybody," he says.

"Not all of them. I told you. Maybe there are a few that give them a bad name but for the most part, they are just like you. I'll just bet you have a pirate or two among you that has gone too far and robbed someone or took something that was not from the System. There are bad people everywhere, you just judge a whole group of people by actions of a few," I say.

He sits in the chair silently for a moment and then stands up, adjusts his uniform, and picks up the newspaper from the table. "You will spend the rest of the night here and then in the morning I will have you and your cat set upon the road to Bryson City. I will have someone bring you some food and a bed to sleep on," he says. He turns and walks to the door to leave.

"Thank you," I say. "You know, the real enemy here is the System not the people it's created," I say.

"Very astute for one so young," he says, looking at me intently, and then he leaves.

Five minute later Mandy comes in with a tray of food for both Boots and me. Two men come in with her carrying a cot and some blankets and set it up on the floor for me. The two men leave but Mandy stays and sets the food down on the floor for Boots. I look at the tray where there's a cup of hot liquid, which smells like tea and a cheese sandwich. I sip the tea, which is very good, and practically scarf down the sandwich. I didn't realized how hungry I am..

"You know you could just stay here and be a pirate with us. We are always in need of good pirates," she says.

"Thanks Mandy but I really have to find my papa. You know you really should be careful," I say.

"Don't you worry about me! I'm one of the best pirates here, I can take care of myself, hobo girl," she says.

"My name is Abby. Please stop calling me that," I say.

"Right. Well I gotta go. See ya in the morning bright and early," she says, and leaves.

I check the door handle after she's gone but I'm not surprised that they still have it locked. Oh well at least I have a safe place to sleep, though I'm sure half the night is over by now. I finish the tea and sit down on the cot to try it out. I look over at Boots who has finished his food but is now prowling all over the room. Finally he stops and squats on the floor and pees. Way to go Boots, that'll teach them to lock us up in here.

I have half a mind to do that myself when I suddenly feel overwhelmingly sleepy. I try to stand up but I feel all wobbly and fall right back down on the cot. I can't possibly be that tired. My head feels woozy and the room looks foggy and fades away from me. I vaguely feel myself lying down on the cot and then a spinning sensation.

CHAPTER 27

My eyes open to clouds floating across a blue sky. I feel the hard earth beneath me and the grasses tickling my skin. A warm breeze blows across my face and I stretch my arms above me. Oh it was all a dream, a terrible, terrible dream and I'm at home by the pond. I sit up and look around.

The first thing that hits me is the pain in my head, throbbing, beating at my temples. The second thing that hits me is the fact that I'm not home and it wasn't a dream. I'm sitting somewhere actually on the side of a road. Boots! Where is Boots? I look around for my bag, which is right beside me, and I open it up but Boots is not in it.

"Boots!," I call out. "Boots, kitty, where are you?"

I'm about to panic when bounding over the grasses comes Boots as happy as a cat can be. If my head didn't hurt so badly I think I should be mad at him for being so happy and scaring me like that. I feel for my satchel and Papa's spyglass and those too are lying beside me. I pick up Papa's spyglass and unscrew it to see if the map is still inside. Fortunately, it is, and I breathe a sigh of relief. At least the pirates are not thieves, or rather, they didn't take anything that is of great value to me. I check my satchel and find my money, knife, compass, and everything else I have still there.

Slowly I stand up feeling each movement as a sledgehammer in my head. I think they drugged the tea. But why did they have to do that? I wouldn't have told anyone where they were, even if I could find my way back, which I probably couldn't. Paranoid pirates.. I look up and down the road. Which way do I go? Cinder told me he would put me on the road to Bryson City which is south, or was south from where I had been. I take out the compass to find the direction and set out down the road with Boots bouncing along, happy to be free again, as I am.

As I walk to where I hope is Bryson City the sun rises, the air becomes stifling, and my walking more labored. Though the countryside is lush, green, and filled with lovely shade trees, the shade offers no relief. The breeze from the north has quieted leaving instead air that seems to stay in one place, hardly rotating within its own circle. I feel as if I'm breathing the same air in and out along with any other creatures that may be in close proximity. Buzzards fly high overhead circling an area close by me so I know that something near has died or is dying, or maybe they're after me.

I can't really tell what time it is other than by judging where the sun is in the sky but I feel like I've been walking for hours, and the sun has not even peaked to noon yet. The road is pretty even and not too many holes which is good because that would just make the traveling all that much worse. I really hope that someone will come along this road and then maybe I can hitch a ride.

I stop to rest for the tenth time since I started out. I know it is taking me longer to get anywhere but I just can't keep going, and my head still hurts. I sit down and watch as the squirrels run around the trees chattering above me. I'm sure they're very unhappy about my invading their neighborhood. Watching them makes me think about the fact that they don't have to answer to the System. Or do they have a System of their own keeping them all in line? Maybe they have soldiers and food gathers and every squirrel has their own task to perform to keep the system running or it will break.

What would break our System? It's certainly obviously that it's already broke if there are people like Ms. Marcs running things. Who gives the System the right to separate families and take homes away? Seems to me the System has created its own enemies like the hobos and pirates. What if the pirates and hobos got together and fought back? What then? Would there be a war I wonder? I s there enough people to fight back? And who would lead the people in this war? Cinder?

A loud squawk startles me and I look up to see vultures circling directly above me. I look down and around and sniff the air but I don't smell anything bad. There must be something dying nearby that's got those birds in a tizzy. Other than that, I don't hear anything except a creaking sound. I suddenly realize that the creaking sound is not a natural sound and I sit up listening intently.

Boots finally relaxes and walks over, flopping himself on his side, and begins to take a bath. I guess whatever it is making that noise, he doesn't think much of it. But as the creaking sound gets closer, I hear a clip clop along with it and finally realize it's a wagon being pulled by horses. By the sound of it the wagon isn't a Crusher Box most Crusher Boxes these days have been modified to steam doing away with the horses. Even if it were an old one the wagon doesn't sound like it's in any sort of a hurry and Crushers are always in a hurry.

The sounds of the wagon comes closer growing louder until at last I see it come around the bend. It's a large square wagon that looks very much like a small box. Its sides are covered with a tarp that has some sort of picture and writing on it but I can't tell what it says from here. An elderly gentleman with a long beard wearing black and white pin striped pants tucked into tall black boots sits in the front of the wagon driving the horses. He has a white shirt on with a yellow vest over it and a red bow tie. The man is strikingly familiar and it comes to me right away. He saved my life from a snake once.

I recall he was a bit of a jovial fellow, this may be an opportunity for me to get a ride. I stand up and dust myself off realizing that I don't look anything like myself dressed as a boy. I wonder if he will recognize or remember me. He does at least see me and the wagon pulls up to a stop.

"Ho there critters," he says tugging on the reins. "How do you do, young sir?"

"Umm," I say taking off my hat.

"Oh pardon me dear lady, quite a disguise. Oliver T. Clark at your service, my dear lady," he says, nodding his head to me.

"Hello again," I say.

"Hello again? Have we met before?" he asks.

"Yes, we have. You saved me from a snake just outside of New Joplin some months ago," I say.

"Are you referring to a real snake, or metaphorically speaking?" he asks.

"Excuse me?" I ask.

"Did I have to step in and defend your honor young lady," he asks.

"No, I don't believe so. I think the snake had honorable intentions, just not to my liking. I simply surprised it I guess when washing up and you set your boot on it. Then you took it off to milk it I think was the word you used," I say.

"Why yes, I believe I do recall an incident of that nature. But that was some time ago and yet here I find you in the midst of nowhere far from the place of our meeting. I feel the winds have fated us together my dear for it is far too an unlikely a place for a chance meeting don't you think?" he asks.

"Well sir, you got that right," I say, looking around at the wilderness around me.

"Well come aboard, my dear lady. Let's not stand in this confounded heat more than we have too. The sooner we continue traveling the sooner we can catch a breeze, however miniscule it may be," he says.

He reaches his hand down to me and I grab it, hoist myself up to the bench, and settle myself beside him, setting my bag and satchel at my feet. He starts to go but I put my hand on his arm.

"Wait, my cat. Here Boots!" I call, patting the floorboard. Boots jumps up at my feet and settles underneath the bench.

"Oh I see so you have a traveling companion to protect you," he says, with a laugh in his voice.

"Yes he's a real protector," I say, laughing a little myself.

Mr. Clark whistles softly and the horses begin again at a soft pace.

"I am at a loss, my dear, for I do not remember your name," he says.

"Abby, you can call me Abby," I say.

"So Miss. Abby, why are you out here in the middle of nowhere and without your cart and pony," he asks me.

I wonder how much I should tell Mr. Clark and decide to play it safe for the moment.

"I had an errand to take care of for my granny, my horse and cart has been sold," I say. There I have not told a lie just sort of a half-truth and I have not divulged too much information.

"I see," he says thoughtfully. "Well I'm just glad your cart and pony were sold and not stolen."

"Yes sir," I say. I in my mind I think that it is one in the same under the circumstances.

"So where are you headed, young miss?" he asks.

"I'm going south to Georgia," I say.

"Oh Georgia, sweet Georgia peaches. Well I've good news for you, you are in Georgia already," he says.

"Excuse me?" I ask. "Peaches?"

"Yes. Georgia is well known for the large juicy peaches that grow here, well, it used to be anyway when I was a boy. I think they still grow them but only for the Richies," he says.

"We have peach trees on our farm, they are just normal size not very big, but Granny cans them," I say.

"Oh canned goods are nice, they save for a long time, get you through the winter," he says.

"Granny sells most of ours," I say.

"I expect you make a right good bit of money," he says, more as a statement than a question.

"Yes sir, it helps," I say. I try not to think about the fact that I may never see Granny again.

"There's a lot of hard working folk here in America, seems you have to be if you want to be left in peace. If you're not working, well then they will put you to work," he says.

"You mean like at the workinhouse?" I ask.

I feel a little flutter inside my stomach as the words leave my lips. I've tried not to think about the workinhouse,, but not a day goes by that I don't think about all those poor souls who died when the boilers blew up. My heart aches when I think about those little children, and those boys down in the boiler room, all of them.

"Oh yes the workinhouse is where they will put you, or a farm maybe. Either way makes no difference, you earn your keep for food and a bed, they keep the rest," he says. I think I detect a slight bitter tone in his voice but I'm not sure.

"They being the System, you mean?" I ask.

"Indeed," he says.

"Did you say we are already in Georgia?" I ask, changing the subject.

"Yes, I did. Crossed the line some ways back," he says.

"I need to get to Bryson City," I say.

"No need to fret. That is my destination as well," he says.

Our conversation falls silent for a time as we both sink into our thoughts. I can see he is working something behind his grey eyes, and he strokes his white beard that comes down just past his chin, but unlike the hair on his head, which is shockingly white, his beard has red highlights that catch in the sun. I feel he must have been a full ginger red in his younger days. Now even his bushy eyebrows are white with age.

I think about Granny and the farm and remember her canning in the kitchen with the walls painted yellow because she said it made the room feel cheery even in the winter. I close my eyes and see our house surrounded by rolling hills of grass. The big oak tree stands across from the house with its leaves turning red in the sunlight. Suddenly I feel a hand grab my arm hard and I open my eyes to see Oliver T. Clark holding my arm tight.

CHAPTER 28

"Whoa! Be careful there Miss, you're going to fall out of the wagon," he says, pulling me back to the bench.

"What happened?" I ask.

"You must have dozed off; you started falling over and I had to grab you before you fell out," he says.

"Oh, sorry," I say.

"No need to be sorry. I nearly fell asleep myself. I've just grown accustomed to sleeping sitting up," he says, winking at me.

"Well I just didn't expect to fall asleep, that's all," I say.

"We're going to be stopping soon," he says.

"Aren't we were going to Bryson City?" I ask

"Yes of course we are but we have to make a stop along the way. I'm an entertainer and marketer you see. Up ahead is a place I frequent to, to not only vend my wares, but also stock up some of my supplies. The good people of the village are always so eager to trade with me. I wonder if you don't mind accompanying me as my assistant in my endeavors at which point I will happily pay you," he says.

"Oh, will we be there for very long?" I ask.

"No more than a mere day, my dear lady, and then we shall be on our way to Bryson City on the very next morn," he says.

"I suppose it couldn't hurt. I mean, it's better than walking," I say.

"Stupendous!," he exclaims.

I find his peculiar way of speech a bit dramatic and almost comical at times, however it does seem quite elegant for the most part. He appears every bit a gentleman. I think about the snake he saved me from and remember he said he was going to milk it, I wonder what he meant by that.

"Sir, what did you mean when you told me you were going to milk the snake you saved me from?" I ask.

"Oh yes, the milking of a snake is indeed a miraculous but very dangerous thing. You see it is a way of extracting the venom from the snake without hurting the snake or, hopefully, oneself," he says.

"What do you do with the venom?" I ask.

"Most of the time I in turn, sell it to medical facilities in the east where they use it to create an antivenin for the poor souls who have been bitten by such creatures," he says.

"You said mostly. What else do you do with it?" I ask.

I am glad you asked that of me. I have been experimenting with a new weapon and have created a shooting iron that does not use gunpowder but air and shoots out snake venom," he says proudly. "I shall show it to you when we stop. I believe you will be highly impressed."

"It certainly does sound impressive," I say. "I've got a Derringer, though I've never shot it and I hope I don't ever have to."

"A Derringer is a splendid invention however, loud and difficult to reload in a hurry especially if one misses," he says.

"Yes I suppose so," I say.

"It's good to be protected, especially if one is on their own," he says.

As the wagon rounds a mountain bend, the road meets up with a river following it for another mile or so before I see a cluster of buildings. I expected a little town but instead see we are entering a small village.

"What is this place?" I ask.

"This is the native village of Yellow Hill, home of the Cherokee tribe. Their chief here is White Owl," says Mr. Clark.

"Native village? I've never been to a native village before," I say.

"Then I suggest that you be polite and do as I do, for the natives are very suspicious of outsiders. I happen to be a friend and they except me without caution. You are just a child but I never know how they will react," he says.

The native village has several small round buildings made of wood, clay, and grasses that all surround a much larger rectangular building made of logs. There are no roads or steam carriages only trails and a coral of horses at the back of the village. Chickens, dogs, and children run wild through the camp and upon the arrival of our wagon, the children descend upon us screaming and laughing.

Mr. Clark stands up in the wagon and gives a low bow of greeting and the children grow silent as they watch him closely. He reaches into his pocket and takes out his handkerchief waving it in the air as he does. As he is doing this, I note the adults of the village are now coming closer but quietly so as not to disturb the show. After waving his kerchief around he removes his hat and showing it to all that it is empty, he stuffs the handkerchief in his hat and taps on it three times before reaching in and pulling out a fat white bunny.

"Oh!" the children exclaim in unison, mesmerized by the magician's sleight of hand. Both children and adults clap their hands with delight as the bunny is placed back into the hat, and magically turned into a pigeon, which takes off into flight. I'm also staring at this magical treat with surprise despite the fact that I know it's all a trick. After the bird flies away, he throws his hands up in the air and candied honey drops seem to fall from the sky. The children scramble around on the ground to pick up the candy as fast as they can, as if they fear it might disappear like the fat bunny.

At the completion of his little show, Mr. Clark gets down from the wagon and offers me his hand. I take it and step down as well. I look over my shoulder at Boots who has retreated far into the recesses of the wagon bench. I lean over and open my bag, and quick as a wink Boots dashes in to hide. How very strange, usually he loves kids, but perhaps there is just too much excitement for him right now. I leave the bag open a little so he can get out if he chooses to later.

I follow Mr. Clark walking to the large building in the center of the village. I get the impression this is the gathering place for the village as everyone is now congregating with us. A man comes out of the door and stands there waiting. His face is weathered and his clothes are simple cotton, cream color garments but he wears a bright red wide belt around his waist and a red turban on his head, and a snakeskin across his chest from his left shoulder.

"A good day to you, Mr. Clark," the man says, greeting Mr. Clark in English. This surprises me because I didn't know many natives spoke such good English.

"And a very good day to you White Owl," says Mr. Clark,

bowing first slightly and then extending his hand to the man and they shake. Not like the usual handshake, I've seen businessmen do, but grasping each other's elbows and shaking the arm once.

"You have a new wife now?" asks White Owl.

"Indeed not sir, the very suggestion of it . . . No sir, this is my young companion and assistant Miss AB'Gale," he says, introducing and pronouncing my name properly, I note.

Mr. Clark turns to me and whispers, "take off your hat."

Obligingly, I do as he asks and take my hat off. I hear a few sounds of astonishment from the villagers behind me but I ignore this and do a small curtsy to Mr. White Owl. I'm not sure if I'm in a society where women should be seen and not heard or children should not speak. I guess it's best to just say nothing in case I say something stupid.

"AB'Gale. That is an interesting name for a young girl. You must have a very strong totem," White Owl says. "Do you know what your totem is?" he asks me.

"A cat," I say before even thinking, because I'm not even sure what he means by totem except perhaps the sprit that guides me which of course is Boots.

"A cat?" he laughs very heartily for a moment. I don't know what the joke is but I'm glad he is happy. "Come in, come in, Mr. Clark and we shall do some business and talk of things," he says to Mr. Clark.

Mr. Clark turns to me, "My dear, this is of no importance to you, why don't you busy yourself at the wagon, maybe see that the horses get some water and food, if you don't mind?" he asks.

"Sure," I say.

I really don't want to hear a bunch of boring talk anyway. I walk back to the wagon. I can now see what is painted on the side of it is a big coiled up snake. Next to the snake in bright red letters are the words, *Oliver T. Clark's Snake Oil Liniment & Tonics to Cure Whatever Ails You.* I wonder if that's true or if he's just a con man. Granny told me that most of the traveling salesman are con artists well versed at stealing people's money. Mr. Clark doesn't seem that sort of person though, he seems like a genuine nice guy, a little strange, but nice.

After some searching, I find a bucket and take it down to the river. I notice that I have a small following of children and from time to time, I catch one of the women looking at me. All I can figure is it must be my red hair. Everyone here has beautiful black shiny hair I suppose they don't see anyone with my color hair very often. After I give the horses some water, I look to see if there is anything around to give them to eat when a splash of color catches my eye. It wasn't just color but color on a woman's hair.

CHAPTER 29

$\mathcal{I}$ get a fluttery feeling as I walk quickly to where I thought I saw the person with the colored hair walk around a house. I see a girl stooping down to pick up a basket and as she stands long strand of blond hair mixed with streaks of rainbow colors fall down her back.

"Raine?" I say, questioningly. The girl spins around to face me and there she is. "Raine, is it really you?" I ask.

"Abby?" she asks hesitantly.

"Yes, it's Abby," I say, taking off my hat so she can see me better. She tosses the basket aside and runs to me throwing her arms around me and I her as we both sob with delight in finding each other. My tears are even stronger, I think, because all this time I thought she was dead. When we at last break apart we size each other up. She looks amazingly well and put together unlike me. She is wearing a long blue traditional Cherokee cotton dress very plain and simple unlike her colorful skirts she had on last time I saw her. Her hair of course, is still a shocking rainbow.

"Raine, we all thought you were dead! How long have you been here? What happened to you?" I ask.

"Well, I fell off the train and into the river, and nearly drowned.

I found some wood to grab onto and floated down the river for a while until I could get ashore where a hunting party from this tribe found me," she says.

"Did they bring you here against your will?" I ask quietly.

"No, they asked me if I wanted to go with them and I said sure," she says.

"But Raine, didn't you try to find us?" I ask.

"Well, no, I figured you would think I was dead so I didn't see any reason," she says.

"We didn't know if you were dead or hurt or alive or anything!" I say, frustrated by her answer. "Why didn't you try to find us? We have been worried sick about you. Lyza went off with Julian to try and find you or your body and we haven't heard from them in a while."

"Who's Julian?" she asks.

"One of the guys who saved us from those ruffians just after you fell. What does that matter? Do you hear what I'm saying? We were trying to find you, and you have been here the whole time and didn't try and send word that you were ok!" I say.

"I'm sorry, how was I supposed to find you?" she asks.

"That's not the point, the point is you didn't try," I say.

"Well, you found me now and I'm ok," she says, cheerfully.

"Yes, I see. But I have no way to tell the others until I see them in October," I say.

"What's in October?" she asks.

"We're all supposed to try and meet up at Hot Springs Arkansas in October," I say.

"Oh. Why?" she asks.

"Because that's what we planned to do. I'm still looking for my papa. Lyza and Julian are looking for you, and Freckles and

Charlotte have gone to Illinois to help Tom get the kids to their families. No matter what the outcome of what we're doing, we're supposed to meet in Hot Springs," I say.

"Oh, ok. Who's Tom?" she asks.

"Oh never mind," I say. It just seems too hard to explain everything to her right now and I'm still mad that she didn't even try to let us know she's ok.

"So how long are you staying here?" she asks.

"Just the night and then I'm off to Bryson City to see if I can find out anything about Papa there," I say.

"Oh, ok," she says.

"Are you going to come with me?" I ask.

"No, I'll stay here," she says.

"Are these your mother's people?" I ask.

"No, they're not," she says.

"Then why are you staying here? Why don't you come with me?" I ask.

"I think the chief's son want to marry me," she says with a smile.

"Marry you? Are you kidding? You're only fifteen," I say.

"That's doesn't matter, I can get married at fifteen," she says.

"I guess if that's what you really want to do. Do you love him?" I ask.

"Who?" she asks.

"The chief's son, do you love him?" I ask. I'm starting to wonder if maybe she hit her head or something. I really don't remember her being such a ditz.

"Oh Grey Hare is very handsome, he's the one that found me," she says.

"Ok, handsome does not mean you love him. You really

shouldn't get married unless you love him," I say.

"I think I do," she says.

"Right, so do whatever you want, have a nice life. I'll let the others know you're alive," I say, frustrated with the whole conversation I walk away back to the horses. I turn back to see what she is doing and she has picked up her basket and continued on her way as if we had never had a conversation at all., What a loon, and I thought we were friends. After all we went through together and she just leaves like that.

I get to the horses and find the children from the village have gathered up some hay for them and they are happily munching away. Boots has been tended to as well, for he has a little wooden bowl of milk in front of him that he is contently lapping from. I wonder who coaxed him out of the bag?

Mr. Clark comes out of the lodge, to the wagon, and with his instructions. I help him set up his table of medicines, ointments, and tonics to cure whatever ails a body. He also sets out a box of snakeskins that have been oiled and stretched until they are flexible for making belts or shoes and such. Then to my horror, he pulls out several small boxes containing various species of live snakes.

"I usually have a big to do and fanfare that I do, sort of a show. People like to be entertained before they commence to purchasing items such as these. But the natives prefer to get down to business and do their trading and then have the entertainment, so we will do a bit of trading today," he says, rubbing his palms together.

During the remainder of the day, I watch the villagers come to his wagon and with a bit of sign language and body language, communications commence between parties as to what ails them and Mr. Clark shows them what medicine or tonic or ointment would be best. What is interesting to me is that he does not deal in money but takes goods and items such as jewelry or food or weapons in trade. At one point, a woman comes to him who appears to me by her actions and private medicine bag, the village medicine women. She and Mr. Clark exchange medicine for medicine. She also purchases a couple of live snakes in exchange for some furs.

By the time the sun starts setting, the trading has ended and we have been invited to supper in the lodge as special guests. I help Mr. Clark put everything away in the wagon first and stow my gear in there as well. Since it's no secret I'm a girl here in the village, I decide to change back into my skirt and am obliged to sit with the women for dinner as is custom. I don't mind. I really don't want to hear a bunch of men talking about hunting and things like that. However, since I don't know the language I sit quietly with nothing to say to anyone and nod politely when they say something to me or pass me food.

Raine comes in and sits down beside me, but I don't say anything to her. I just keep eating because I'm still so very frustrated and angry with her that I just don't know what to say. She must know I'm mad at her because she doesn't say anything to me either all through dinner. Then the entertainment starts and several women get up to dance to the beat of drums. I watch the dance mesmerized by the movements.

I'm taken in by the graceful movements of the dancers, their bronze skin glowing in the firelight, their long black hair twisted and braided about their heads like crowns. I focus on their features and note the distinct almond shaped eyes and prominent high cheekbones. They are a decidedly beautiful people and proud of their heritage, yet the System has driven them to the edge of extinction. I suddenly realize the dancers are telling a story and find myself wondering what it's about.

"They're telling the story of how the first human being was created," says Raine, as if reading my mind.

I just nod my head and keep watching. I don't see why I should even bother talking with her if she is just going to stay here and get married anyway. We will never hear from her again. Like she said 'she just figured we thought she was dead so she didn't bother,' why should we bother if she doesn't care? I just don't understand.

I leave the lodge before the party is over; I just want to be alone for a while with my thoughts. I miss the other girls and seeing Raine is like having part of them back again, only her strange attitude toward me makes me feel worse. Now I really know what a fair weather friend really is. I get my gear and open the carpetbag all the way out. I lay it under the wagon and make my bed there for the night. It's still warm enough to sleep outside though the mountain air is a bit cooler.

I lay down, and Boots comes to snuggle with me. I wonder what he has been up to, hunting rodents no doubt. Sometimes I wonder if maybe it would be better to live as a cat than as a human in this world. I lay in the dark listening to the rhythm of the drums and wonder what the rest of the girls are doing. Are they safe? Will I ever see them again? If I do see them, will they be like Raine and not really care? Something inside me hurts and it's not just the loss of Granny or not knowing where Papa is, or even not having a home anymore, it's an empty feeling inside me like a hole. I feel so alone.

CHAPTER 30

$\mathcal{M}$orning greets me with a new day and the sound of Mr. Clark singing. I get up and take a deep breath of fresh mountain air. I hadn't really realized how mountainous this area is we are in. I guess I just didn't pay attention enough to notice the lush green trees now starting to turn colors. Mr. Clark is by a small fire with a coffee pot sitting on a rock in the middle of the fire. I walk over to him.

"Good morning, little miss sunshine. You missed quite a party last night," he says.

"I was there for a while but I didn't feel very well," I say.

"If you'd like a cup of coffee there's another cup hanging just inside the door of the wagon to the left," he says.

"Ok, thank you," I say, running to the wagon. I haven't had coffee in a good while and it smells wonderful.

I bring the cup and he pours me some coffee and offers me some sugar. There's no milk or cream so I will have to just make do with the sugar. I take a sip and the warm liquid goes down my throat soothing me and taking a chill away I didn't even know I had. I sit down to enjoy this moment and watch the village as the people go about their business doing laundry, sweeping their doorways, and cooking their food. The children chase chickens, and the dogs chase the children, playfully nipping at them. I think about how peaceful their life is. I find it comforting.

"I saw you talking with that girl yesterday, the one with rainbow hair, it looked like you know each other?" Mr. Clark asks

"We did, I mean do, but . . ." I let my voice trail off. I don't really feel like explaining Raine to Mr. Clark right now. I think he understands this because he doesn't press the issue.

"White Owl told me that things have gotten so bad around here that they don't dare step foot off their land anymore. Some of his people have gone missing from the last hunting party he sent out," says Mr. Clark.

"Missing?" I ask.

"It seems so. He's restricted the hunting to the reservation now but he fears that the System agents are deliberately chasing or luring the game off his land so his people will have no choice but to hunt elsewhere," says Mr. Clark.

"I bet they're taking his people and throwing them in workinhouses," I say.

"Don't let anybody else here you say that," he warns.

"Sorry, but I think it's true," I say.

"That friend of yours, if she doesn't belong here and the System knows she's here, that just might be a way for them to come on White Owl's land and take all his people," says Mr. Clark.

"She belongs here, sort of anyway. Her mother was a Native but I don't know what tribe, I don't think she knows either," I say.

"But she's only part Native?" he asks.

"Yes, half," I say.

"That's enough to cause problems," he says.

"I tried to get her to come with me but she won't. She thinks she's going to marry the chief's son," I say.

"Who? Gray Hare? That's not going to happen, he and the daughter of another chief have already been promised long ago when they were younger. He can't break that for anything," says Mr. Clark.

"I've got to find Raine and let her know, then," I say.

"We'll be heading out in about an hour. It'll take us about two to three hours to get to Bryson City from here," he says.

"Oh that's wonderful, I feel like it's taking me forever to get there," I say.

"The roads we travel tend to have hiccups along the way," he says.

"Yes they do, sometimes great big ones too," I say.

I go into camp searching for Raine. I don't know what the rules are about going into the lodge so I don't look for her in there. I just walk around the village smiling at the people when they smile and say something to me that I have no idea what they are saying. Finally, I find her by the ponies. I really don't want to talk to her again and have half a mind to go ahead and just let her get her heart broken. On the other hand, she is endangering these people and I have to let her know that.

"Raine, I need to talk to you," I say.

"Oh, now you want to talk to me when you're leaving. You didn't want to talk to me last night at dinner when we had time to talk," says Raine.

"No, I didn't because I was mad at you, and I still am, but I have something to tell you and you need to listen to me," I say.

"Why? Why should I listen to you?" she says in a day dreamy voice.

"Because, you're putting these people in danger being here. If the System finds out you're here they may just come on this land and take you and all these people and throw you and all of them into workinhouses," I say angrily.

"That's not going to happen. Gray Hare and I are going to get married and we'll leave here and go into the mountains where they can't get us," she says.

"That isn't going to happen, Raine. Gray Hare is betrothed to someone else," I say.

"You don't know what you're talking about," she says.

"I do. This is your chance to leave with some dignity. When we leave today, come with us. You don't have to come with me you can go wherever you want but you can't stay here, it's not safe," I say.

"Nowhere is safe," she says.

"That's true. There's something else, Raine. The System has put up wanted posters for my papa and me/ If you're known to be with me you may not be safe," I say.

"Then I should go as far away from you as possible," she says.

"I guess so, but not here, ok? Just leave this place. If you change your mind about wanting to be with us, Freckles, Charlotte, and Lyza, we're meeting in Hot Springs Arkansas in October," I say. I don't have anything else to say so I walk away, back to the wagon where I find Mr. Clark putting out the fire.

"You look a little down in the mouth, my dear lady," he says.

"Things didn't go so well with Raine," I say.

"I'm sorry, is there anything I can do to cheer you up or get your mind off it?" he asks.

"I doubt it, let's just get going," I say.

"I'm waiting on a few more supplies from the villagers before we go," he says.

"Oh, well I'll just umm, I'll just look for Boots then," I say, not sure what to do to kill time.

"Hey! How would you like to see my invention? You know the one I told you about, the snake venom iron shooter?" he asks.

"Sure," I say, trying to sound enthusiastic.

"Come on, it's in the wagon," he says.

"We go to the wagon and he opens the door up. Yesterday I saw inside just a little as he handed things to me to set up outside but today we go inside. It's a lot bigger inside than I thought it would be. It's half the size of a boxcar but has room enough for a bunk with cupboards above it on one side. A secretary desk opens down from the wall on the other side and a chair is pulled up to it, I suppose it's where Mr. Clark does his bookkeeping.

In the back is a line of crates I recognize from yesterday, some still with live snakes in them. Above them are several shelves with boxes of medicines and ointments and tonics all fortified with ropes so they won't fall while the wagons moving. Snakeskins, various pots, pans and tools I'm not sure do what hang from the ceiling. In the back corner is another table, which appears to be nailed to the floor.

"This is my work bench," he says, proudly pointing to the table. He pulls a box out from under it, and he places the box on the table taking an item out of the box and handing it to me. I take it carefully and examine it.

It looks like an old flint gun but the barrel is made of some sort of metal I don't recognize; it's not iron because it's too light. Along the top of the barrel is a long glass tube with some sort of liquid in it. The trigger isn't curved like on a gun but flat and appears to pull back rather than down when pulled.

"Let's take it outside and I'll show you how it works," he says.

He grabs another glass tube from the box and we go out the door.

When we get outside, I watch as he takes the one glass tube off and carefully lays it down and then removes the top of the other tube and pours water in it. As he pours the water, I notice that there is a small hole at the bottom where it fits into the gun. Then he puts that tube back on.

"I don't want to waste the venom so we'll use water, but when you load the gun you must be very careful to keep the hole up so the venom doesn't leak out until you're ready to slide it into the top of the barrel. Once that is done, the venom will drain into the reserve when you pump the trigger and shoot out. See here there's an intake where air is taken in for pressure to push the venom out," he says, showing me the intricate of the weapon. He then aims at a leaf on a nearby tree and a small spurt of water shoots out in a long stream.

"Wow," I say. "There's not a whole lot that comes out is there? I mean it looks like a long stream but it's very thin and quick."

"Yes, just like the spitting cobra. You don't need very much venom to be deadly," he says.

"Is it deadly?" I ask.

"That depends on the venom you use. I use a diluted mixture that not only stings but also can cause some nerve damage, but unless a person is allergic it won't kill them. It's merely a deterrent or a means to get away. I don't like to have to kill someone. It just seems so final," he says.

"Yes, I know. I hope I never have to use my Derringer," I say.

"Here, try shooting this," he says, handing the gun to me.

I take the gun and again am amazed at how light it is. I aim for a different leaf on the tree and pull the trigger. My aim is true. I try it again and again I hit my target with no kick like a regular gun would have and an easy pull to the trigger.

"This is almost too good to be real," I say.

"I've been working on this for some time now. I've made about five of them so far, I keep one on me as well," he says pulling his coat away for me to see the gun strapped to his side.

"But will it work if you just hit a person or animal or do you have to get it in their eyes or something?" I ask.

"Well that was indeed the problem at first, so I mixed a bit of acidic elements into the venom so it burns through clothing, skin, hair, fur, even leather if you shoot enough on it," he says.

"Hmm, interesting. Have you used it on anyone or any living thing?" I ask.

"No, I haven't and I hope I never have to, but I'm absolutely sure it will work," he says.

"Are you sure?" I ask.

"Allow me," he says. Mr. Clark takes the gun and replaces the water tube with the venom tube. Then he aims it at a tree stump and shoots. Instantly the venom shoots out and hits the stump which begins to smoke. We go over to the stump to inspect and see a hole burned through several layers of the wood.

"I guess it burns through wood too," I say.

"Indeed," he says.

We return to the wagon to clean up camp and get ready for our journey to Bryson City. While Mr. Clark says his goodbyes to the villagers, I look for Raine hoping maybe she will change her mind or at least come out to say goodbye but she is nowhere to be seen. Maybe I hurt her feelings by leaving last night and I kind of feel bad about it but on the other hand she hurt mine so fair is fair.

I climb up on the wagon with Mr. Clark and a little girl hands

Boots up to me. Of course, that's why he hasn't been around. Boots is a sucker for little girls, but when it comes down to it he doesn't stay. Like me, he's a traveler. I only hope our days of traveling will be over soon and that Papa is in Bryson City.

CHAPTER 31

$\mathcal{T}$hough it's only a few hours, the trip to Bryson City seems to take forever. The beauty and colors of the mountains are breathtaking, but after a while I lose interest in the scenery as I think about my plan of action. I want to check the train station but I'm afraid to. Maybe dressed as a boy no one will recognize me. I've changed out of my skirt and back into the breeches again, but I still have the problem of the shoes; they are a dead giveaway if anyone looks at my feet.

If I don't get any information at the train station then I guess I will do what I did in New Joplin and check the hospital and the Crusher station. Other than that I'm not really sure what else to do or where to go for information. Except, perhaps if there is a mine nearby, I could check there; Papa has a lot of mining towns marked on his map so I feel like maybe he is looking for something or collecting. I just can't imagine what he could be working on.

"Mr. Clark, have you ever been to Bryson City before?" I ask.

"Why yes, my dear lady, it is one of my regular stops," he says.

"Are there any mines there?" I ask.

"Yes, as a matter of fact there are several mines in the

surrounding area," he says.

"What do they mine?" I ask.

"Oh there are a lot of secrets around here and some say there's gold in the hills being mined but the real truth of it is simply feldspar and diatomite," he says.

"Dynamite?" I ask.

"No diatomite, though that is used in dynamite, you are correct," he says.

"What is diatomite?" I ask.

"I believe that it's some sort of plant fossil turned to dust, it can be used for lots of things, but I only know of its use as filler in dynamite," he says.

"Who runs the mines? The System?" I ask.

"The mines are owned by Mr. Grugen but I'm sure he partners closely with the System. Yes that is how it works," he says.

"Grugen," I say under my breath.

"Not a man to reckon with, little miss. It would be best if you stayed clear of such a man and his dealings. You don't have business with him do you?" he asks.

"I hope not," I say.

When we at last arrive in Bryson City or at least the outskirts of it, I'm a little let down; Bryson City isn't much of a city at all and in fact is no better than a Jasper. Well, maybe a little bigger than Jasper, but not by much. Mr. Clark sets up camp on the edge of town due to needing some sort of permit or something he mumbles under his breath. I gather he can only sell his wares outside the city limits.

"I need to go into town, Mr. Clark, on some business," I say.

"Very well, I do hope you will be back in time for my show, and if you can help that would be very kind," he says.

"Of course. I'm leaving my bag and Boots here with you," I say, looking over at Boots perched on top of the wagon, and he doesn't seem the slightest bit interested in leaving anyway.

"That is fine. They're both completely safe with me," says Mr. Clark, tossing a piece of bacon on top at which point Boots pounces on it immediately.

Bryson City has a neat little downtown area with a post office, general store, dinner, saloon, apothecary, a few other little miscellaneous items businesses, a train station, and a clock tower standing in the middle of town. I also notice the telltale smokes stacks of a workinhouse on the other side of town, actually pretty far back from the town up on a hill. I have to wonder what they have going on in that workinhouse and if there is some terrible woman running it like Ms. Marcs.

I pull my cap down over my eyes and tuck my hair up inside and aim for the train station first. I'm not sure what I expect to find there but it's at least a start and I have to start somewhere. The train station is a little box of a building with a platform and water tower. Inside the station is a small ticket booth, which no one is manning right now, and a few benches. On the wall beside the ticket booth is a list of the train times, very easy but I suppose someone must have gotten tired of telling people so it's posted. The list simply states: *North bound 10:00 p.m.; South bound 10:00 a.m. no West or East bound trains from this station.* I read the rest of the board which lists rules about riding the train and what is allowed as luggage, free reining chickens are not allowed. There are also items for sale, posted by people in the town I suppose, and the wanted posters. I've seen wanted posters before in Jasper, at the post office, but never had I before seen Papa's or my face on them.

I just stand there like a dodo bird staring at the posters, which pretty much read the same as the newspaper article. I just can't believe that Papa is a wanted man or even more absurd is that I'm a wanted girl. The System wants me and I'm listed as dangerous. Why? What did I do to be so dangerous? I just don't understand it.

The sound of the clock tower striking the time brings me back from a daze. I realize I have just been standing here staring at the wall for a while now so I look around but there is still no one in the room. This is a good time to leave before anyone sees me. I don't see anyone around so I pull the posters off the board and shove them in my coat pocket. Maybe they're the only posters in town and no one has noticed them or looked at them very closely.

Pulling my cap down tight and making sure all my hair is still tucked up inside, I slip out the door and head down the street toward the other side of town. I'm not sure why I am going this way but I just letting my feet take me right now while I think about what to do. Pretty soon I find myself just down the hill from the workinhouse.

I stop and look at the sign posted at the base of the road: *Grugen Mining Company # 328*. Geez, how many mining companies does this Grugen guy own I wonder, at least 328 I guess. I look up at the twisting dirt road that leads to a building on the side of the hill. It looks just like an ordinary mill with a waterwheel spinning slowly on the side and a spoke stack rising from the middle of the building.

"Hey! What are you doing here?" asks a voice behind me, startling me so badly that I think my heart just jumped into my throat.

I turn around and see a boy about ten or twelve years old. He's wearing the uniform of a messenger which is the tan jumper suit tucked into brown boots and a brown jacket over the suit. He has a riding hat and goggles and is standing next to a steam cycle. I've never seen one of these but I had heard of them. I think Papa had discussed making one at some point but never got around to doing it.

"Wow," I say. "That's pretty cool."

"Yeah, they only give these to messengers of high grade," he says.

"Really? How do you rate high grade?" I ask.

"You wouldn't understand. It's too complicated to explain, but the point is not everyone gets a steam cycle, most get horses, or if you're in town you gotta walk or run," he says.

"Oh I see. Well then you've come a long way and must have a very important message to deliver," I say.

"This one's not so important, and the lady don't even tip. It's the next one I go to that's the most important and the mayor tips the best," he says. An idea suddenly comes to me.

"I bet it's really an experience to be a messenger," I say.

"What do you mean?" he asks.

"Well, it's such an important job and people treat you with respect. I've never experienced that. I work for a traveling salesman who never treats me with respect and kicks me half the time. I wonder what it's like." I ask.

"Being respected is not something you can explain. You just have to experience it to know what it is. Maybe someday you will," he says. He starts to get back on his steam cycle.

"Wait! Why not today? Why don't you let me take this message up? After all you said she doesn't tip so you're not missing out on anything," I say.

"Naw, I can't do that. This is my job," he says.

"Who would know? Besides, didn't you say you'd rather go the next one anyway?" I ask.

"What if someone finds out?" he asks.

"How would anyone find out? I'm just going to walk up there and give the message to the lady and leave. How is anyone going to know? I ask.

"I don't know," he says.

"Tell you what, I'll give you fifty cents," I say, reaching into my pocket. I know I should ration my money but I think this is a good time to use it. I don't know why but for some reason I feel like I need to get into that workinhouse.

"What's in it for you?" he asks, eyeing me suspiciously.

"I told you, I just want to know what it feels like to have a respectful job if only for just one minute," I say.

"Your boss makes you wear them girly shoes?" he asks, looking down at my feet then back at me grinning.

"Yeah," I say sheepishly. "I told you he's kind of mean to me, this is one of his ways of making me feel like I ain't nothin'," I say.

"Poor, kid, alright here, you can take the message. Gimmie the fifty cents though," he says, holding the message in one hand and his other hand out for the money. I drop the money in his hand and take the message.

"Thanks," I say.

"I ain't staying around though incase, I don't want to get into trouble. If something happens I'm gonna say you beat me up and took it. You got that?" he asks.

"Sure, I got that," I say.

He smiles at me and then gets on his steam cycle, pulls his goggles down, starts the cycle up with the crank on the side, and takes off leaving a billow of smoke behind him. I trudge up the hill toward the front door of the workinhouse wondering if it will be possible for me to even walk in the front and walk back out without being caught. I didn't think this through very well. I don't even know what I'm looking for or why I'm doing this.

CHAPTER 32

 $\mathcal{T}$ he front door isn't locked and I find this is very odd. Ms. Marcs always kept the door locked in fact all the doors were locked. I go in and find myself in a small hallway with a door to my left, a door at the end of the hallway and an opening to the right. I go to the opening at the right past the left door and see that it's just an entryway to a set of stairs. I'm not sure where to go from here.

"Hello!," I holler. The door I past to the left opens and an elderly petite lady comes out.

"Yes, boy?" she asks.

"I have a message," I say in my deepest boy voice.

"Come with me," she says walking down the hall to the door at the end. I follow with caution, there's always a chance of a trap. I find myself always being afraid someone will recognize me and grab me.

We go through the door and walk into a very large sitting room with an archway that leads to another room we walk through as well. This room looks like a large dining room but not as large as the one at the workinhouse I was in. Of course, this could be for the staff since the room is decorated nicely; the workers are never put in nice rooms, not even to eat.

We pass this room and through another door that goes outside behind the workinhouse. We are now between the workinhouse and the mountain. I can see now that the placement of the building from the front is deceptive because here is where the real workinhouse is. Laid out before me are ten long troughs with about five chairs on either side of the troughs set at different spots. The troughs are filled with rocks on either end of them and there is a girl sitting at all the troughs but one. I can't quite make out what they are doing but it looks like they are sorting through the rocks.

Why do they have girls sorting through the rocks I wonder? The troughs are perched on a deck up against the mountain where there are tons more rocks piled up against it, I think I remember Tom or maybe even Papa telling me these are called tailings from mining. A gaping hole from where all the rocks must have come from is higher up the mountain with a trail coming down to the deck. A small roof covers all of this but no walls.

Standing where there should be walls are several Matrons overlooking the whole procedure. There are two or three men located on the mountain with guns. I'm guessing these are guards. I suppose they are very serious about not letting anyone escape, I guess that's why they didn't need the front door locked. The main Matron, known only by the different uniform and the sour look on her face, is sitting in a chair beside the door we just came through.

The old lady takes me to her desk. "There's a message for you sent by delivery," she says.

The woman looks up and reaches out her hand. I hand her the message and wait in case there is a reply. Not that I'm going to deliver it, but I think that is what a messenger boy would do.

While I wait I glance down at the girls sorting rocks again. They don't look very happy, and they don't look very well fed either, or clean. I turn back to the woman reading the message. Like all the other Matrons her hair is pulled back tight and the glowering look on her face reminds me of a constipated frog. She reads the message very slowly, and carefully, and then she smiles revealing nasty black and yellow teeth. I look down to hide my revulsion.

"They are sending us more girls, finally Mildred," she says to the old woman.

"Well. That's a relief. We can't keep our quota up with these ten," she says.

"You may go boy, there's no reply," she says to me dismissively.

I turn and go back through the door and it closes behind me. I stand there a moment before I realize that the old woman is not going to show me out. That's very lucky, I think. I head back down the hall through the rooms where there really is nowhere else to go but to continue on until I'm almost at the front door when I remember the stairway. I look back behind me to see if I'm being followed but there's no one there. I go to the front door and open it, then close it again, just in case there is some sort of bell or something that notifies them to whether I actually left the building or not.

I turn back and head up the stairs as quietly as I can. At the top of the stairs, I find another hallway with doors on either side, reminiscent of the sleeping quarters where I once slept. I walk by each room finding the doors open and empty. At the end of the hall, as I expected, is the stark and lifeless dining hall with long tables and chairs. There is nothing here. I still don't understand why I'm here. How is being here going to find Papa? I walk back out and down the hall when it occurs to me that the woman said she only had ten girls to make their quota but I only counted nine, I wonder where the tenth girl is?

I pass a closed door I hadn't realized was there before and turn the knob. The door is not locked so I open it and see another set of stairs going down into the dark. On a shelf next to the door is a lantern and I'm about to grab it when I think better of it. I reach into my satchel, pull out a candle, and light this instead. J always carry my satchel with me as it has many useful items including candles and matches.

I close the door behind me, making sure I can open it again before I do, and then start a mindful walk down the stairs. The stairs keep going down and down and I wonder when they are ever going to stop when I suddenly see the bottom stair meeting up with the dirt floor. So I must be in the basement if there is a dirt floor here. I see a faint glow ahead of me that might be the firebox for the boiler. I hold the candle up as high as I can to see what is in here, when I hear a sound like a small cough.

"Ms. Mildred is that you?" comes a week female voice from the dark.

"No, I say. I'm not Ms. Mildred. Where are you?" I ask.

"Over here by the boiler pipes," I hear her say.

I walk toward the sound of her voice, and the glow that becomes larger as I get closer. Indeed it is the boiler that runs the house, and there is a girl chained to one of the pipes coming off it. She is sitting down next to a pile of coal with a small shovel in her hands and I can tell she's been tending to the firebox. How very cruel this is to chain a person to a hot boiler in the dark. She could get burned, or worse, the boiler could blow up. I close my eyes a moment to shake that thought out of my mind.

"Are you ok?" I ask.

"I guess, just a little thirsty," says the girl.

"Here," I say pulling out my canteen and helping her to drink some of the water.

"Who are you?" she asks, after she is done drinking.

"Abby," I say.

"That's a funny name for a boy," she says.

"I'm not a boy. I'm just dressed like one so no one will recognize me," I say.

"Oh. Are you here to let me out?" she asks.

"Maybe I am," I say. "Why are you down here?"

"They said I was stealing but I wasn't. It was one of the guards who took some stones and he almost got searched so he dropped the stones in my pocket, but they won't believe me," she says.

"Stealing? Stealing what? Rocks?" I ask.

"Those aren't all rocks; we pick through the rocks to find the emeralds and rubies from the mine," she says.

"Oh, that explains a lot," I say.

"How long do they plan on keeping you here?" I ask.

"I think my time is almost up. I think I've been down here for a long time, and Ms. Mildred should be coming to get me. They can't afford to leave me here for too long, even to punish me because they are behind in their quota," she says.

"Yes, I heard that," I say.

"The Matrons say they can't let the natives sort the rocks because it's too hard to explain to them what to look for," she says.

"Natives? They have Natives here?" I ask.

"Oh yes several. They usually have an Native tending the firebox but because they wanted to punish me, I'm doing it. They also have the natives bring the rocks down from the mountain for us to sort," she says.

"Where are the natives now? I didn't see any," I ask.

"They usually keep them chained in the mine," she says.

"That's horrible," I say.

"It's not a very nice place here at all, but the worst part is when you're old enough or too wild for them to handle they sell you to a brothel," she says.

"Yes, I've heard of workinhouses doing that. My friends and I escaped one just before they tried to send us to one of those places," I say.

"You escaped?" she says, wide eyed.

"Yes, and I'm going to get you out of here too. Do you know where your family is?" I ask.

"I have a brother working in the mine about a mile from here. Our parents are dead now," she says.

"Do you know anything about the man who owns this place?" I ask.

"No," she shakes her head.

I look at the chain on her ankle trying to decide how I'm going to get this off her. I don't have any tools with me, and even if I did, what kind of tool would I need? Didn't Mr. Clark say something about acidic properties? The snake venom gun has something in it that burns through things, I wonder if it would burn through metal? I hear the door up stairs open and close and I blow my light out quickly.

"I will try and find your brother," I whisper to her. Do they lock you in your room at night?"

"Yes," she whispers.

"Can you open your window?" I ask.

"Yes, but it's too far down. There is no way to climb down," she says.

"Don't worry about that. I'll figure that at out. Which room do you sleep in?" I ask.

"The last one at the end of the hall. They cram us all into one room so we don't have to waste time cleaning," she says.

"Ok, I'm going to try and find your brother and come back tonight. What's his name and what does he look like?" I ask, worried that we are running out of time as the Matron makes her way down the stairs.

"His name is Frederick and he's short with blond hair and has a birthmark on the back of his hand," she says.

I give her a kiss on the cheek, I'm not sure why, maybe for encouragement, and run around to the other side of the boiler. Finding an indent in the wall I squeeze in thinking this is the best place to hide. It's pretty hot and I think maybe this isn't such a good hiding place after all, but it's too late to move now.

CHAPTER 33

Sweat runs down my body while I try to hold still and remain quiet as the Matron approaches. I can hear her agonize down to the last step and then shuffling across the floor to her prisoner. I try to breathe quiet and steady. I lean hard against the wall behind me as far back from the boiler as I can and keep myself steady. The last thing I want to do is pass out right now.

"Well Grace, I hope you have learned your lesson down here in the dark.," says Ms. Mildred in a crackly voice, but no less menacing. I realize now that I had forgotten to ask the girl her name, but I guess her name is Grace.

"Yes ma'am," says Grace.

"You know, next time you get caught stealing we are going cut your hand off?" says Ms. Mildred.

"Yes ma'am," says Grace, in a shaky little voice.

"You are just luck that we need you to have both hands right now. But if we have to cut your hand off and you can't work here, well, there is nothing wrong with a one-handed brothel worker," she chides. "Now fill the firebox one last time before we go so I have time to fetch your replacement."

Grace does not say anything, I can only imagine the horror

she must be imagining right now. I hear her shoveling the coal into the firebox and shutting the lid. Then I hear keys and the chain being worked as Ms. Mildred releases her bonds. Then I hear them moving about the room and watch the light form the lantern dance across the walls as they ascend the stairs.

Once the light has faded completely and I hear the door shut upstairs. I crawl out from behind the boiler but as I do I accidently touch one of the hot pipes. Searing pain rocks my body as the flesh is burned from my arm. I yank my arm away quickly but not quick enough. I have to sit down and tuck my head between my knees to keep from screaming from the pain. I hold my arm rocking back and forth until the initial shock passes. For a moment I think I'm going to pass out. No time for that now. I have to work through this.

With the light of the furnace I look at my arm and see that I really only have a small burn about as long as my thumb and as wide as a pencil but it still hurts horribly. I pull my scarf from my bag and wrap it around my arm, I will have to deal with this later. I have to get out of here first. I dash up the stairs as quickly as I can without making any noise.

At the top I listen by the door for any noises but hear none. Then I slowly open the door and peek out. The way is clear down either side of the hallway so I come out and close the door silently behind me. I listen again for any noises but hear nothing. There doesn't seem to be anyone in the house. I walk down to the end of the hall where Grace said she and the other girls sleep. I need to get my bearings if I'm going to help them.

Inside the room, just like she said, are ten beds all crammed in the tiny room every which way they can fit. I go inside the room and go to the window. I don't want anyone from outside to see me so I stay to the side and low just in case. The window looks out into the woods and not the back of the house where the girls are working and the guards are watching. I judge the distance down to the ground is only about ten feet, but that's ten feet too high for anyone without a rope.

I check the latch just to make sure it works and that the window will open and it does. I leave the room and go back down the hallway, when something in one of the other rooms catches my eye, a box of shoes. No doubt these shoes are for the new girls. I shouldn't take the time but I run in and rummage through them until I find a pair to fit me and take them with me. No time to put them on now. I practically run down the hall and the stairs while still trying not to make any noise. At the foot of the stairs I check the hallway, but there's still no one around. I dash to the front door then out the door closing it gently behind me.

I don't run down the road but head for the trees in case my opening the door has triggered any alarm. I duck down behind some shrubs and wait but nothing happens. While I sit here, I switch shoes. It's not that they are any more comfortable, it's just that I can't pull off being a boy while wearing these dainty ones. I'm surprised the Matrons never noticed them.

I sit here a while in the bushes but still no one comes out of the building so I guess I'm safe. I get up and head down following the road but sticking to the trees just in case. At the end of the road to the Grugen's Mining Company # 328 is the main road. Grace said her brother works at a mine about a mile up the road, but which way? I don't suppose it would be back through town. It would have to be past the workinhouse.

I follow the road with the idea I will go only about a mile to see where it takes me. I've tucked my other shoes in my satchel, just barely. My arm hurts badly but I don't have any ointment with me. I know Mr. Clark probably has something that will help make it feel better, but I will just have to try and deal with the pain for now. I pull my sleeves over the scarf and the pressure at first nearly makes me scream, but after while it turns into a dull pain.

I'm tired of walking and think about the fact that I have to walk back too. I'm just about to stop and turn around when I see a sign just around the bend. I run up and see a short little sign pounded into the ground at the end of a road that reads: *Grugen Mining Company # 320.* Well isn't that interesting? I wonder where the rest of the mines are.

I start down this road and suddenly get the urge to walk through the trees which is a good thing because right when I get into the tree line I hear an engine. I stop and duck down in the bushes and watch a steam carriage drive by leaving a trail of white smoke. I wait until it turns a corner out of sight before I stand back up. I continue on but more quickly now. When I get to the corner where I saw the carriage turn, I proceed with more caution until I see the compound. An entire mining set up with tents and processing machines of some sort.

I'm startled by a loud whistle and hide back behind a tree. That whistle sounded very odd, not like a train whistle. I can hear a lot of commotion going on in the camp and risk another peek. I see several people coming out of the mine, actually they look like young boys about my age, some probably a little older. I watch as they all go to a tent and get in a line. I smell food. It must be dinnertime, and that's what that whistle I heard means.

I watch as the boys get their food and sit wherever they can such as rocks, tree stumps or even just the ground. I guess Mr.

Grugen is too cheap to supply enough dining tables for them. I don't see how I'm going to find her brother unless I get a little closer. I don't see any guards and if there are any they must be in the tent getting food too. I inch my way closer until I get up close to a boy sitting on a tree stump eating. He is the closest to me and there is a tuft of bushes near the stump. I stealthily advanced to the bushes.

"Psst, hey boy," I whisper, just loud enough for him to hear. "Don't look over here just listen," I say.

"What you want?" he says without even looking up.

"Do you know Frederick?" I ask. "Can you get him to come over here? I have a message from his sister,"

"Yea, stay there I'll get him," he says.

He gets up and walks slowly over to another boy sitting on the ground with a group. The boy sits down, and after a while a shorter boy with blond hair gets up, and meanders over to the stump and sits down.

"I'm Frederick, Joes says you got a message from my sister for me," the boy says. I see a large splatter of dark skin on his hand and I know he is telling me the truth.

"I've talked to Grace," I say. He sits upright as if excited but slumps back down as he realizes not to show any emotion.

"How is she? Is she ok?" he asks under his breath.

"She's ok. I'm going to bust her out tonight, but I need help, are you in?" I ask.

"Of course," he says.

"Will it be difficult for you to sneak out?" I ask.

"No. There's hardly any guards after we go to bed," he says.

"When is that?" I ask.

"About 8 on the dot every night," he says.

"That's pretty early," I say.

"Not if you're up at 2 a.m.," he says.

"Oh, sorry," I say. "We need some rope. Can you get some?" I ask.

"No problem," he says.

"This will be cutting it close, but if we can get everyone out in time there's a train heading north at 10 tonight," I say.

"Why didn't I think of that?" he says.

"Don't beat yourself up. Just meet me at the end of the road of the workinhouse by 8:30. Ok?"

"Yea, ok," he says.

"One more thing, do you know anything about the man who owns this mine?" I ask.

"No," he says.

"Have you ever heard of Bishop Steel?" I ask.

"That name sounds familiar, maybe. There's a guy named Bisket comes out here now and again. Sometimes he brings people with him and they go into the mine. I don't know what they do in there," he says.

"Where can I find this guy?" I ask.

"I think he's in town somewhere," he says. The whistle blows again and it sounds louder than ever.

"I got to go," he says.

"Hey Frederick, if you can figure a way to close this mine down after you leave without getting caught or getting hurt, that would be a good thing," I say, thinking of the saltpeter mine and how it won't be used again.

"I'll see what I can do," he says, getting up and leaving.

The boy leaves with the rest of the crew after returning their plates to the tent. I wait until they've gone and start to leave when that same steam carriage starts up and drives back down the road. Maybe that's the cook but he must be a good cook if he's driving one of those. I wonder what happened to Papa's steam carriage. The thought of those railroad men hiding it from me just makes me angry all over again.

I get up from my hiding spot and catch sight of a box of dynamite. Well now, there's an interesting item. I could do a bit of damage with that myself. I look around the camp wondering if it would be possible for me to get that dynamite from where I am, and not be seen. I don't see or hear anyone around. Maybe this mine is so far off the beaten path, the Overseer doesn't think anyone would steal anything, including a stick of dynamite. What am I thinking? I don't even know what to do with dynamite or how long to give it before it blows up. That's just way over my head, and what if I get caught?

I look around the camp again. Everything is quiet except for the wind and the birds chattering. I can't help myself for some reason and find myself running over to the box of dynamite. I grab what I can and then run back to the trees and duck down into some bushes and wait. Nothing, no one, not a sound. This is too easy, and it scares me that it could be a trap. I look down at the sticks of dynamite in my hands. I can't believe I just did that. I look around again guiltily and shove them way down into the bottom of my bag.

CHAPTER 34

$\mathcal{I}$ get into town finally. The walk has cooled my heels a bit so I don't feel as reckless as I did a little while ago. I feel a bit giddy about helping these kids escape. They are going to need supplies and a place to go. My plan is to send them north. I can tell them how to get to Momma Sampson, she'll help them, I'm sure of it. But they are going to need food. How am I going to get them supplies? I still have money, so I suppose I could buy them some supplies. Should I go into the general store? Maybe I would be pressing my luck if I go in there. On the other hand, that's the place for information. That and the saloon and I'm sure not going in the saloon.

I take a deep breath and go inside the general store. A bell rings over my head as I open the door announcing my entrance; so much for not being noticed, just about everybody in the store turns to see who's coming through the door. No one is interested in a kid, so they all turn back to what they are doing. Two ladies discussing some material, two gentlemen are sitting by a kettle stove playing checkers, and a clerk is filling an order for another lady standing at the counter.

I go to a small rack of newspapers and dime books and

pretend to be interested. Actually, I am. I scan the front page of the newspapers, but nothing looks to be that important to me. I'm thankful my face and Papa's is not on the front page. I take this time to think about what I want to get. I have to know exactly what I want to buy or they might be suspicious. On the other hand, maybe these people don't even care and I'm just being paranoid.

The lady at the counter leaves with her goods. I look around and see the other two ladies are still discussing the material. I adjust my cap and go up to the counter, I think I have an idea of what to get but I peruse the shelves behind the counter anyway. The clerk turns around and smiles at me.

"What, can I do for you, sonny?" he asks. "Would you like some penny candy?"

"Yes, sir about twenty please," I say, stalling for time.

"Very good," he says, and turns to the jar of candy dishing some into a bag.

"I have a list of things I'm supposed to get," I say in my boy voice.

"Ok, where's your list?" he asks.

"It's in my head," I say.

"Ok then, let's hear it, lad," he says, laughing.

"I need a dozen apples, a quarter wheel of cheese, a box of crackers, a jar of peanut butter, and three jars of those peaches, please," I say.

"Alright then. You got something to put all this in?" he asks.

"No sir. I could use some potatoes too, then you could just put it all in the potato sack," I suggest.

"So I got about six potatoes in this bag here, will that do?" he asks, holding up a gunnysack.

"Yes sir, that will do," I say.

"This will be six ninety eight. Do you have money, son?" he asks, with a scrutinizing look in his eye.

"Yes sir," I say. I start to dig in my satchel for the money when the shoes fall out. I pick them up, shove them back in the bag quickly, and hand him the money.

"Those are some pretty shoes you got in there," he says, while handing me my change.

"They're my sisters. She wanted me to see if I could get them shined. She scuffed them. She's a bit of a priss," I add, thinking quickly.

"There's a boy sometimes at the train station who shines shoes," the clerk offers.

"It's ok, thank you. I'm going to do it myself and keep the money," I say. This response triggers a burst of laughter from the entire store which I'm thankful for. I grab my sack of supplies and leave them laughing so there is no time for anyone to ask any more questions.

I have to carry the sack with my right hand because my left arm is just throbbing horribly now, so bad I can hardly stand it. I'll have to try to find this Bisket guy later. Right now I need to go see Mr. Clark and hope his ointments are real. The pain in my arm makes me feel like I'm walking forever to get to the wagon. When I finally do get there through my tears of pain I see a small crowd has gathered about.

"Oliver T. Clark's remedies from the Far East are guaranteed to cure whatever ails you. From the tonics that cure dysentery to the ointments that sooths aching muscles you will find these miracle cures to be better than anything any doctor has ever prescribed. And! For you ladies we have creams to sooth those

wrinkles, for men, tonics that cause hair growth. So step right up and get a bottle or two of these amazing products," Mr. Clark is suggesting to the crowd in a vibrant tone.

I must say he does look the part in his bright fancy suit standing in front of the wagon with the snake and bright red letters painted on it. I'm sure he has already done his magic tricks. By the looks of the crowd though, he is not impressing anyone. No one is moving to purchase anything and it seems to me that Oliver T. Clark is either losing his touch, or never had it. Some of the crowd is starting to turn away when an idea comes to mind. I push my way through the crowd and bump into a lady as I do, falling at her feet. The woman makes a strange little astonishing cry and then reaches down to me.

"What is wrong with you young man, have you no manners?" she asks.

"My arm ma'am, it hurts so bad," I say.

She looks at my arm and sees the burn, "Oh dear child come with me, I'll take you to the doctor," she says.

"Wait!" says the man next to her. "Let Mr. Clark Quack give it a try," he says.

"Oh do be serious. You can't let that man experiment on a child," she says.

"Ooh it hurts," I say rocking a bit though I really don't have to exaggerate my pain.

"Oh alright, but he better help or the SPDL will hear about it," she says.

My heart drops into my stomach; did she mean that the System Police Department of Law is here, in Bryson City? I had better make this good, no matter what Mr. Clark does I will pretend it works. The man and the woman help me up and walk me over to Mr. Clark.

"What have we here?" asks Mr. Clark.

"This boy has been injured, see?" says the woman, pointing at my arm.

"Please sir, do you have anything that will help? It hurts awfully bad," I say.

Mr. Clark grabs my arm, examines it for a moment, and then, nodding his head, reaches for a bottle off the table. He opens the bottle and scoops out a finger full of white ointment and rubs it on my arm. Almost instantly my arm feels cool and stops burning. The throbbing stops too.

"How does that feel, young sir?" he asks me.

"Much better sir," I say, my surprise very genuine.

"Really?" asks the woman.

"Yes ma'am, it does feel a lot better," I say.

"The properties in the ointment cause a soothing effect while prompting healing of the wound. It will not heal overnight, of course, but it will heal much quicker than the most common treatment of a burn," says Mr. Clark.

"This certainly is something to have around the house isn't it? How much is a bottle of this?" asks the woman.

"Since you allowed me a fair demonstration of my product on your son, I will let you have this bottle for half price, Madam," says Mr. Clark.

"Oh dear me, this is not my child," says the woman.

"Well then for your honesty Madam, I shall sell you a full bottle for half price," says Mr. Clark.

"In that case I'll get one of your wrinkle creams as well," says the woman.

"That is so thoughtful of you to think of your mother, Madam," says Mr. Clark.

"But my mother is dead . . . Oh! My, sir, you flatter me so," says the woman blushing once she realized what Mr. Clark meant.

"Boy, why don't you sit here a while I tend to these good folk, and then I will escort you properly to your family," says Mr. Clark to me, winking at me.

"Yes sir, I say, and settle myself on the ground against the wagon wheel while for the next hour Mr. Clark sells his products nonstop. My guess is that after some of the people bought their items they went back to town and spread the word around until everyone came to purchase something, including the good doctor himself who examined my arm and proclaimed that it was not a hoax and that I truly have a real burn on my arm. At this revelation even more people come to see Mr. Clark until it appears to me that he is almost out of supplies and the people stop coming.

"My dear lady, never before have I done this much business in one day," Mr. Clark says, as he sits down next to me wiping the sweat off his brow.

"I thought you said you've been to this city before?" I ask.

"I have, but I've never done very much business here. They always think I'm a phony and merely an entertainer," he says.

"Didn't you ever think of having someone pretend to be sick and curing them before?" I ask.

"No, because I don't want to labeled a flim flam man, and because I don't want to be tar and feathered. I would rather be thought of as a bad entertainer than have that stigma put upon me," he says.

"Completely understandable," I say.

"I don't suppose you're going to tell me how you got that

burn?" he asks.

"No sir," I say.

"Very well, that is your business, as long as it doesn't interfere with mine," he says.

I don't say anything but just nod my head.

"Is there anything I can do to repay you for today?" he asks.

"Yes, there is as a matter of fact. Would you mind going to the saloon and seeing if you can find out about a man called Bisket? He apparently knew my papa. Only you need to keep my papa's name secret from people because he is wanted," I said.

"I understand, and what is your papa's name?" he asks.

"Bishop Steel," I say. I take this chance because something tells me I can trust Mr. Clark and there is no reaction of surprise or knowing from him when I tell him Papa's name.

"Very well then, I believe I have no problem wetting my whistle after a long hard day of work. However, you must keep out of sight now or the jig is up, got it?" he asks.

"Got it," I say.

"Good, then let me make sure no one is looking before you go into the wagon," he says.

We stand up and I pick up my gunnysack of supplies and satchel while Mr. Clark gathers his things up while surveying the area. When it appears it is all clear, he ushers me back into the wagon with instructions on putting everything away. He leaves with a satisfied look of a man who has had a profitable day. I on the other hand, have a long night ahead of me.

CHAPTER 35

$\mathcal{I}$n the wagon I rearrange my carpetbag adding the shoes and the sticks of dynamite. I wonder if it's safe to travel with dynamite or if it could explode by accident. I need to make sure and ask someone. Thinking about this, I change my mind about keeping it in the carpetbag, I wouldn't want Boots to get blown up. I put the dynamite back in my satchel wrapping the sticks very carefully in my scarf and shoving them way at the bottom.

Thinking of Boots, I wonder where he is. I can't go outside to look for him until it's dark. I'm sure he's fine though, he's been taking care of himself long before I ever came around. I sneak some of Mr. Clark's jerky into the gunnysack I plan on giving Grace and her brother. I think I have enough supplies to help for a while but they will need to learn to fend for themselves as I have.

To kill time I think about my overall plan of finding Papa. If Mr. Clark is unable to find this Bisket guy then Bryson City has been a total wash. I need to plan out my next move. I take the spyglass, open it up, and take out the map. I lay it out on Mr. Clark's worktable and look at it, smoothing it down with my hands, holding the corners down with some jars from a box under the table. I can almost smell Papa's aftershave and hair cream from the map. I close my eyes and think of home for a moment, but all too soon the moment is gone and I'm back here in a wagon in the middle of the North Carolina mountains.

"Where can you be, Papa?" I whisper, looking hard at the markings on the map.

Charlotte had said she noticed a mark on the map near Hot Springs Arkansas and that's why we were all meeting there. I look closely at the area near Hot Springs again and a big V with the number 23 written next to it. I can't begin to imagine what that means but it's Papa's hand writing. I look over at Rome, Georgia. I'm tempted to go there. But it is has a big X over it. I can't determine if that indicates that Papa was crossing this place off or if X marks the spot. I roll the map up and put it away again.

I wish I had a watch. I have no idea what time it is but it's not dark yet. I take a peek out the door and see that the sky is growing dim at last. I'm about to close the door when I see Boots running up to the steps. I let him in and after some exchanged affection I give him some jerky to chew on. That will keep him busy for a while.

I think about everything I plan to do tonight, and how to do it. The boys from the mine are on their own to escape, they just have to meet me at the workinhouse and then I'll show them where the girls are. We'll get the girls out and head over to the train station and I'll help them get into a boxcar and give them the supplies. I feel like I'm forgetting something. Then it hits me. White Owl's people. The natives being held captive in the mine up on the mountain, those must be White Owl's people. But regardless of whose people they are, I have to help them don't I? I can't just leave then there.

Grace said they are chained up in the mine this means I have to go back underground again. I can't do it. I just can't do it. I can't save everybody. I can't help everybody. I have to find my papa. I'll get one of the other boys to go in there and get them, they should be used to going in mines right? I mean, someone has to do it. The big question is how to get the chains off without a key?

I look around the wagon for tools but I don't see anything of much use until I come across Mr. Clark's venom shooting irons. I had thought about this before when I thought about getting Grace's chains off. There is something in the liquid besides venom, some acidic property Mr. Clark said. I don't know if it will go through metal though. I grab the shooting iron that appears loaded, I hope it has venom and not water. I'll test it somewhere outside to make sure.

I peek out the door and see it's twilight, dark enough for me to go. I have a lot to do in a very short time. I look around to make sure there is no one about and then leave making sure the door closes tight, I don't want Boots following after me he might get hurt. I stick close to the trees carrying the bag with the supplies, my satchel, and spyglass of course. By the time I get into the actual town it's dark enough that if I keep in the shadows no one will see me, but I stay around near the back side of town.

Most of the excitement in town seems to be centered in the saloon as far as I can hear. Music, laughter, and merriment echo through the streets of Bryson City. I hope Mr. Clark is having some luck finding Bisket. Either way I'm sure he is having a good time. Adults really do love drinking liquor and playing cards or whatever it is they do in saloons.

I slide out of town through the shadows and behind buildings like a ghost toward the workinhouse, that most dreaded wicked place. If I could figure out a way to get everyone out of there I'd blow the place up, but I don't want to be a murder.

I get to the workinhouse, up the road, and around the back. I'm wondering where the guards are? Do they go inside or leave at night? I don't see them anywhere. I look up that high steep hill and sigh. I have to climb up to the opening. I thought I would wait for the miners to come so I could have them go up there and rescue the natives. Now I feel I might as well go ahead and go up there myself. Who knows, the miners may not be able to get away, or their escape may turn out for the worst and alarm the whole town before I can help anyone.

I stash the sack of supplies in a bush and reluctantly start the climb the hill. I find that it's not as bad as I thought it would be, just steep and tedious. I manage to make it up to the opening without loosening any rocks or slipping. At the entrance of the mine I wait and survey the area, but I don't see anyone guarding the entrance. They must believe that once they lock the natives up they don't have to worry about them anymore. Now I realize I forgot to test the gun out on something to make sure it really has venom in it and not water, I just hope it works.

I go into the mine, I cannot believe I'm going into another mine. This is just crazy, I think. I hate mines. After stumbling in the dark for a while I turn to see that the entrance is no longer visible. I light a candle so I can see where I am going and find that I'm in a narrow shaft going down. I keep walking and I just hope Grace is right about this because I don't want to be going down here for no reason. I remember in the saltpeter mine they had all those people confused in a secret side room so they couldn't get out. But this is a mine not a cave so if there is a secret room they would have had to dig it out.

I smell something and stop. There's another smell in here other than the smell of earth, something different but not horrid like the trolls. It smells like sweaty humans actually. I raise the candle up so I can see the area better. Ahead of me are five men sitting on the ground looking at me very strangely. They are definitely Natives because even with the dirt from the mine I can see their golden bonze skin.

"I've come to help you," I whisper, but they just stare at me. Maybe they think I'm a ghost. I look down at their chains which are actually all linked together on one long chain. I follow the long chain to the end where it's attached to a metal ring driven into the ground just out of their reach. I take out the venom shooting iron, aim it at the metal link that is hooked into the ring, and shoot. Instantly the metal starts to smoke but it doesn't look like it's enough so I give it another couple of shots.

As the chain smokes I think the natives are starting to get the idea of what is going on and they start to tug on the chain quietly. After a few minutes of this the chain breaks free and I can see the men are about to holler in celebration so I turn to them very quickly and put my hand over my mouth and shake my head. I am fortunate that my limited sign language is understood because from that moment on they are so quiet I would hardly know they are there if I'm not looking at them.

Once they pull the chain from the loops attached to metal cuff on their ankles, their legs are free. I don't want to risk burning their skin so I don't offer to try to shoot the cuffs off. I'm sure they will find a way to get them off later. I motion for them to follow me and we head back up the shaft. When I see a peek of the entrance I blow the candle out.

With the help of the surprisingly agile natives, we make it back down to the ground soundlessly and I have a newfound admiration for them. I must learn how to be as quiet as an Native. That kind of stealth could go a long way. I motion to them to squat around me in the woods while I draw a map in the dirt with a stick. It's crude, but it serves its purpose, I think. I draw the workinhouse and point up to it, then I draw the town and point to the direction of the town. Then I draw another circle past the town and point to the natives hoping they will understand that there is a reservation not far from here.

"White Owl," I say, pointing at my crude reservation circle. Then I realize that the native language for White Owl is probably completely different. However, despite my naive and stupid attempts trying to help, they all nod and act as if they know what I'm talking about. They probably already knew where they are and how to get back home. So I wave goodbye and turn to leave when one of them grabs my arm and stops me.

He points to each of the natives counting on his hand the five, then he holds up a sixth finger and points to the workinhouse. I don't understand what he is trying to say to me. He makes the motion again counting each man then adds another finger and points to the workinhouse again, and then it dawns on me, there's someone inside, the workinhouse.

"Oh no, how am I supposed to get him out of the workinhouse?" I groan.

Off in the distance I hear the sound of the clock tower strike eight, I don't have much time to sort this puzzle out. the missing man must be in the basement with the boiler. They probably have him down there keeping the firebox going all night. The only way I know how to get into there is through the front door. I can't imagine the front door would be unlocked. I feel a little panic start to well up inside me. I take a deep breath to calm myself. This is all I can do. I know there's nothing else for it. I've got to go in.

CHAPTER 36

$\mathcal{I}$ put my hand up to them in a signal to wait. I hope they understand what that means, but I guess that's a standard sign in any language. They must understand because none of them follow me when I head for the front door. I go to the front door, keeping close to the shadows and bushes so no one will see me from a window if they are looking out. I wonder if maybe I should wait until we get the girls out before I try to go in the house. I think that might be a better idea, because if I mess this up going inside those girls will never get free. I back away from the door and run to the right side of the building and just in time as the front door opens and several men come out.

I'm lucky they didn't see me, and I stay low watching and listening. I can't hear what they are saying, but it seems as though they are leaving for the night, because I do hear one of them yell goodnight as the door closes behind them. I watch as they walk toward the town and disappear down the road. I let my breath out that I didn't know I had been holding. I move around to the back of the building where the girl's window is and look up just as the light is turned out.

I Imagine right about now the Matron is locking the door to

the girls' room with a smirk on her face. How do does the System always get such maniacal people to run workinhouses? Maybe that's in the job description when they apply for the job.

A few minutes go by when I hear something behind me. I turn, dreading that I have been found out. Heart thumping in my throat I duck down into the shadows as far as I can and wait. Suddenly out of the dark comes several dark shadows haphazard through the bushes. As they come closer, I recognize the blond haired Frederick.

"Over here," I whisper. They follow my voice.. "You're a little early, and loud. Do you want to draw attention?" I ask.

"Sorry, and I don't have a watch," he whispers back.

"How many are with you?" I ask.

"There's just three of us here, but fifteen of us all together. The rest are hiding in the trees," he says.

"Fifteen! There are ten girls up there, how can twenty-five people … wait, no, thirty counting the Natives … how can thirty people escape the System all at once? We'll get caught for sure," I say.

"The Natives?" he asks.

"They had them chained in the mine," I say.

"Where are they?" he asks.

"Hiding over there in the tree, except one of them is inside the basement," I say. I want to tell him that someone has to get him out, but there really is no point because I realize that someone is me since I'm the only one who knows where it is.

"Well, now what?" he asks.

"Did you bring the rope?" I ask.

"Yeah, we got it," he says.

I look up at the windows and point to the one on the end. I

pull a berry from a nearby push and throw it up to the window where it hits the glass lightly. I'm afraid at first maybe too lightly because nothing happens. I start to feel around on the ground for something else to throw when Frederick nudges me. I look up and see the window slowly open and a head peek out.

"Abby, is that you?" comes a small whisper from above.

"Yes, and friends," I call back.

"How are we going to get the rope to them?" asks one of the boys.

"Can't you throw it?" I ask.

"I don't think so, it's pretty high," says Frederick.

"Sure you can, you just need a little momentum," says one of the other boys, and grabs the rope.

He steps back a little from the building and swings his arm with the rope in his hand a couple of times before he lets go. The rope flies up to the window. Graces reaches to catch it but misses it and the rope falls to the ground. We all stop and wait to hear if anyone else inside the building heard anything but there's no sound. The boy grabs the rope again and tosses it up but this time Grace catches it. She disappears from the window with her end of the rope, I hope she is smart enough to tie it to something strong and she knows how to tie a knot well. A few minutes pass before Grace sticks her head back out the window with a thumbs up sign. Frederick tugs on the rope hard and gives a nod of approval. Then one by one the girls come out of the window and down the rope.

It's obvious that none of these girls have climbed up or down a rope before, but in a situation like this they give it their best. We are only fortunate that it's not too far down since some of them end up falling a few feet. This whole process takes an agonizingly long time or at least it seems to me it does but we manage to get everyone out by the time the clock in town strikes the ninth hour. I pull Frederick and Grace aside to explain everything to them, not because they are the oldest but because I know them, that's all. I don't really care who takes control of the group from here as long as they are able to escape.

"Frederick, Grace, you have to get everyone as quietly as you can, and without being seen, over to the train station and lay low until the train comes in. There's a burlap bag with supplies in that bush over there. Take it with you, but ration it, because unless you know how to get food on your own, it's all you have for everyone. Once the train comes in sneak onto one of the boxcars while they are watering up the train, don't let the break-man or engineer see you or you'll get caught," I say.

"We understand this is our one chance to be free," says Frederick.

"Yes, be smart, be quiet, be careful," I say.

"Where are we going to go?" asks Grace.

"I don't know. But I do know there's a woman, her names is Momma Sampson, she lives in a house by the river outside of Smithland, Kentucky. If you can make it that far she might be able to help you or tell you where you can go. Be careful of hobos. Not all of them are friendly, but if you meet an older guy named Jim who says he knows me, he can be trusted." I say.

I wish I have more to tell them; I wish could I tell them a safe place to go to get away from the System for good. I also wish that I knew for sure they would get away for good, but nothing is for sure, and the only hope I can offer them now tonight is their freedom, at least for now.

"Thank you Abby," says Grace, hugging me hard.

"We'll never forget you, and by the way, the mines been taken care of, so they won't be using it anytime soon," says Frederick, with a sly smile on his face.

Then suddenly they are gone, shadows vaporized in the dark. I return to the trees where I left my Natives friends, wondering if they are still there, or if maybe they have left as well. I duck down into the trees looking around but see no one. Well that doesn't change anything, they may have left their friend inside there but I'm not going to. I half cock the Derringer for the ready, put it in my boot, and shove the venom fire iron in my belt. I take a deep breath and let it out steeling myself against my fear, I can do this.

Back to the workinhouse I go right to the front door. I wait and listen but I don't hear anything. I grab the door latch but it's locked. I should have known. What am I going to do now? I can't go through a window unless I break it. Maybe I can lift the latch with my knife like Mandy Moon did on the train with her hatchet. I take out my pocket knife but it's way too small and hardly reaches through the crack of the door. I'm so frustrated I don't know what to do, when I feel someone behind me.

I spin around quickly my hand on the fire iron and find one the Natives standing behind me in the dark. Up close I can see it's the man who explained to me about his comrade in the house. He points to the venom fire iron and then points to the door. Of course, what am I thinking? Holding the fire iron, I take careful aim through the crack where the lock is, and pull the trigger. Instantly the metal starts to smoke. I do this a couple more times for good measure before I gently push on the door.

The door opens easily since the metal in the lock is not as strong as the metal of the chains that held the natives hostage. I peek through the door and see the hallway is dark. We both enter and I shut the door quietly behind us. Now of course the door does not want to stay shut since I have essentially melted the latch. I take off my boot and lean it against the door and it keeps it shut. I take the other one off because it will make it difficult to walk with just one boot on. I will just have to go barefoot.

I motion for my native friend to follow me to the stairway and up. Then we go down the hall as I remember, all the while I'm listening for any sound of other people in the building. All I can determine from the silence is that the Matrons are on the other side the building where the fancy parlor and dining room is, they must have their private rooms on that side of the house as well.

We get to the door of the basement and go in. The lantern is there on the shelf but I leave it and use one of my candles instead. No sense in breaking habit. Down the long staircase we go and into the dark basement where there is only one glowing light and one half naked man shoveling wood chips and coal into a firebox. The man with me whispers something in his native tongue and the other man stops, lays his shovel down and turns around.

The two men great each other and the man with me rapidly explains things to the other as I find the best part of the chain to melt. I point the gun and shoot at the metal, instantly smoke appears as the venom burns through the metal, I can only imagine what this would do to a person's skin. I get down on my knees and without touching the liquid or sprayed metal I tug and pull at the chain. I've almost got it free when my satchel swings down from behind my back and down in front of me getting in the way. I throw it over my back in irritation because every minute we spend down here is a chance we will be discovered. Not to mention it's so hot I feel like I'm going to burn up. At last with all of us tugging we get the chain free. We go back up the stairs, careful not to make any noise. I'm wondering how long our luck is going to hold out.

We get to the hall and I peek out and see no one there, so we race down the stairs. I grab my boots as we race out the front door as fast as we can and straight for the trees. The Native is rambling something to me and I don't understand a word he is saying. We stop on the outskirts of town and he grabs my arm and points up the hill. Then he points to all his friends and I understand now that this where we part ways. I nod in understanding and point to myself and then to the town. He nods and then he touches his fingers to his lips, then his chest and makes a low bow to me. They turn and leave and I'm again left alone in the dark.

CHAPTER 37

$\mathcal{I}$ sit down briefly to put my boots back on. My feet hurt from stepping on rocks and brambles but m adrenalin must have prevented me from noticing at the time. I walk back toward the wagon on the outskirts of town when I hear the train whistle as it comes into town. I hope those kids find a way on that train. I wonder how twenty-five people are going to be able to get on a train without anyone noticing? When we got on the train in New Joplin the yardmen were distracted by the workinhouse explosion. There is just no way, unless there is something distracting everyone. I sudden strange urge comes over me to blow something up. Maybe I could just blow something up just outside of town where no one will get hurt.

I stand at the edge of town near the train station, indecisive. The train has pulled into the station and since there are no passengers it won't be long before the train leaves again. Should I just go throw some lit dynamite in the woods for a diversion, or should I actually blow something up and cause damage or a fire. I need a big something up for a distraction. I reach in my bag for the dynamite and instead I find a hole in my bag and the dynamite is gone. I examine my bag more closely and see that it's not a rip but it looks like a burn. Oh no, I think when my bag flipped over it must have touched some of that venom stuff and it burned a hole in the bag. I wonder what else I've lost?

Suddenly there's a distant rumble and the ground shakes a little. I have no time to wonder what that is when I realize where I lost the dynamite as I hear a loud explosion closer than the prior rumble. I turn to see in the distance the workinhouse sliding down the side of the mountain. Oh criminy! I know where the dynamite fell out. This is not good at all.

Panic and fear take over my body all at the same time; I'm not sure if I need to run or hide. Maybe both is a good idea, I see the people in the town run to the street in marked confusion and I use this mayhem as my cover dodging the crowd when I can all the way to the wagon. I open the door and there is Mr. Oliver T. Clark sitting with another gentleman wearing a brown leather suit.

"Well howdy young Miss, did you see them fireworks out there?" asks Mr. Clark in a drunken slur.

"Who's your friend?" I ask.

"This here's your man Mr. Bisket," says Mr. Clark.

"That's Bisqué," says the other man in a slurred accent.

Oh geez, this is what I need right now, inebriated fools, absolutely no help at all. Boots just stares at me from Mr. Clark's bunk. I slam the door shut and leave them in their stupor. Now what do I do? Well at least this has made a good distraction for those kids to get away but sooner or later they will find out that they're gone. Or maybe they will think they're all dead, that should buy them some time. I think the best thing to do at this point is to leave this place but Mr. Clark is in no condition to drive the wagon.

I hitch the horses up to the wagon. It's not much different than hitching the ponies to the cart really. I get it done as fast as I can so we can get out of here before anyone starts asking questions. Once I get everything attached and hooked up, I make sure the camp is clear of everything and the fire is out and hop up in the driver's seat. I haven't driven a big rig but how much harder can it be?

Before I know it I'm driving a wagon full of drunken idiots, snakes, and a cat. I hear the train whistle blow as the train pulls out from the station. *The train must always be on time*, I remember Papa saying to me. The engineer has a thing about keeping the train on time no matter what, even if a building blows up I suppose.

I can't believe my luck. I know for sure they're going to blame this on me and then what will they do, lock me in irons? Hang me? This is just great, and I don't even know which way I'm going. I stop the wagon a moment to try and get my bearings. But it's dark. I need to go south. It's too dark for me to figure out and I just need to keep going. I slap the reins again and get the horses moving despite the verbal resistance inside the wagon. I keep traveling through the night away from the town and the burning workinhouse.

It's nearly daylight by the time I stop the wagon, I have no idea where we are, but I hope we are far from Bryson City. I stiffly get down off the wagon and stretch my aching muscles. I open the door to the wagon and Boots dashes out. Mr. Clark is passed out in his bunk snoring away and the other fellow is asleep on the floor.

"Sorry Boots. I shouldn't have left you in there with them," I say.

I'm exhausted, but there is nothing else I can do but set up camp. I build up a fire pit and set everything up including a pot of coffee, which wakes up Mr. Clark who comes out of the wagon.

"Good morning my dear young Miss, how do you fare this fine day?" he asks.

"Fine," I say.

"You know I had the strangest dream that I was floating across the prairie and then I come out here and my scenery has changed," he says.

"What do you mean?" I ask.

"Where pray tell is the illustrious Bryson City?" he asks.

"I'm not sure?" I say, looking around. "It must be around somewhere."

"Quite the jokester you are this morning, Miss Abby. I am confounded by your trickery and yet far more intrigued by your reasons than your actions. I must say I was bit taken by the spirits last night but not too so that I did not realize a great explosion had taken over Bryson City at which point we decamped quite suddenly and ended up here, wherever here is," says Mr. Clark. He takes a deep drink of his coffee and studies me a moment.

"Umm, would you like me to make breakfast?" I ask, stalling.

"I think we have come to a point in our traveling relationship where we must either part ways or you need to give me a little information as to why we so hastily left last night. Did you have something to do with that explosion?" he asks.

"Well sort of, but not intentionally," I add quickly.

"Sort of?" he asks raising one eyebrow in question at me, the same way Papa would when he knew I had done something wrong and would question me about it. That look that adults give children when they already know the answer, or at least they think they do.

"I guess I should start at the beginning," I say, sitting down on a large rock near the fire.

"That is usually where one starts when they start a story," says Mr. Clark seemingly more relaxed.

As accurate as I can remember, I tell Mr. Clark all that has happened to me since Papa disappeared. I leave out the part about the map of course since Jim told me to be very careful who I let know about it. I explain to him about the explosion at the workinhouse and how that has bothered me ever since it's happened.

"Well now, things happen in those workinhouses, those old boilers get over heated, or expand or, well just about anything can go wrong. It doesn't sound like it was your fault. As far as warning those people or helping them get out, how could you have known? You might have been killed yourself and then who would look for your father?" he asks.

I close my eyes, feeling the hot stinging tears run down my face and I can't stop them. I try to wipe them away with the back of my hand. Mr. Clark offers me his handkerchief from his topcoat pocket and I take it and dab at my eyes and nose. I'm shaking so bad now that I have to stand up and cross my arms in front of me.

"It doesn't matter if it was my fault or not, the System blames me. They are holding me responsible for that I think. There's a wanted poster of me," I say.

"Yes, I saw that in town. I was very surprised at the accusations for such a young girl to have done all they say it's incredible. What I want to know is how does all this factor into last night?" he asks.

"I got a clue about Papa to go to Bryson City but I didn't know where to start. For some reason I was drawn to that workinhouse and I just couldn't leave well enough alone. I bribed a messenger boy to let me deliver his message so I could get in and when I saw those girls and how they were being treated, it was just awful. I couldn't stand it. They had one girl chained up in the basement to the boiler. They had some of White Owl's people chained in the mine above," I say.

"White Owl's people, are you sure?" he asks.

"Yes I'm sure. That's how it all happened," I say. I proceed to tell Mr. Clark everything that took place the day and night before leading up to me braking camp and bringing us here, wherever here is. I couldn't just leave them there, not like that, not in those conditions, not after . . . well I just couldn't," I say, a note of defiance in my voice.

"Maybe I plan too much, or think too much about what could happen but then when I'm not thinking things do happen. Now they are going to blame this on me too but I couldn't leave those people there," I say. I'm near hysterics now but I try to hold it together the best that I can.

Mr. Clark takes out a tobacco pouch. I didn't even know he smoked a pipe. I watch as he packs the pipe and then lights it, taking deep long puffs. Swirls of smoke rise above his white hair and I'm reminded of a wizard in fairy tale, only this is no fairy tale and Mr. Clark is no wizard. I sit back down on the rock, taking advantage of the silence to control my emotions. The air around us fills with the smell of baked apples and tobacco blended with the pine and cedar wood from the fire. The aroma relaxes me, comforts me, and brings me back to myself.

CHAPTER 38

"It seems to me," says Mr. Clark breaking the silence. "That you need to get your priorities straight. Are you looking for your pappy or are you trying to save the world?" he asks.

"I'm not trying to save the world," I say.

"No, no you're not. You're guilt riddled with something you had no control over and now you're trying to make amends by saving everyone," he says.

"I'm not trying to save everyone, just trying to help people when I can. The System has labeled me already so it doesn't really matter, now, does it? No matter what I do it's going to be wrong," I say.

"You had no cause to go up to that workinhouse, yet you felt yourself drawn to it, knowing full well what you would find." he says.

"No I didn't. I thought maybe not all workinhouses were the same as the one I was in? I was hoping that these people, people like Granny and me and whole families who lose everything don't really have it so bad. Like maybe if their struggling then the System takes over and helps them," I say.

"Were you really?" he asks.

"No, I guess not. I guess I know better. I guess I should blame the System for all those people dying in that workinhouse and feel lucky I got out, but it doesn't seem fair that I lived and they didn't. Why did I live?" I ask.

"Because you're smart and you figured a way out. Because your pappy didn't raise no fool, and you weren't going to stand for what was being done to you. Because you have a mission to find your pappy; don't lose sight of your goal," says Mr. Clark.

"No, I'm going to find Papa, but if I have to tear down walls and workinhouses along the way while I do it then I will. They got no right to take everything from people and make them work the rest of their lives so the Richies can have a fine one," I say.

"Now that sounds like the makings of a revolution and it's dangerous talk in any company," he says.

I hold my tongue because he's right. I don't want to start a revolution. I just want my family back. Let someone else change the world. I'm just one girl and that is nothing up against a whole country. Mr. Clark has a very valid point I should just concentrate on finding Papa, getting Granny back, and hiding out somewhere safe.

"Sacré Bleu! I av been keednaped!" says the man stumbling out of Mr. Clark's wagon.

"You're ok, Mr. Bisket. We just took a little road trip while we was sleeping last night," says Mr. Clark.

"It is Bisqué, I keep telling you. So dis place, quoi faire?" he asks, looking around.

Something about this man makes me very nervous. He has shifty eyes and I can't determine where he is from because his accent is so very odd I don't understand half of what he says. He might be from another part of the world like the guy I met on the train. I only hope it's the same guy Frederick talked about and that he knows something about Papa.

"Mr. Bisqué, I'd like you to meet my companion Miss Abby," says Mr. Clark, motioning to me.

"AB'Gale Steel," I say, taking off my hat and letting my red curls fall from my head, hoping this will trigger something in his mind. If he knew Papa perhaps Papa talked about me.

"Sacré Bleu! Your papa, he is not Monsieur Bishop Steel?" he asks, coming toward me.

"Yes sir. You know my papa?" I ask.

"But of course, Monsieur Steel is my friend, we together work in di mountains. But where is he I not see heem in a long time?" he asks.

"Well I was hoping you could tell me that," I say.

"Mon chagren, I cannot. We parted company some time ago," he says.

I sigh long and deep, another dead end. I can't believe this. At every step and every place I go it turns out to be a dead end. I put my hands in my face and shake my head trying to think. I should at least ask this man what they were doing in the mountains. I sit up composed again.

"Can you tell me what you and Papa were doing in the mountains?" I ask.

"Ma jolie fille I can do more den dat, I can take you there," he says.

"Really? Is it far from here?" I ask, excited about actually finding a clue.

"Non, not far but I am ungry can we eat first?" he asks.

"Yes, of course, I'll make some breakfast I say jumping up excitedly.

I rush to the wagon and grab the two frying pans, some cornmeal, water, sugar, and some of the bacon Mr. Clark traded for at White Owl's camp. In no time at all we have corn pone and bacon for breakfast. I did notice while I was cooking that Mr. Clark and Mr. Bisket are talking quite a bit and away where I can't hear them and that bothers me. I want to know what they are talking about and if it has anything to do with me.

"So what were you two fellows discussing while I made breakfast?" I ask.

"We were discussing our options," says Mr. Clark.

"Options, what do you mean options?" I ask

"Ma jolie fille, you see Monsieur Clark must continue on with ees journey, but I dake you to dat place yor papa was working" says Mr. Bisket.

"I have a prior engagement I must attend to west of here in Chattanooga. I wish to accompany you to this place Mr. Bisqué is taking you but I'm not sure I will have the time. I suggest that you continue on with me as it is clear that Mr. Bisqué has not seen your pappy in some time and therefore he will not be at this . . . where exactly did you say it was Bisqué?" asks Mr. Clark.

"Dat place is maybe a day north to the foot of the mountain where we go," says Mr. Bisket.

"A whole day! You said it wasn't far," I say.

"Dat is not far," says Mr. Bisket..

"Too time consuming for me, we must move along," says Mr. Clark.

"But Mr. Clark I have to go, I have to see if there is some sort of clue Papa left me or something, I can't not go, I'm just too close," I protest.

"My Dear, I cannot in good conscience let you go traipsing off into the wilds of North Carolina with a man you just met," says Mr. Clark.

"I thought we were friends Monsieur Clark. I would not let anything urt er," says Mr. Bisket.

"No offense Bisqué but we have only just met, and being the fatherly type I just feel a might protective of the young lady," Mr. Clark.

"What about me? Don't I have a say in the matter? I've been taking care of myself long before we met, Mr. Clark and as a matter of fact, I don't know you very well either," I say.

"Oh, don't us fight, I will take ma jolie fille to the place er papa and I worked, then I will bring her safely to you in Chadanooga, oui?" asks Mr. Bisket.

"That's a great idea right? And then I will continue west with you until Hot Springs, I mean if you're going that way of course," I say.

"Well I don't much like it but you are your own so I cannot stop you, only advise you to be careful. I believe you have been very lucky up to this point, don't you think?" ask Mr. Clark

"Yes sir, but I'll be fine," I say.

"Maybe we find a 'orse and dat will make et much faster, no?" says Mr. Bisket.

I can see that Mr. Clark is still not convinced but there is no way I'm not going to a place where Papa has been. I guess whatever it is that Mr. Clark has to do in Chattanooga that he can't wait one day must be very important. I wonder if perhaps Mr. Clark is planning to turn me in and that is why he is so anxious to keep me with him. I didn't think he would be the type but then I haven't been a very good judge of character. On the other hand, I don't relish the idea of traveling alone with a strange man with a funny accent wearing an entire suit made out of animal skins.

Maybe he's a native from somewhere south. That would explain his accent and attire but his skin is too white. Even Raine had a bit of tint to her skin though her hair was as white blond as corn silk. Mr. Clark doesn't seem to trust him much but he was out drinking with him all night. I'll just be on extra guard, I've got my Derringer and I still have the venom fire iron, which actually might be out of venom come to think of it, I'll have to remember to reload.

After I wash the pans out in a nearby creek, I clean myself up and then head back to the wagon where the men have broken camp. I'm greeted by Boots who I haven't seen all morning. He must have been out hunting but I've saved him some bacon and I give it to him just before we leave. He seems happy to have it but like me, anxious to be on our way.

"I will take you as far as the pass and drop you off," says Mr. Clark. I can tell he is still fuming a bit about my decision.

"Thank you that'll be great," I say as pleasantly as I can.

Mr. Bisket rides on the bench seat with Mr. Clark while Boots and I ride in the back of the wagon. I take this opportunity to sew the hole up in my satchel and pack it with only the essentials. I plan to leave my carpetbag with Mr. Clark, that should make him feel better knowing that I have to meet him in Chattanooga to get my bag back from him at least.

After inspecting everything, I find the only item I lost from my bag besides the dynamite and my scarf was the pocketknife. I'm very sad about that since Tom had given it to me after we fought off the trolls. It also worries me because it has initials on it and if anyone ever finds it they might think he had something to do with the explosion. I wonder if the System really does have a log of every person they have working for them. That's a tremendous job I would think, having to keep track of everyone's name and where they all are or where they should be anyways.

It occurs to me that it's just Boots and myself in the wagon, I need some extra protection and though I know I shouldn't take things that aren't mine. My guess is if Mr. Clark is so worried about me, then he won't mind if I take another refill of venom and just keep the fire iron a while longer. I'll give it back to him when we meet up again. I'll also help him get more venom if I can.

I carefully switch out the venom tubes like he showed me, feeling very proud of myself for not getting any on me or anything else. I put the fire iron in my satchel on the outside pocket where it's easy to reach if I need it. For now, the Derringer stays in my boot. I just think about taking a nap when the wagon stops. I jump out right away to see what the matter is.

CHAPTER 39

"What's wrong?" I ask.

"We have arrived at the pass, my dear," says Mr. Clark.

I look around again and then I see it, the bare outline of a trail going up through the trees. I hope it's not going to be a horrible walk uphill continuously but I get the feeling that it is. Mr. Bisket has already jumped down off the wagon. I notice that he does have a small leather satchel at his side that I didn't see before. I guess the guy travels light, unlike me and my satchel which seems filled to the brim but only because I have food and weapons in it.

"Please think carefully about our discussion, my dear. I hope you find some information about your pappy too," says Mr. Clark.

"Thank you," I say to Mr. Clark.

"Bisqué, remember what I told you," says Mr. Clark.

"Oui," is all Mr. Bisket says to Mr. Clark.

I watch as Mr. Clark's wagon continues down the road, and I wonder if I have just made a bad decision. I turn again to the path and see Mr. Bisket standing on it waiting for me. Boots sits at my side waiting to see what I do. Do I go up the path or chase after the wagon? No, I'm going to see what Papa was up to and find him. I walk up the path and follow Mr. Bisket and Boots follows me.

The sky seems a bit cloudy unlike the sunny weather we had earlier. I'm concerned we may end up walking this trip in the rain before too long. I wonder where it is we are going anyway? After walking for a while my curiosity is killing me and I just have to know where we are going.

"So what is this place?" I ask.

"Eet is a place where dey mine dat gold," he says.

"Gold! Papa was mining gold?" I ask.

"Not exactly, eet may be ard to explain but ee made a deal wit dat Moon Eyed peoples," he says.

"Moon Eyed people? What are you talking about? I never heard of any kind of people called Moon Eyed. Is that a tribe of natives?" I ask.

"Of a sort, but not like dey natives, dey have been ear longer," he says.

"Longer than the Natives, who's been here long than them? That's just not possible," I say.

"Anything is possible," he says.

We keep walking up and through this mountain pass and to be honest, I was really liking riding in a wagon and on the train, I hate this walking everywhere especially up hills and mountains. It's ok for short distances but if we are going to be traveling for a whole day there and then all the way back to Chattanooga, well that's just a lot of walking. We are just going to have to find some means of transportation.

We get to a spot on the trail that keeps going up, but to the right is a valley that juts down. Here Mr. Bisket turns down into the valley and walks through the trees. I don't see a trail anywhere and I'm a little reluctant to follow him.

"Come, come, ma jolie fille, eet is dis way," he says.

"Are you sure? I don't see a trail anywhere," I say.

"Come on, I make dat trail," he says continuing on and blazing a trail for me has he goes.

I adjust my satchel so that the fire iron is within my reach and follow Mr. Bisket. In to the valley. One would think that going downhill should be easier than going uphill, but when it's very steep it makes it more difficult. After we travel down the valley for about an hour my legs are aching and I'm about to ask him to stop for a rest, when we come out into a clearing.

The scene I behold is breathtaking; we are standing on a rock ledge overlooking a small valley surrounded by mountains on all sides. The trees are sparse but rocky cliffs edge a stream flowing south. There are several dark spots on the sides of these cliffs, and I peer at them for a moment before I realize they are holes. Maybe not holes but mine entrances, several of them scattered all over the edges of the valley.

I look for a way down and see to my right a path but it's rocky and rugged. It could be a dangerous climb up or down. In any case, I presume that this is where we must go and so I head for it and Mr. Bisket grabs my arm.

"No, we must wait," he says.

"Wait, for what?" I ask.

"You must see for yourself what dey do at night when dey come. Eet will be dark soon, we can wait, ear, seet ear," he says, making a spot on the ground for me with the grasses.

Reluctantly I sit down but I'm relieved that at least he wasn't lying to me and that there really is a place here where he and Papa worked.

"So what was the deal Papa made with these Moon Eyed

people," I ask.

"Ee made something for dem, we put long wires down in the mines. I elped put dem up all over, dey hooked up to some machine but I don't know what dat do," he says. "Maybe you know?" he asks.

"No, how would I know?" I ask.

"You know your papa and de tings he can do, I tink maybe you have an idea what eeh was doing?" he asks.

"No, I have absolutely no idea, that's why I came here with you to find out," I say.

It's getting dark and the night air is cool, a little colder than I had anticipated. The wind is picking up a bit too, but luckily, it hasn't started raining. I'm wondering if there's anything in my bag I could have brought that would have been warmer. I do at least have my blanket and I suppose I could make a fire. I get up to start collecting firewood.

"What are you doing?" he asks.

"I thought I would get some wood to start a fire," I say.

"No, no fire, dey can't see us," he says.

Suddenly I hear a strange droning or humming sound. I look around but it has grown so dark so quickly that I can't see very far. The humming gets louder, and I look up to see the bottom of a very large gondola. It is so large it looks like sailing ship but it's an airship. I stare up at it mesmerized as it passes overhead, humming as it goes.

"I didn't know dirigibles could be that big and fly," I say.

We both sit in the dark watching the thing fly over to the valley and then stop. I'm amazed because it just stops and hovers about ten feet over the ground; this big zephyr-like balloon with a big boat underneath is just hanging in midair over the ground.

Then something flies over the edge and hangs, then another one and another one. I'm not sure what they are, weights maybe.

Little round lights glow from the side of the gondola, probably windows. I can't make out what the ship is made of because it shines a little like brass but I can't imagine anything as heavy as brass could fly or even hover as it does. I can't tell what they use for propulsion if there are propellers attached or what. I need a closer look.

"I got to get closer I can't see well enough from here," I say. I head for the rocky path and start to go down it.

"No, ma jolie fille you do not go down. You give me da map," he says.

I freeze. Did he just tell me to give him the map? I didn't tell him about the map. I didn't even tell Mr. Clark about the map. I decide to play stupid.

"Map? What are you talking about Mr. Bisket? We came here to find out about my papa, I want to get closer and see what they are doing," I say.

"Eet is Bisqué you stupid cow, why can't you get dat right? Now you give me da map," he says again.

"I don't know what you are talking about, I don't have a map," I say.

"I didn't want to do dis da hard way but you give me no choice, instead of killing you quick I will do eet slowly and painfully unless you give me da map now," he say.

"What map?" I ask. Before I know it, he reaches out and slaps me, and I fall back and almost lose my footing.

"Why did you bring me all the way out here, if all you wanted was some map?" I ask.

"I ave business eer besides you, and I needed to get you away from dat stupid old man. Now you stop acting like you don't know what I talking about, and give me dat map of your papa's?" he says.

"How do you know about Papa's map? What is it? Why do you want it?" I ask.

"You ask too many questions. I don't got time for dat," he says, and reaching at his waist, he pulls out a big hunting knife. "Dat old man tink he is clever taking my gun but I got dis to cut you up," he says, coming at me.

I turn to run but the path is steep and rocky and it's dark making it slow and difficult. I feel him getting closer no matter how fast I try to go. I keep going as fast as I can down that path. Even though I don't know who is in that dirigible anyone is better than this guy cutting me to pieces. I don't think he will let me live even if I do give him Papa's map.

Suddenly I feel his hand wrapped around my arm, pulling me, and I don't think, I just grab the fire iron, turn toward him, aim it at him, and pull the trigger. Like in slow motion I see his knife go down across my arm cutting me, and at the same time the venom shoots out of the gun and into his face. He drops the knife, grabbing at his face, screaming, and falls to the ground wreathing in agony.

I feel a burning sensation on my arm and at first I think I may have gotten venom on my arm but then I remember he cut me. Stunned, I back away. I'm light headed and sick to my stomach. I feel myself falling, but there is nothing I can do. I can't seem to make my arms or legs work to stop myself and for a moment I feel myself rolling down the hill before it all goes black.

CHAPTER 40

$\mathcal{I}$ open my eyes to a strange little face of a man staring down at me. He has an old wise face but it's very small. He smiles at me and I suddenly think I'm dreaming only I've never had a dream like this before, not the kind of dream where your body hurts all over.

"I'll tell Gunter you're awake," says the man, and leaves.

Gunter? Who is Gunter, and why was I asleep? I look up at a ceiling of wood finely put together in long strips. There is a gentle rocking and it almost feels like I'm on a ship at sea, only that couldn't be because I was in the mountains.

"Boots!" I yell sitting up suddenly. I am greeted warmly by my feline friend who apparently has been lying by my side. I nuzzle him thankful that for whatever reason he is here with me.

I look around the room and see I'm in a small berth built into the wall along with several others all along the other walls of the room. In the middle a small table appears to be set into the floor, not crudely nailed in like Mr. Clark's, but almost as if it were built into the room or the floor as one. A tiny little round window on the other side of the room reveals nothing to me but blue, blue like the sky.

On the floor next to the bed are my things. I pick up Papa's spyglass and unscrew it to see if the map is still there. I breathe a sigh of relief to see it rolled up inside neatly as it always is. I quickly screw the spyglass back together and place it around my shoulders where I know it's safe. I have no idea what has happened. I only remember shooting Mr. Bisket and then I think I fell. My arm, he cut my arm. I look at my right arm and see a bandage wrapped around it. So I know it really did happen.

A door I hadn't noticed, opens, and two little men step in the room. They are both maybe only three feet tall, it's really very hard for me to judge but it's clear that they are much smaller than any ordinary man. They both have long white beards and white hair, and in fact, their skin is very pale and they have wide eyes.

"So you're awake now, you took a terrible spill once the poison set in," says one man.

"Poison?" I ask.

"Yes, that other feller must have had his blade covered in some kind of poison. It numbs the nerves. If we hadn't gotten to you in time you would've stopped breathing," he says.

"Oh goodness, he really was trying to kill me," I say.

"Well, it's seems you had a likewise match in the poison department. Very dangerous weapon, very dangerous indeed," says the little man.

"Yes, I know, but I only used it because I had to," I say.

"Yes. Well, understandably. But why would you have such a weapon in the first place? Where would one get such a thing?" he asks.

"I'm sorry, but who are you, and where am I? I ask.

"Oh, yes, manners, yes. I am Gunter, First Mate of the ship Moon Star, and this is Clint, he's the ship's doctor," says Gunter.

"Am I on the dirigible?" I ask.

"Yes. I said the Moon Star," says Gunter.

"Oh that's amazing. I mean, I've been in a balloon with pirates but now I'm in a real dirigible with, with . . ." I look at the two men because I don't know who or what they are.

"Some call us dwarves, some call us little people, the locals call us the Moon Eyed people, but we like to call ourselves the Sky Riders," says Gunter.

"Ok," I say.

"You know, because we ride the sky," he says.

"Yes, I understand," I say.

"So we need to know who you are and why you have such a weapon. We are very particular about who rides in our ships, you know. If it hadn't been for the cat we would have left you," he says.

"Boots? How is that?" I ask.

"Well he just didn't leave your side and kept howling. It was a horrid noise, so the captain said maybe we better help you, beside you're just a young'un, aren't you?" he asks.

"I'm fifteen. Well, I will be sixteen soon, but yes, I'm young," I say.

"So, what is your name?" asks Clint, finally speaking up.

"My name is AB'Gale Steel. I believe you know my papa, Bishop Steel?" I ask. Of course, this is exactly what got me into trouble and nearly killed the last time but what am I supposed to do?

"Really?" asks Gunter.

"Yes really, and I'm trying to find him," I say.

"What do you mean trying to find him?' asks Clint.

"Papa has been missing for about five months now," I say.

"That's not good, that's not good at all," says Gunter.

"You better tell the captain right away," says Clint to Gunter.

"Why? What's going on? Do you know something about my papa?" I ask.

"You better talk to the captain about this," says Gunter.

"Where are we going, by the way?" I ask.

"West. We're heading west, pretty much the same way you need to be going if you want to find your papa," says Gunter, as he and Clint leave the room.

West? Papa is going west? All this time I've wasted going in the wrong direction, I can't believe it. I think about the map, I want to take it out so very badly and look at it but I don't dare until I get more information out of these little men. They seem very concerned about Papa and they have taken care of me so I guess they are good people. After I talk to the captain and find out what he knows about Papa and why he's going west I'll be able to work out a plan.

If the captain knows where Papa is or where he's going then everything will be ok. I can send word to Papa that I'm fine and coming to him. I'll meet up with Mr. Clark in Chattanooga like I promised. Boy won't he be mad that he was right about Mr. Bisket or I guess Bisqué? I wonder who he was and how he knew about Papa's map. I guess it doesn't matter now that he's gone. Did I kill him? Those men didn't really say. Well if I did then I've saved Papa from him as well as myself, so everything should be ok now. Maybe we can even straighten things out with the System. Maybe Papa was only hiding because of Bisqué.

After I see Mr. Clark I'll have to go and meet up with the gang in Hot Springs before I go to Papa or they will worry about me. It's on the way anyhow and maybe they'll want to come with me. Then I can head west to Papa. I lie back in the bed and relax at last comforted by my own thoughts that everything is going to work out fine. The ship sways gently on a breeze carrying me toward my papa. Boots curls up in my arms purring, and at this moment I feel safe, at least for now.

CHAPTER 41

The rain came pelting down on Detective Reese Walker as he arrives at the train station in Bryson City. Since no one is there to greet him at the station, he finds himself walking in the rain to the SPDL. The SPDL office turns out to be little more than a tiny office with two closet cells in the back. With a name like Bryson City he expected a larger facility. Once he established contact, the SP insists on driving him to the first explosion site, a mine. Riding in the mayor's own steam carriage with a makeshift roof to cover them from the rain, Detective Walker surveys the area.

The mine site proves to be little more than a soggy hole in the ground. The foreman and overseer are both very cooperative and express their deepest concern about the individuals that may be trapped in the mine. Detective Walker makes a note that the foreman seems confused as to why any of the miners were in the mine at the time of the explosion. He is adamant that he sent the boys to bed and retired himself. The only thing the foreman and the overseer can determine is that maybe the boys were trying to get a head start since they had a quota to meet. They had promised the boys a treat into town if they met it by a certain time. When Detective Walker asks the foreman and overseer why they feel the miners are in the mine and not elsewhere, the overseer becomes quiet. The foreman seems confounded simply saying that the tents are empty, and asks, "Where else would they be."

The next explosion site, which they passed on the way to the mine, proves just as fruitless but more mysterious and interesting. The SP explains that the only bodies recovered after the fire burned out were those of the two Matrons who ran the place. No bodies of the girls who worked in the place could be accounted for. He also mentioned the fact that the Matrons had several natives working but none of them were found either. Detective Walker inquires as to whether the natives are employees or hostages. The SP just smiles and says he doesn't know, becoming very quiet after that part of the conversation. It is no secret that several companies have started taking natives if they are found off their land. However, it is highly irregular and seriously frowned upon.

After these two fruitless trips, Detective Walker finds himself standing quietly in the general store taking notes. His whole reason for this trip in the first place is to determine if these explosions were set on purpose, and if they could be traced to Bishop or AB'Gale Steel. He has been working on capturing the Steels for some time and now he might actually have some leads. He received several notifications of sightings of them on trains and at railroad stations but here was something much more substantial.

"So you say there were no bodies found in the rubble?" He asks the clerk.

"No sir, not except them Matrons up there, but none of them girls' bodies was found," says the clerk.

"Yep and all them miners run off too, left that mine high and dry. Mr. Grugen ain't gonna be too pleased about that neither," says an elderly man sitting by the stove. Detective Walker notes this as well; the fact that this man probably sits in this store day in and day out, collecting all the town gossip.

"We're there any strangers in town?" asks Detective Walker.

"No sir, none that I recollect," says the clerk.

"There was that boy, Finis, remember that boy who bought the supplies while I was showing Naomi Wilks the material," says a woman, clearly the clerk's wife.

"A boy?" ask Detective Walker.

"Why yes, I remember because later that day I went to see Oliver T. Clark's show and that boy showed up with a burn on his arm. Well I don't usually buy anything from Mr. Clark's but I like to watch his show, but when I saw how that ointment helped that burn so well and quickly, I was just amazed and decided that maybe that old snake oil salesman might actually have something worth buying," says the woman.

"Same boy huh? And you're sure it was a boy?" asks Detective Walker.

"Detective, I think I know the difference between a boy and a girl, really," says the woman.

"He was dressed like a boy anyways, I remember him," says the old man.

"Yes, I remember him, bought a lot of supplies," says the clerk.

"Such as?" asks Walker.

"Oh like lots of penny candy and cheese and crackers and such, you know, ready foods. But he paid with money," says the clerk.

"What was this boy wearing?" asks Walker.

"The usual I guess, brown pants and shirt and jacket," says the clerk.

"Was he wearing a hat?" asks Walker.

"Yes, he had a flat cap on," says the clerk.

"Have you seen this girl?" asks Walker, holding up a poster with the title Abigail Steel under the picture.

They all shake their heads, saying no they had not seen the girl. Detective Walker then takes his pencil and sits down at the table next to the old man and starts scribbling on the picture of Abigail Steel. The people in the store just watch him wondering if he is doing something constructive or if he's just crazy. Then the detective holds the picture up again for all to see.

"How about now?" he asks.

They all look at the picture and see that Detective Walker has drawn a flat cap on top of the girl's head, and scribbled all over the long hair from her shoulders and now there is a picture of a boy, a very familiar boy.

CHAPTER 42

Oliver T. Clark sits on the wagon bench and braces against the cold wind as the wagon rolls toward Chattanooga. He wonders if he's made a mistake in letting the little girl go off with that Cajun. All he can do is hope she shows up in Chattanooga like she promised. But what if she doesn't, what can he do about it? Since she's wanted by the System, he can't very well tell the authorities. In fact, he realizes there is not much he can do at all. He's so deep in thought that he almost runs over the boy walking down the road and just catches a glimpse of red hair.

"Whoa there, how did you get here so fast?" he asks. The boy turns and Oliver T. Clark see a young freckle-faced lad, wisps of red curls protruding from his hat.

"Excuse me, sir?" asks the young man.

"Terribly sorry I thought you were someone else," says Mr. Clark.

"That's ok. Since you're stopped anyway do you think you could give me a lift? I've been walking for a long while," asks the young man.

"Sure, sure, climb aboard lad. Oliver T. Clark is the name," says Mr. Clark.

"Thank you kindly sir. My name's Joey," says the young man, as he climbs up onto the wagon.

"What pray tell brings you out into this wilderness on this windy day Joey?" asks Mr. Clark.

"Well sir, I'm looking for someone," says Joey.

"Oh, you too huh? Please don't tell me it's your pappy," says Mr. Clark.

"No sir, I'm looking for my girl," says Joey.

"Your girl?" asks Mr. Clark.

"Yes sir. The Crushers took her and I tracked her to a workinhouse but it blew up. Well I thought she was dead. Then I found this poster of her tacked up and I got the feeling she's in a lot of trouble and I gotta help her, cause she's my girl," says Joey.

"Let me see that poster," says Mr. Clark.

Joey takes a folded up piece of paper from his pocket and carefully unfolds it revealing the face of AB'Gale Steel.

"They spelled her name wrong but this here's my girl Abby," says Joey.

"You don't say?" says Mr. Clark, pulling the wagon to a stop.

"Yes sir," says Joey.

"Well Joey, today is your lucky day and not mine," says Mr. Clark.

"What do you mean sir?" asks Joey.

"I will miss my appointment dear lad, but you are going to get your girl," says Mr. Clark as he turns his wagon around.

While an old man tells his story of his meeting with AB'Gale Steel to a young man in love, the sky darkens over Oliver T. Clark's wagon as it rolls back down the road from whence it came toward the mountain pass. Forgoing his prior plans, Oliver T. Clark sets his mind to return to a young girl's assistance for the sake of love, friendship, and duty.

Far north the train from Chicago heads to Little Rock. The train engineer is unaware of the three stowaway passengers in one of its boxcars. Huddled together for warmth, Tom, Freckles, and Charlotte make their way to Hot Springs to a reunion for the sake of love, friendship, and duty.

A steamship rolls up the Mississippi river carrying two heartsick souls who sit on the deck watching the darkened landscape pass by. Their hearts saddened by the loss of a friend they could not find, Lyza and Julian console each other. With the receipt of a message, they journey to a designated meeting place for the sake of love, friendship, and duty.

Acknowledgements

I would like to thank my family and friends for their support, love, and understanding. My thanks to Seventh Star Press and all who are a part of it for their work, help, and support. Many thanks to the people who have inspired, encouraged, and who have explained technological facts to assist me. Most of all I would like to thank my readers for reading the stories I write. I hope you continue to enjoy the adventures.

ABOUT THE AUTHOR

A California native born in Hollywood, J.L. Mulvihill has made Mississippi her home for the past seventeen years. Her debut novel was the young adult title The Lost Daughter of Easa, an engaging fantasy novel bordering on science-fiction with a dash of Steampunk, published through Dark Oak Press in 2011. The sequel to this novel is presently in the works.

Her most recent novel, The Boxcar Baby of the Steel Roots series, was released in July 2013 through Seventh Star Press. Steel Roots is a young adult series based in the Steampunk genre and engages the reader into a train hopping heart stopping adventure across America.

She is also the co-editor of Southern Haunts; The Spirits That Walk Among Us which includes a short story of her own called Bath 10, and a fictional thriller involving a real haunted place. Her poem, The Demon of the Old Natchez Trace, debuts in Southern Haunts part 2, Devils in the Darkness.

J.L. also has several short fiction pieces in publication, is very active with the writing community, and is the events coordinator for the

Mississippi Chapter of Imagicopter known as the Magnolia-Tower. She is also a member of the Society of Children's Book Writers and Illustrators (SCBWI), Gulf Coast Writers Association (GCWA), The Mississippi Writers Guild (MWG), as well as the Clinton Ink-Slingers Writing Group.

J.L. continues to write fantasy, steampunk, and poetry and essays inspired by her life in the South. You can find some of her short stories at

Dark Oak Press www.darkoakpress.com

as well as

Seventh Star Press www.seventhstarpress.com

and at her websites:

www.elsielind.com

jlsbooks.blogspot.com/

home.comcast.net/~mulvijen/site

Check out the following pages
to see more from

 SEVENTH STAR PRESS

All Seventh Star Press titles available in
print and an array of specially priced eBook
formats.

Visit www.seventhstarpress.com for further
information

Connect with Seventh Star Press at
www.seventhstarpress.com
seventhstarpress.blogspot.com
www.facebook.com/seventhstarpress
www.twitter.com/7thstarpress

Transcend Reality!

An Anthology of Animal Companions
from Editor Scott Sandridge!
Available in print and eBook!

Hero's Best Friend
Softcover ISBN: 978-1-937929-51-0
eBook ISBN: 978-1-937929-52-7

How far would Gandalf have gotten without Shadowfax? Where would the Vault Dweller be without Dogmeat? And could the Beastmaster been the Beastmaster without his fuzzy allies? Animal companions are more than just sidekicks. Animals can be heroes, too! Found within are twenty stories of heroic action that focuses on the furries and scalies who have long been the unsung heroes pulling their foolish human buddies out of the fire, and often at great sacrifice-from authors both established and new, including Frank Creed, S. H. Roddey, and Steven S. Long. Whether you're a fan of Epic Fantasy, Sword & Sorcery, Science Fiction, or just animal stories in general, this is the anthology for you! So sit back, kick your feet up, and find out what it truly means to be the *Hero's Best Friend*.

16 Tales of the Paranormal and Ghostly from editors Alexander S. Brown and J.L. Mulvihill!

Softcover ISBN: 978-1-937929-12-1

eBook ISBN: 978-1-937929-14-5

From the shadowed realms of the paranormal comes 16 chilling tales that dwell in the South and South West. From 16 authors, learn of haunted homes, buildings, landmarks and roads where restless entities from beyond the grave desire acknowledgement amongst the living. Become acquainted with the aftermath of an eclipse that awakens the dead in a Memphis cemetery, see what horrors dwell in the woods at Hell's Gate, learn the dark secrets of Sidney's Cotton, and dare to travel down Ghost Road. These and many other tales are sure to keep you awake as you are introduced to what makes the South and South West so unique.... History and GHOSTS!!!!! So, sit back, dim the lights and prepare yourself to face the spirits that walk among us.

Action-driven Fantasy from D.A. Adams!
Begin your journey into The Brotherhood of Dwarves, the popular YA Fantasy series from D.A. Adams. An action-filled saga where the dwarves are not just sidekicks!

Softcover ISBN: 9781937929916   Softcover ISBN: 9781937929923

eBook ISBN: 9781937929930   eBook ISBN: 9781937929-947

Softcover ISBN: 9780983740254   Softcover ISBN: 9781937929787

eBook ISBN: 9781937929909   eBook ISBN: 9781937929770

YA Fantasy From Jackie Gamber!
The highly-acclaimed Leland Dragon Series from Jackie
Gamber! Strong character-driven YA Fantasy for those who
enjoy authors such as Christopher Paolini.

Softcover ISBN: 9780983108672

eBook ISBN: 9780983108696

Softcover ISBN: 9781937929893   Softcover ISBN: 9781937929404

eBook ISBN: 9781937929817   eBook ISBN: 9781937929435

Dystoptian Anthology *Perfect Flaw* Now Available!

Softcover ISBN: 978-1-937929-11-4

eBook ISBN: 978-1-937929-13-8

Readers everywhere are invited to experience adventures of a dystopian nature in the anthology Perfect Flaw, from editor Robin Blankenship! Featuring seventeen speculative fiction tales, spanning many genres, Perfect Flaw explores the subject of societies gone wrong. From "utopian" societies masking an underlying controlled state, to stories of people fighting back against repression, in hopes of a better world, the flaws that create a dystopian atmosphere are brought to light. Thought-provoking and entertaining, Perfect Flaw will be a welcome addition to any reader's collection of dystopian literature.

Softcover ISBN: 978-1-937929-47-3
eBook ISBN: 978-1-937929-48-0

The Fey have been with us since the beginning, sometimes to our great joy but often to our detriment. Usually divided (at least by us silly humans) into two courts, the first volume of A Chimerical World focuses on the Seelie Court: the court we humans seem to view as the "good" faeries. But "good" and "evil" are human concepts and as alien to the Fey as their mindsets are to us.

Inside you will find 19 stories that delve into the world of the faeries of the Seelie Court, from authors both established and new, including George S. Walker, Eric Garrison, and Alexandra Christian.

But be warned: these faeries are nothing like Tinker Bell.

Softcover ISBN: 978-1-937929-49-7

eBook ISBN: 978-1-937929-50-3

The Fey have been with us since the beginning, sometimes to our great joy but often to our detriment. Usually divided (at least by us silly humans) into two courts, the second volume of A Chimerical World focuses on the Unseelie Court: the court we humans seem to view as the "evil" faeries. But "good" and "evil" are human concepts and as alien to the Fey as their mindsets are to us.

Inside you will find 19 stories that delve into the world of the faeries of the Unseelie Court, from authors both established and new, including Michael Shimek, Deedee Davies, and Nick Bryan.

But don't be surprised if these faeries decide to play with their food.

Olde School, a new take on the world of fairy tales and folklore from Selah Janel!

Softcover: 978-1-937929-65-7

eBook: 978-1-937929-67-1

Kingdom City has moved into the modern era. Run by a lord mayor and city council (though still under the influence of the High King of The Land), it proudly embraces a blend of progress and tradition. Trolls, ogres, and other Folk walk the streets with humans, but are more likely to be entrepreneurs than cause trouble. Princesses still want to be rescued, but they now frequent online dating services to encourage lords, royals, and politicians to win their favor. The old stories are around, but everyone knows they're just fodder for the next movie franchise. Everyone knows there's no such thing as magic. It's all old superstition and harmless tradition.

Bookish, timid, and more likely to carry a laptop than a weapon, Paddlelump Stonemonger is quickly coming to wish he'd never put a toll bridge over Crescent Ravine. While his success has brought him lots of gold, it's also brought him unwanted attention from the Lord Mayor. Adding to his frustration, Padd's oldest friends give him a hard time when his new maid seems inept at best and conniving at worst. When a shepherd warns Paddlelump of strange noises coming from Thadd Forest, he doesn't think much of it. Unfortunately for him, the history of his land goes back further than anyone can imagine. Before long he'll realize that he should have paid attention to the old tales and carried a club.

Darkness threatens to overwhelm not only Paddlelump, but the entire realm. With a little luck, a strange bird, a feisty waitress, and some sturdy friends, maybe, just maybe, Padd will survive to eat another meal at Trip Trap's diner. It's enough to make the troll want to crawl under his bridge, if he can manage to keep it out of the clutches of greedy politicians.